I0825307

GO GENTLE

ALSO BY MARIA SEMPLE

Today Will Be Different

Where'd You Go, Bernadette

This One Is Mine

GO GENTLE

-a novel-

MARIA SEMPLE

G. P. PUTNAM'S SONS
NEW YORK

PUTNAM
— EST. 1838 —

G. P. Putnam's Sons
Publishers Since 1838
An imprint of Penguin Random House LLC
1745 Broadway, New York, NY 10019
penguinrandomhouse.com

Book design by Lorie Pagnozzi

Library of Congress Cataloging-in-Publication Data
Names: Semple, Maria author
Title: Go gentle : a novel / Maria Semple.
Description: New York : G.P. Putnam's Sons, 2026.
Identifiers: LCCN 2025033471 | ISBN 9798217176632 hardcover |
ISBN 9798217176656 epub
Subjects: LCGFT: Fiction | Romance fiction | Novels
Classification: LCC PS3619.E495 G6 2026
LC record available at https://lccn.loc.gov/2025033471

Printed in the United States of America
1st Printing

The authorized representative in the EU for product safety and compliance is Penguin Random House Ireland, Morrison Chambers, 32 Nassau Street, Dublin D02 YH68, Ireland, https://eu-contact.penguin.ie.

For Poppy Meyer,
because everything is

"Do not go gentle into
that good night,
Old age should burn and
rave at close of day;
Rage, rage against the
dying of the light."

—DYLAN THOMAS

GO GENTLE

—PART ONE—

THE COVEN

I slid the fried egg—extra crispy, embedded with cracked pink peppercorns—onto a nest of baby arugula centered atop a slice of toasted sourdough. I sharpened my paring knife with a few satisfying slashes and sliced four cornichons thin enough for light to pass through. Those I placed across the warm egg, chevron-style. I capped it all off with a second piece of toast, this one thick with lemon aioli.

Or: I made a fried egg sandwich.

But how you do anything is how you do everything, and one might say my life's work has been chasing the Platonic ideal.

Viv appeared wearing that day's iteration of short-shorts, baby tee and sneakers. Her alarm had gone off at six. Evidence indicated she'd devoted the past hour to awesome lashes and beachy waves.

"Good morning!" I couldn't help but sing out.

Gorgeous, shallow creature, Viv! Reliably irritable, bereft of interests. Scroller, consumer, influencee. That Fate gave me Viv as a daughter provides a daily fountain of dismay and delight.

I encased the sandwich in glass, snapped shut the lid and presented it to Viv. She looked down and back up in dawning, victimized bewilderment.

"I'm not shivving you," I pointed out. "I'm handing you your favorite sandwich."

"But . . ." she began.

"But all my friends go out to lunch? But bringing lunch from home makes me look poor? It's okay, you can say it."

Viv narrowed her eyes, swiped the sandwich and pivoted back down the hall to her room. For punctuation: ye olde door slam.

A scrape in the lock. Our dog walker, Ziggy, returning Mr. Man from his morning constitutional.

Ziggy, there's a kid: freshman at LaGuardia, he just had three pieces in the student art show. He's a dedicated runner, has a dog-walking business and in his free time is watching all of Bret Easton Ellis's movie recommendations. Added bonus, he's besotted with me.

Mr. Man, unclipped from his harness, shot past me and straight to his bowl without a hello.

"Hey, Ziggy," I said, positioning myself outside Viv's room for maximum effect. "How's photography?"

Also, as an infant, Ziggy had contracted meningitis, which resulted in progressive hearing loss. He grew up in the building and is a fan favorite. When we learned he was saving for eardrum surgery, we put up flyers in the elevator. Within a week, residents and staff had raised enough for two surgeries; we threw in one for his pal from camp. Not one to let a skill go to waste, Ziggy gets paid princely by gossip sites to lip-read clips of celebrities bad-mouthing other celebrities at awards shows.

"Or," I said, loudly enough for Viv to hear, "is photography on pause because of cross-country?"

“I can do both,” Ziggy answered, hopping up and down while standing still, which is his lovestruck way.

“How do you find the time? You must never be on your phone.”

“You can stop trolling me,” a muffled command from within.

“Hey, Viv!” Ziggy stared at the closed door, hanging for a response. None came.

Or: maybe it’s Viv he’s besotted with.

Mr. Man, seeing his bowl was sans treat, returned and gave me an abject look.

“Don’t you worry, Mr. Man,” I said, all cute. “You’ll be dead soon enough. We’ll all be.”

“Oh!” Ziggy said. “Seven-sixteen. I saw them talking in the elevator.”

“For real?”

Ziggy poked his head into the hallway and indicated they were still there.

I whipped the dish towel over my shoulder.

At the far end of the hall, a luggage cart—the brass cage type, a remnant from when the Ansonia was New York’s grandest hotel—was stacked and strung with Fairway bags.

A blonde in her twenties, who I’d seen in the trash room (sweet-faced but notably unfriendly), came out in stocking feet and hoisted a case of IPA onto one knee.

“Hi!” I called as I approached. “You’re selling your apartment—”

At the sight of me, the girl became skittish as a bird.

“How did you know?” she half-gasped.

“I live down the hall, and—”

A handsome man with loose curls and strong captain-of-the-lacrosse-team vibes appeared and stood, shoulders flat against the door frame. At well over six feet, he looked down on me in more ways than one.

"Why, hello," I said, and returned to the girl. "I'd like to talk to you about buying."

"Hold on," the guy said. "Are you—"

"Matt!" the girl whispered. "No—"

"—in the coven?" A grin broke out across his cherub-hued face.

Mention to one doorman, in passing, that you're starting a coven, and soon the whole building is looking at you askance!

I chose to ignore.

"We can do it off-market," I told the girl. "Save you the hassle and stress of listing."

"I'm not really sure," she said, eyes darting at Matt.

"How much?" he asked.

"We can get it appraised," I answered. "If we don't use a realtor, it saves you commission."

"Not bad," mused Matt. "We'll get back to you." He tossed a laughing look my way. "Now, if you'll excuse me. Duty calls."

Matt returned to a big screen television. He dove onto the couch, pulling off a midair half-rotation to land him flat on his back and aimed at the TV. This, he unmuted to "Breaking News."

"TERRORISTS HIT THE BRITISH MUSEUM," read the chyron.

". . . No casualties have been reported," blasted the anchor. "But we can confirm the Rosetta stone has been badly damaged."

I was beginning to reassess my man Matt, the news lover, when the screen went black and switched to a crude animation of the back alleys of Baghdad.

Matt clutched a videogame controller with both hands and, elbows dug into his sides, began the grim business of annihilating soldiers, prostitutes and fruit merchants alike.

“He’s in commercial real estate,” the girl offered, starry-eyed. “We’re moving to Phoenix for his job.”

“Call me before you decide anything,” I told her. “I can think of five people who’d be interested.”

Just inside, I spotted a Sharpie on the counter. I popped in and wrote my number on a jumbo bag of Cool Ranch Doritos.

“Wait!” said the girl, as I turned to go. “Are you saying that the coven . . .” She was doing some kind of math.

“Yes?”

“Has a waitlist?”

Inside her apartment, Matt (shoes-on, doing the couch luge) was gunning people down with an intensity I reckoned he never applied to learning her love language. A statement bong dominated the coffee table. Meanwhile, out in the hallway, bag handles had begun to cut off circulation to his beloved’s ringless fingers.

“You’ll see,” I said.

I entered Central Park at Seventy-Second Street with amazement that this was my route to work. Even after five years, I took in the city with the mawkish wonder of a recent arrival. On the upside, tourists never stopped me to ask directions. On the downside, I tripped and fell more than your average New Yorker.

Passing the Dakota with its lit torches: each step I took as if through history itself. Approaching the Imagine mosaic and its unceasing soundtrack of buskers: my ears peeled through the din of car horns and helicopters to name that tune. Today, a deep cut, "Savoy Truffle." Not even a John song! Descending the dogwood-flocked path: the majestic clomp of distant horse hooves sent a reliable thrill. Beholding the crazy quilt of budding magnolia blossoms, lime-green chutes and cutesy crocuses beginning their annual prison break: spring had sprung, baby!

The reflexive next move would be to stop and breathe it all in. But I've learned the hard way. Central Park, no matter how fresh-smelling it may look, you take one whiff and it's piss all the way down.

I crossed the park, my pace juiced by the recent bomb-drop. (Not your bomb-drop, British Museum. Sorry, Rosetta stone, you were fun while you lasted!) The available apartment. Who would I ask to join . . .

Whatever you'd call our trio of highly competent, accomplished women (theater director, lawyer, philosopher) of a certain age (divorcee, widow, divorcee) who'd bought apartments on the same floor of the Ansonia so that down the line we could age in place and go out in a blaze of independence?

An unimpeachably intentional, highly curated, feminist old folks' home? Nah, not much of a ring.

A tragic, estrogen-free trio trying to put our best face on the realization society is done with us and we're destined to die alone? No, and bite your tongue.

It had started innocently enough. I'd moved to the Upper West Side after my divorce. Weeks in, I went to see chamber music with my friend Emily Ann (widowed lawyer), and on the way home said I had to stop at the market.

Emily Ann did, too. "What are you getting?" she asked.

(Now see, looking back, I already want to spend the rest of my life with that person: someone genuinely interested in my shopping list.)

"I've been craving tuna," I said. "But the celery comes prepackaged in two heads, and I only ever want a couple of stalks." I hated waste. Emily Ann did, too.

"It's why I never make tuna," Emily Ann put in ruefully.

"What are you getting?"

"Bread for sandwiches."

Sliced bread. That, too, I hadn't bought because I only ever needed a couple of pieces at a time. (Viv was away, summering with her dad.)

Right then, in the fusty cavity between the inner and outer doors of Morton Williams on Fifty-Seventh, inspiration struck.

I grabbed Emily Ann by both arms and dug my fingers in.

"You buy celery!" she cried, reading my mind. "And I buy bread, and we give each other half!"

A runaway train couldn't have stopped us. On the aggressively narrow dining counter, I broke off celery stalks and slipped them into her Dave's Killer Bread bag. Into my celery bag went six pieces of her twenty-one-grain bread. It was divine, if spinsterish—

Strike that.

It was divine *and* spinsterish.

When I attempt to define happiness and understand its place in the hierarchy of the human project (divorced philosopher), my mind leaps to those five minutes in the market with Emily Ann. (Sorry, marriage-to-Hal! Sorry, birth-of-Viv!) They were marked by spontaneity, creative problem-solving, lawlessness, laughter and kinship. I existed vividly and exclusively in the present moment. The universe was harmonious and it had my back. I felt wide and well.

Obv, the next day Emily Ann and I texted each other pictures. Her tuna: rough chunks of celery and onion drowning in mayonnaise. My tuna: finely diced celery, onion, fresh dill, parsley, kalamata olives, capers and Mama Lil's Peppers, undetectable mayonnaise, generous lemon juice. Her arms: fingerprint-bruised from being dug into. Mine: not.

I recounted the story to our friend Minna (making her the divorced theater director). She wildly wanted in.

Thus began Fridays at Fairway. A meetup of single women who purchase and divvy celery, carrots, basil, muffins—anything we want but comes packaged too much for one. We've been known to bring

Tupperware and Ziplocs. I call it a meetup because when other women see what we're doing, they instantly get it and want in. Sometimes it's a dozen of us. Other times it's just me and a bag of Mexican limes, ten for a dollar. I'm still surprised *The New York Times* hasn't gotten in touch; isn't that all the Style Section is, breathless reporting on trends that barely exist?

We kicked it up a notch when an apartment became available on my floor. I mentioned it to Minna, who'd turned on her longtime East Village neighborhood for getting overrun by bougie NYU students. So she escaped to the suburbs of Manhattan, aka the Upper West Side, followed by Emily Ann a year later. The idea being to pool our resources and, when the time comes, we'll take care of one another.

Women. You can't accuse us of not being practical.

Whenever I mention this arrangement to married couples, I'm met with one of two responses neatly divided along gender lines.

1. "Wait, you can do that?" (Said with wheels turning and fond memories of Ding-Dong Ditch.)

2. "Keep away from my wife."

I took out my phone and texted Minna and Emily Ann.

716 available. I'm on it.

In immediate response, not just the shriveled witch, but an outbreak of shriveled witches floating across my screen.

So, yes: coven.

As I waited to cross Fifth Avenue, I bid good morning to the private security guard who patrols the block.

"Morning, Tony! Catch any crazies?"

"Whatever you're on," he said, red-eyed and nursing a Greek diner coffee, "I need some."

"A life of the mind," I answered, and headed towards the steps of one of the few remaining Beaux-Arts mansions from the Gilded Age.

I have one of the weirder jobs. I'm the recipient of a fellowship from the Lockwood Library, you know, the museum on Fifth Avenue. Once home to steel baron Leo Lockwood, it's now among New York's swankier museums and houses the Lockwood collection. If you haven't been, run-don't-walk to check out the rare books, art, and whatever show is currently up. It's a can't-miss experience and the price is right: free, plus unlimited apple cider. At the very least, now you know where to pee on the Upper East Side.

In exchange for health insurance, an office overlooking a formal garden, and a cushy (for a philosopher!) income, I'm asked to research and write in the Library and, four days a week—here comes the weird part—provide moral training for Lionel and Layla Lockwood's twin tween sons.

Today it's weird. Back in the day—way back, we're talking Ancient Greece and Rome—it was all the rage to have a philosopher on staff. Alexander the Great was famously tutored by Aristotle. Marcus Aurelius, future emperor of Rome, attributes his swoon-worthy character to his Stoic teacher, Rusticus. Philosophy, it wasn't just for rich people! Socrates walked the streets of Athens hectoring all he came across into debating right from wrong, so vexing the powers that be they sentenced him to death by hemlock.

I admitted myself through the employee entrance, scanned into the turnstile and dumped my bag onto the conveyor belt.

"Oh, Doctor!" came a voice.

It was Hannah, the first assistant to Lionel and Layla Lockwood. Hannah was early thirties, with curly hair and severe, blow-dried bangs which left a neat runway of forehead above her chunky black glasses.

I entered Command Central, the eyes and ears of the Lockwood Library. A cramped space, it was barely big enough for Hannah. One wall was devoted to video surveillance monitors.

"The family returned from Paris early," Hannah said, slicing mail with a letter opener. "There was an incident with the boys, and Mrs. Lockwood requested you today after school."

I was supposed to meet Emily Ann at five, before the ballet—

"I'll be there," I told Hannah.

"I am drinking the yummiest latte right now." She spoke slowly, emphasizing every word.

I never knew when she was done. Time passed.

"It's from Blue Bottle," she added.

As I waited for the next piece of information, or not, my eyes wandered to Hannah's desk. On it was a visitor badge. The woman in the photo had dishwater hair. It sat atop her head like a bird's nest.

I must have been giving off question marks.

"She's back, all right," explained Hannah. "Mr. Lockwood wants to put in a hydroponic garden and she got a sudden opening in her schedule. They're meeting at four."

Of course! The landscape architect.

When I started my fellowship, a massive renovation of the Lockwood residence—not to be confused with the Lockwood Library, but where the family lives, across Seventy-Sixth Street—had just been completed, and she'd designed the garden. I hadn't thought of her for years.

No.

The opposite was true. I did more than think of her. Every time I stepped into that house and looked out the window, I felt her. Her playful genius became my playful genius.

"This is really good almond milk," Hannah said, taking a close-eyed sip. "I wonder if it's barista blend."

Didn't the landscape architect live in Los Angeles?

Hannah, noting my interest, added, "She's moving here, you know."

At that moment, Ravi entered. Ravi Bhardwaj was the elegant and aged curator of the Lockwood Library. He wore a tweed jacket over mahogany sweater and collared shirt. In other words, three layers.

I dug my fingers into Ravi's arms and let out a rapturous growl.

Ravi, no questions asked, growled back. Which is why we love Ravi.

I felt wide and well.

I would ask Blanche Falk to join the coven.

The "incident" of which Hannah had spoken involved the Lockwood boys acting like spoiled little shits.

While in Paris, the eleven-year-old twins had learned of a flash drop of Louis Vuitton sneakers happening the next day. Lucien had woken up at six and, braving the spring dawn, stood in line for five hours and scored a pair. Lorenzo slept in. By the time he rolled into the Champs-Élysées flagship, the €2,500 limited editions had sold out.

If only Jesus were around, he'd make hay.

But none of this was considered the problem. That occurred later, as was being explained to me by their mother in the third-floor sitting room of the Lockwood residence.

Layla Lockwood was a young, natural beauty who was nevertheless doing more than her part to keep thriving the injectable economy.

Layla wore a one-shoulder workout crop top and matching leggings in persimmon. I knew from experience it would only be a matter of weeks before that particular hue trickled down to the hoi polloi and Viv would refuse to go on living unless I bought her something in that exact color.

Layla stood scoldingly over the boys, who were sunk into the bulbous cushions of a wood-trimmed settee. Lucien was forlorn, his face the tragedy mask turned to flesh. Lorenzo stared menacingly at the wall.

"As Lucien slept," Layla said for my benefit, but looking at Lorenzo, "this one took a knife to Lucien's brand-new shoes. And destroyed all the beadwork!"

At the reminder, Lucien tipped sideways and began bawling into the silk ikat.

On the coffee table sat a pair of beaded high-tops, so garish they made me want to avert my eyes. Upon reluctant inspection, indeed, beading was missing.

Lorenzo relocated his scowl to me. "Not all the beads."

Lucien raised his head long enough to wail, "Pharrell's signature!" and tipped back over.

"Where this one got a knife," Layla said, shaking her head, "I'll never know."

"I ordered it from room service," replied her son.

"Gee, I guess all I had to do was ask." Layla turned to me. "Lucien has been a wreck ever since. And who can blame him? These boys have to wear uniforms all day. Shoes are the only way they can express their little personalities. There was a presentation about it at parents night."

"You were supposed to wake me up!" Lorenzo said accusingly.

"Dad did wake you up! To go to the Louvre. That's another thing. And this applies to you, too, Lucien. Lucien. Look at me."

Lucien pushed himself up and looked at his mother with big, sad eyes. Dry eyes, for those keeping track.

"The whole point," she said, "of our trip to Paris was to go to the Louvre. Three days I tried to get them to go. Three days they refused."

"I hate the Louvre," Lorenzo said.

"That is not an option," returned his mother. "You know if it weren't for the Louvre your father would be dead."

Lucien parlayed the morbid sentiment into another anguished collapse.

The elevator dinged. Out popped Hannah, tapping her watch. Layla acknowledged her with a nod.

"Lucky for you," Layla told the boys, making a rainbow with her index finger, "I have aerial arts." She turned to me. "They're all yours."

Layla disappeared into the elevator, leaving me alone with the boys.

Lorenzo gave a look of complete boredom. Lucien, of semi-boredom.

Sulking rudely in their monogrammed sweaters, cerulean ties, moussed hair and emitting the nauseating odor of ruinously expensive body spray . . . I did kind of love them.

"Today is my lucky day," I said. "You gremlins have given me a lot to work with."

Where would I take this? Natural versus unnatural desires? Nonattachment equals freedom? Want what you have? Shop in your closet?

"I already know what you're going to say." Lorenzo came at me in full-on brat.

"Yeah," said Lucien.

"So tell me."

Lorenzo went. "You're going to ask what are the four virtues."

"And what will you say?"

"Wisdom, courage, justice and temperance," Lorenzo sneered.

"Can we go?" asked Lucien.

"Not until we find the real culprit."

“It’s Lorenzo!” Lucien said. “He wrecked my Frontrows.”

“Or,” I said, “there’s another culprit. One that came before.”

“Hee-haw,” Lorenzo said, and delivered his brother a noogie.

“You know what has its fingerprints over all this?” I asked. “Not Lorenzo. Not Lucien.”

Both boys leaned in. I paused for effect.

“Desire.”

They instantly deflated.

“Specifically, desiring externals. What’s an external?”

“Anything you don’t have,” said Lucien by rote.

It was subtler and more complex than that, but I took the win; the kid was eleven.

“Let’s think of some. I’ll go first. Louis Vuitton sneakers. What’s something else you want that you don’t have?”

“Artist passes to Coachella,” offered Lorenzo.

“A Cybertruck,” said Lucien, liking where this was going.

“A Mercedes-Maybach S 680!” Lorenzo added with glee.

“A backstage meet and greet with Kendrick Lamar!” Lucien shouted.

“A day with Sydney Sweeney!” cried Lorenzo ecstatically.

“Okay, okay!” I said. “What you’re displaying here? This is what I call irrational joy. Which might sound good. But actually it’s bad. You know why it’s so bad to get this jacked over wanting things you don’t have?”

“You might not get them?” said Lucien, already on the comedown.

“Yes! And want to hear the real mindblower? Even if you do get them, they’ll still make you unhappy.” I pointed to the shoes. “Look at all the misery those puppies caused.”

“Only because he wrecked them!” Lucien said.

“Let’s say Lorenzo didn’t wreck them,” I countered. “You could step in mud and ruin them. Someone else at school could show up wearing the same exact pair. Pharrell could go on an anti-Semitic rant and the shoes become radioactive. And for certain, you'll grow out of them. How happy are they going to make you then?"

The boys were a different kind of silent. That's what I was going for, the barely perceptible shift.

"Externals," I said. "They make for a highly unstable existence. They put you in a constant state of fear that your happiness will be taken away."

"So you can't want anything?" Lucien asked.

"He who wants nothing is the richest man in the world," I said, paraphrasing Seneca. "The less you want, the happier you'll be."

"Don't you want anything?" Lorenzo asked in a rare display of inquisitiveness.

"Not if I'm doing it right. The only thing I want is good character. Another word for good character?"

"Virtue," said Lucien.

"Available to you anytime, anyplace. You don't have to stand in line for it. Nobody can deface it. Tell me again, what are the virtues?"

"Wisdom," said Lorenzo, counting off, starting with his thumb.

"Being smart about things," I said. "Always an available option. Always makes you feel good."

"Courage," Lucien added.

"Having the strength to do the right thing. It might be hard in the moment, but man, you feel good after."

"Justice," Lorenzo put in.

"Treating other people with respect. No world in which that's a bad thing. What's the last one?"

"Temperance," said Lucien.

"Or self-restraint," I said. "Which you two have displayed magnificently. You're officially excused."

The boys registered shock for about one second, then shot to their feet and sock-skated down the glass ramp.

"Nice try," quipped a voice. "Ten bucks it won't stick."

It was Blanche Falk. I had no idea she'd been listening.

She wore a black T-shirt stretched at the belly and mustard Carhartt pants. Her skin was sun damaged; her hair wild straw. Her breasts, uncaged, pointed down and out. She was the type of woman you never saw in New York, certainly not on the Upper East Side: one who'd stopped trying. Her whole air was a throw-down that said, "Come at me, haters."

Blanche was in poking-around mode, inspecting the garden through the third-floor windows. She spoke half to me, half to details only visible to her.

"What was that?"

"With the boys?" I said. "Tutoring."

"Weird-ass tutoring."

I stood up. Blanche took me in.

"Shall we dance?" She offered her hand. "It's a *King and I* reference."

To her point, my style did lean towards the marmish.

Years back, I'd made the executive decision to waste no brainpower fussing over what to wear each day. So I came up with a uniform: blue, long-sleeved dresses I could put in the wash. Blue to match my eyes. Long sleeves for sun protection. Machine washable because have you seen what they charge for dry cleaning?

Today's dress was from Cos: navy cotton, boat-necked and A-line with a hem that hit above the ankle. Adding to the effect, on my feet were ballet flats.

"Moral training," I explained. "Every day after school, I walk over and attempt to instill values."

"How's it working out?"

"I choose to enjoy the journey."

"I was once walking down the Strip in Vegas," Blanche said. "Outside the Mirage there was a billboard. It read, 'The Mirage Buffet. Imagine it. Eat it.' I thought, that's rich people in a nutshell. Imagine it. Eat it."

She went to a wall of glass and slid it open. "I'm not judging. I'm just saying Lionel and Layla sure know how to kick it to the next level."

Lionel Lockwood was the left-leaning, black-sheep son of right-wing scion Loren Lockwood.

The family name had gotten Lionel into Harvard, where, judging from the photos on the wall, he majored in ultimate frisbee, rock climbing and anything not requiring a shirt. (If you're carved from marble, why not flaunt it?) His gentleman's Cs were no impediment to admission to Harvard Law. After several failed attempts at the bar, Lionel decided to become an "angel investor," which translated into being hit up by anyone with coke and a startup.

At Burning Man, Lionel's camp was legendary for being the biggest—forty-five RVs paid in full and stored in Reno the other 355 days—and the most dialed: illuminated bicycles with vanity plates for each guest, vegan chef, DJ flown in from Ibiza, masseuses galore, art concierge, psilocybin trip-sitter, nightly X-rated burlesque shows and ecstasy-laced apple cider.

Layla Lee-Howard—who'd been camping in a single tent in the outskirts of Black Rock City—heard there was Cereal Milk soft serve at Nepo Camp on the corner of Genuflect and Eighth.

She and Lionel locked eyes across his *Austin Powers*–themed outdoor living room. Lionel knew her from a past life, he was sure of it. (More likely it was from her supporting role on a campy, long-running drama. But who was Layla to correct him?) That was a Wednesday. Saturday they were exchanging vows in the Temple while behind them, the Man burned.

They returned to Lionel's childhood home: five combined townhouses across the street from the Lockwood Library. Nine months later, the twins were born. Lionel and Layla continued to live large, if discreetly. Lionel came from the kind of money where you paid to keep your name out of the paper.

When the twins were five, the family was summering in Aspen. One afternoon, Lionel and his coach went free-climbing up Independence Pass. They'd reached forty feet when, in a true freak occurrence, an aluminum camp chair got caught in a gust of wind and came sailing towards Lionel. He reflexively shielded himself. It was a miracle he survived the fall.

During an all-night, touch-and-go surgery to save his shattered left arm, Lionel suffered several strokes. He emerged with his left arm amputated and right side paralyzed.

Layla, who'd been written off as a featherheaded gold digger, rose up. Her first order of business as the self-appointed CEO of their new life was to get Lionel back home. The townhouses, while taking up a quarter of a city block, were a warren of low ceilings, claustrophobic hallways and narrow staircases. Layla needed to think big.

She'd read about an architect who'd won awards for a research station at the South Pole. In an interview, the architect described herself as having "a soft spot for the logistical nightmare."

Layla called her up. "Have I got a job for you."

The logistical nightmare being that the Landmarks Preservation Commission wouldn't let Layla touch the façades of the townhouses.

The architect solved this by turning the façades into a true façade. She tore down every wall but the ones facing the street. On the now-empty and sizeable lot, she plopped a glass box.

The final product is an astonishingly successful marriage of form and function . . . but you're too gobsmacked by its whimsy and elegance to notice.

The first trick happens when you enter. It feels like there's more natural light inside than outside. It's all glass ramps and elevators, nary a stair to be found.

At one design meeting, Lionel had an attack of phantom limb pain so severe all he could do was scream. The architect watched helplessly as he writhed and howled. This was a common occurrence, one that terrified the already-traumatized boys. Layla expressed consternation that all the king's horses and all the king's men couldn't fix something as simple as phantom limb pain.

The architect lit up. Her husband once worked at Microsoft. In his lab, there'd been a soundproof room where they brought device prototypes to test for buzzing. It had been declared by Guinness World Records as the "quietest place on earth." The architect popped one into the middle of the second floor. It's where Lionel went at the onset of phantom limb pain. The boys called it "Daddy's screaming room."

To me, the best part of the house, the part that made me laugh out loud, was that the façade was four stories, and while the glass house was the same height, it was only three stories. This meant the floors of the glass house didn't line up with the townhouse's. Standing inside and looking out towards the street, you could see through the façade's windows, but they'd hit above your head or below, never at eye level.

The only problem, and it was a big one . . .

When the family moved in, all they could see through the other three sides of glass were the barren, scarred walls of the surrounding buildings.

Enter Blanche, whose work Layla had admired from an Aman resort where she and Lionel honeymooned.

When Blanche arrived, she trudged around the muddy backyard and checked out the light. Her first move was to design and install three enormous metal trellises, one for each neighboring building. Her second move was to "do nothing and see what happens."

Layla pitched a fit. She'd gotten so carried away by visions of helicopters lowering mature trees into her backyard that she'd already contacted the mayor's office for permits.

It's a testament to Blanche's steely will that she went up against Layla and won. The Lockwoods agreed to give it a year.

What a year it was! The backyard began as a desolate eyesore of hoary mud. Still, you could sense a life force at work. When spring arrived, Blanche's trellises exploded to life with multifarious vines, all vying for dominance. With summer's direct sun came a symphony of flowers—lacy jasmine, deep-throated trumpets, spikey passions, weeping wisteria, snowy clematis—and these invited a riot of opportunistic wildlife. By fall, every fairy-tale forest creature in the book—squirrels, raccoons, chipmunks, rabbits, frogs—was calling the walled sanctuary home. The capper was the birdlife. (As of this writing, 193 and counting.) Lionel could go birding without leaving his wheelchair . . . and he didn't need binoculars!

"Parrots swallow hollyberries whole," Blanche said, having observed just that. "Now we know."

"The best show in town."

"The rat wall? It turned out way better than I thought. I can hardly take credit."

"You've provided a lot of joy," I said.

"As any garden should."

"But this one. It makes me feel good about myself. And others."

"I'm going to use that line on my students."

I launched in. "I'm going to go for something big right now—"

The elevator dinged. It was Hannah, pushing her mail cart. In the top basket, the letters she'd screened. In the bottom, a vase of heirloom roses, the kind that actually smell.

"Hello, gals," she said, swapping out a vase of day-old flowers. "My mother taught us never to go up or down the stairs empty-handed."

Blanche looked affronted that she was expected to engage in this conversation. Me, I settled in. It's only bad if you fight it.

"I just heard," Hannah continued as she popped into Layla's office and placed the mail on her desk, "that it was sixty degrees today."

After a fat pause, she turned to me. "I hope your session with Lorenzo and Lucien was productive."

This was Hannah pulling rank and telling me my time in the residence was up. I found it endearing. Blanche, not so much.

I watched her cycle through possible responses for the one most cutting. It took two seconds.

Blanche looked at me and said, "Helpful, isn't she?"

Hannah's eyebrows lifted, breaching her bang line. "Okey dokey." She did a U with the mail cart and exited.

"Am I high right now?" Blanche said. "Did I get hotboxed on the crosstown bus? Sixty degrees? What does that even mean? Is that hot? Is that cold? Do I care?"

"You," I said, in half-admiration, "are on tilt."

"With irrational joy," Blanche said. "Isn't that what you called it? You were going for something big."

"You teach at Columbia," I said, taking a stab off the references to students and the crosstown bus. "So you probably have a place to live."

"Go on."

"I live in the Ansonia—"

"I know the Ansonia," Blanche said, locking in. "I went to school on the Upper West Side. We'd go to the lobby to see the Ziegfeld girls. They'd be lounging in their paste brooches and tatty furs, sitting on the round sofas waiting for Godot."

"They're long gone," I said. "But Flo Ziegfeld's great-grandson, Ziggy, walks my dog."

"Is it still a massive dump?"

A fair question.

The Ansonia, built in 1904, was once the largest and grandest residential hotel in the city, home to Enrico Caruso, Stravinsky, Toscanini, Mahler and Rachmaninoff who prized its thick walls. And Babe Ruth(!). And gangsters galore. The lobby fountains once boasted performing seals. Its heyday was brief, and the building went into steady decline. The basement pools became, in the '60s, home to the Continental Baths, one of New York's first gay bathhouses. (Where Bette Midler got her start with Barry Manilow accompanying on piano.) When too many straight looky-loos started showing up, the Continental Baths moved downtown to be replaced by the notorious '70s swingers' club Plato's Retreat.

Let's say there's history.

"The Ansonia got converted to condos thirty years ago," I told Blanche, "but it's still a quarter rent-stabilized, which is what makes it so great. It's very high-low. Tiny servants' quarters that haven't been touched in a hundred years come on the market for a relative song. Then one day you're walking past a newsstand, and on the cover of *Architectural Digest* you see the ridiculously nice, impossibly chic lady on sixteen who turns out to be a fashion CEO who's combined five apartments. Hallways wider than *The Shining;* thirteen-foot ceilings. No modern amenities; doormen everywhere. You either get it or you don't. To those who don't, we say, 'Boy, bye.'"

Blanche: "I am extremely interested in where this conversation is going."

"An apartment just came up on my floor."

"And you're thinking of buying it?"

"I'm thinking of you buying it."

"Gee!" said Blanche.

"Are you single?"

"I am."

"So am I. Two of my friends, single women, have bought apartments on the same floor. The idea is to grow old in curated company."

"How lesbian are we talking?" Blanche asked.

"Not lesbian at all. It could be, I suppose. But it's never come up. Are you a lesbian?"

God, I hoped Hannah was downstairs eavesdropping.

"After my divorce," Blanche said, "it seemed like a solution. I tried it, so yes. But ultimately, no. Turns out, I like dick. Even though the only way I'll get any at my age is if one falls out of the sky into my vagina. How much socializing is required?"

"None. Minna, Emily Ann and I can go weeks without seeing each other, and often do."

"My kind of friends." Blanche gave me a hard look. "This seems like a big move. Asking me to come live with you."

"True," I said. "And I could make a spreadsheet listing your pros and cons, comparing them to everyone else's pros and cons. But that would be an illusion. I've learned the hard way that when life leaves you for dead, it's always the thing you never saw coming."

"Gee," she said. "What happened to you?"

"Astute of you to ask."

She waited for me to say more. I didn't.

"You're fun," she said. "When did you decide I was the one?"

"This morning. When I saw your badge."

"Spontaneous you! Must be nice."

"It is," I had to admit. "Every morning, I open my eyes and say to the universe, 'Surprise me.'"

"Out loud?"

"It convinces the brain."

"So, literally, if it was someone else's badge, you'd have asked her?"

"No, no, no. Intuition tells me you'd be perfect. We want women like us. Women who present as scary, but have good hearts. Women who know how to get shit done. Women who, despite our age, share a dirty little secret: we're just getting started."

"Blanche Falk," she said, sticking out her hand.

"Adora Hazzard," I said, taking it.

When your mind is popping and all you want to do is think, nothing beats the ballet. And nothing makes you feel more blessed to be a New Yorker than Lincoln Center at 7:25.

With its central fountain gaily splashing, pocked marble sheath ghostily aglow and retro-chic architecture dripping with Sputnik chandeliers that give off light so cozy it never fails to surprise. That night, the philharmonic, opera and ballet were all in residence, making my harried bob-and-weave through the plaza a choreography worthy of Jerome Robbins at his cheekiest.

Adding gas to an already sublime evening? Emily Ann had cancelled on me. I was deliciously alone to unleash my lunatic imagination on its drug of choice: coven logistics!

Here's how it works. There are Fridays at Fairway, as discussed. In addition, Minna, Emily Ann and I have a joint account into which we contribute $650 per month to cover all expenses. These include: Ziggy to walk the dogs; Julio to clean—pro-tip, hire a man because you return home not just to a clean house, but everything is fixed; Minna only needs her assistant Monday through Thursday, so we can request her on Fridays for errands, gratis.

We split subscriptions to the ballet, symphony and theater. A pair of tickets among us, as not all can or want to go to everything. (Bored yet? Too bad!) We sign up on the family plan for streaming services, cell phones and museum memberships. Emily Ann came with a car. We share the cost of a parking space in the Ansonia basement. (An extravagance out of reach for mere mortals, but split three ways? Move over, Gods!) Because we can guarantee three appointments, the hairstylist does our roots at home—at salon prices. I thought it was a bridge too far when Minna insisted on a seamstress once a month. Until the first thing she did was go through my dresses and add pockets. Now? Can't live without.

For the ghoulish eventualities: we'll need to fold in a nurse, physical therapist, cook and someone to hold us by the arm as we take our final shuffles around the block. When Ziggy heard this, he said, "I got you. I'll walk you for free." Love that kid.

Plus, we get to die at home. Plus, we're not a burden to our kids. Plus, no Florida. Plus, compared to nursing homes, it's a huge money saver.

Covens: you can't afford not to!

I entered the packed lobby to blinking lights.

What to do with my extra ticket? I knew from experience that the box office workers shout you down—through their little speakers!—when you try to sell or give away extras. Tonight was a much-ballyhooed program so the standby line was a doozy. The last person in it was safely out of the sight line of the theater staff; I approached.

"Excuse me," I said to a man's back. "If you need a ticket . . ."

He turned.

"This is unbelievable." He looked me up and down in guileless astonishment. Under his camel hair coat he wore a suit and open-collared shirt.

The lights flashed again.

"A Justin Peck premiere to boot." I presented him my extra. "My gift to you."

"What are the odds?" For a man in his fifties, his hair had impressive flow. "What do I owe you?"

"No need."

"This hasn't happened since 1991. Oakland Coliseum, New Year's Eve."

"A Deadhead are we?" I said.

He took the ticket.

"You are not miracling me." He reached for his wallet and searched the ticket for a price. His eyes landed on my name.

"Adora Hazzard?" He looked up. "You're not the . . ."

"Philosopher?"

To the extent people knew me, it was from my three books of Stoic translations. My name is on the cover, but most people only pay glancing attention.

This gentleman—well-off, judging from his Rolex and Italian loafers—looked like my typical reader.

"Right," he said, piecing it together.

"If you're going to go in . . ." came a helpful voice. It was the lady behind the gift counter.

The lobby had drained of life but for the blinking grid of overhead lights. The man and I bounded along the red, velvety carpet.

"Big ballet guy?" I asked.

"My enjoyment of ballet is inversely proportional to how badly I have to pee."

"Aren't you all-woman?"

"Compliment accepted."

I pulled open the door to the auditorium, dark but for the amber glow of the hotly lit curtain. The Voice of God was reminding us to turn off our cell phones. We arrived at our seats.

"Take the aisle," offered my seatmate in a low voice.

"Your legs are longer," I said, slipping past.

The oboe sounded its A, and the rest of the orchestra followed suit.

"I'm paying for this ticket," the man leaned in to whisper. He smelled of fig.

Staring ahead, I smiled wickedly, refusing to engage.

"I always prevail," he said from the side of his mouth.

"No, I do."

A "shh!" from behind.

Naughty energy crackled between us as our eyes remained locked on the curtain.

My program slid off my skirt onto the floor. I bent over to pick it up. As I did, I snuck a glance back. The man's face looked expensively moisturized. I could see through his glasses. The prescription verged on legally blind.

The conductor's baldpate appeared to ringing applause. I jumped at the opportunity to speak and leaned over.

"Buy me a parking-lot burrito." It was a Dead show reference.

Looking straight ahead, the man nodded and smiled in multifaceted approval. Instead of answering, he dropped his eyes to the armrest.

Both my hands were squeezing his cashmere jacket! I had no memory of doing it; it was as if my arms were detached from my body. Mortified, I quickly released my grip.

The curtain rose to a scrim lit so beautifully purple it was worth the price of admission. A pair of dancers took the stage, a bare-chested man in flesh-colored tights and his partner in diaphanous nude chiffon whose crystals shot colored light. They appeared more naked than if they'd been unclothed.

A cello played. Bach. One of the Cello Suites. I knew it from Yo-Yo Ma, and was grateful for the grounding effect of the familiar.

I settled down and settled in.

The male dancer stood statue-still, offering his hand. The ballerina, pretending not to notice, teased him with a solo that was delicate, fanciful, precise.

Heat rose within me.

The ballerina finally took notice of the male dancer. She stepped tentatively towards him. One, two, three, and paused. She reached for his hand. He tenderly took it.

They began a pas de deux, their bodies flowing in and out of each other. It was sensuous. Too sensuous. I'd somehow forgotten the mechanics of breathing.

I took small, shallow sips so as not to draw attention, but my heart had gotten loose in my chest. I pulled in one huge breath.

I felt the man's sideways stare. I gave him nothing. He turned his head and waited for me to do the same.

I dropped my chin and looked at my lap.

One of my hands was palm-down on my program. The other, the hand closer to him, rested palm-up, fingers curled . . . as if asking to be held.

Desire in the form of my hand.

Did the man see this, too? Is this why he was still looking at me? What would he do? Take my hand in the ballet? This handsome stranger I'd just met?

He returned his attention to the stage.

The male dancer was now dragging the ballerina across the floor. She was folded in on herself, like a wounded fawn.

I went to dig my fingers into my leg—but the one hand was stuck to the program. The sweat on my palm was like superglue. I attempted to pull it free—

Riiiip!

The sound of tearing paper shot through the auditorium. At the exact moment of a pianissimo. A dozen heads swiveled.

"Excuse me," I whispered to the man and climbed over.

I hurried up the dark aisle and burst into the dead calm of the lobby. The only sign of life was a pair of ushers watching the Knicks on the bar TV.

I stood there trying to process what the hell had just happened.

I'd lost my center, that's all.

I labeled it, "Nervous reaction to a stressful day."

Between the news of an apartment becoming available, the bombing of the Rosetta stone and asking Blanche to join the coven, I'd arrived at the ballet depleted and off my game.

Nothing more, nothing less. My only available option was to put it behind me and do better tomorrow.

I sighed and headed for the exit.

In the glass, a school matron fresh off the schooner in 1950s Siam.

Blanche had me pegged. Even my hair was in a bun!

Beyond my reflection, in the plaza: a familiar figure on the fountain, leaning back on his elbows, legs splayed.

Ziggy! On his free nights he comes down and tries to score a ticket from someone leaving at intermission. I should have thought of him as soon as Emily Ann cancelled. This whole debacle could have been prevented.

A puff of Bach. Behind my reflection, the approaching man.

I pushed open the door and raced into Ziggy's eye line. His face opened sweetly.

I let my ticket do the talking, pushing it into his hand.

"Whoa?" he said. "Really?"

"Adora!" came a voice through the thunder of the fountain.

I skittered across the plaza and stole into the shadows of the symphony portico. I rode it around the corner to the lesser-known side steps leading to Sixty-Fifth Street.

On Broadway, I mixed in with a human mass crowded around a halal truck. Only then did I dare turn. The man was gone.

I headed uptown doing the math in my head: with Blanche joining the coven, we'd need Julio one more day, but could offset the cost by dividing the parking spot by four instead of three. . . .

Up ahead, where Broadway takes a gentle curve, the Ansonia loomed above its puny brethren. Solid, ornate as a wedding cake, and turreted to boot.

—PART TWO—

SURPRISE ME

The next day I was in my office on the second floor of the Lockwood Library, buried in the lecture I'd be giving in Paris the following week, "The Blight of Hope: the Stoics, Nietzsche and a New Inner Freedom." I was in the process of working in a favorite quote . . .

Hecato: *Cease to hope, and you will cease to fear.*

Which is to say, I was wide and well, and who knows how long pebbles had been pinging my window before I finally noticed.

Below, in the garden, Blanche.

She waved for me to come down. Lionel was with her, in the process of transferring, with nurse Sylvia's help, from his wheelchair to a standing frame. (The padded contraption allowed Lionel to stand upright, vital to maintaining bone density and muscle strength.) Lionel beckoned me to join with a rear of the head and mischievous glint.

This was a radically different Lionel than the one I'd first met.

I'd just moved to the city when I received a mysterious call summoning me to the Lockwood Library for a job interview. That I'd never applied for a job was irrelevant to the person on the other end. As a firm believer in the benevolent universe, I showed up.

Layla greeted me. At first, I thought she was on her way to a photo-shoot or awards luncheon. I later learned we simply had vastly different concepts of "daytime casual." That day, she donned a wooly pink Chanel suit (vintage, handed down by Lionel's mother) adorned with so many gold-chained accessories she could have been a pickpocket hawking his plunder.

From Layla, I learned of Lionel's accident and current depression. A recent suicide attempt was hinted at.

I still didn't understand what I was doing there.

"You wrote a book," Layla said. "On happiness."

"Epictetus did. I translated it."

"Something in your introduction. It was the first time since the accident I saw a light in my husband's eyes."

"What part, do you know?"

"I asked," she said. "But he put the book down and refused to pick it up again."

"So, the job . . . ?"

"Is to sit with him for an hour."

Layla handed me an envelope. In it, hundred-dollar bills. I got the sense they'd come from a large stack, and she'd stuck her fingernail into a random spot. (Indeed, when I got home, I counted seventeen.)

"All you need to know about me," Layla said, "is that I will stop at nothing to make my husband happy."

I chuckled, assuming it was an arch line from the villain she once played in her prime-time soap.

Her cold stare corrected me.

"Noted," I said.

We exited the Lockwood Library, security discreetly trailing, and headed for the family residence across the street. As we waited for the light to change at Seventy-Sixth, Layla searched for small talk.

"So," she smilingly asked, "do you consider yourself part of a religion?"

"Technically," I explained, "Stoics are pantheists. We reject the existence of a personal God but believe God exists in all things, which isn't to say—"

Layla hadn't heard a word. She was too busy giving me the up-and-down. That day: ankle-length navy dress and black tights. I was covering so much skin Layla had pegged me as a member of a sect!

"No," I said. "I just dress this way."

I had to smile: excellence withers without an adversary. And adversaries come in all shapes, sizes and interpretations of day-to-night.

In the row of mismatched townhouses was a wooden door, giant enough for a robber baron's carriage to pass through. Layla swiped her wrist across an indiscernible scanner and gave the hunk of ancient wood the gentlest push. It glided open, as if on magic hinges.

We stepped through, tinily. It was hard not to feel like I was entering *Alice in Wonderland*. . . .

Which morphed into *Silence of the Lambs* when I beheld the glass box surrounded by mud and foreboding concrete walls. (This was just after the house had been completed, during Blanche's "do nothing and see what happens" era.) The newly installed, fifty-foot steel trellises on three sides made me feel like a penned-in Lilliputian.

"I thought this place would help Lionel snap out of it," Layla mused. "But it just seemed to make him worse."

As basic communication had proven not to be our jam, I rode out the awkward silence.

We took a glass elevator to the top floor. Layla led me to a bedroom where Lionel lay, his half of a mechanical bed in the upright position.

Lionel was preposterously handsome. He wore crisp, monogrammed pajamas in sunflower yellow. His left sleeve had been hemmed and folded below the shoulder like origami. The sheets were so starched they looked as if they'd been ironed with him in them.

A uniformed nurse stood at attention. I'd come to know her as Sylvia.

The air was thick with the buttery scent of lilies. Stacked on a nearby table, books by self-help all-stars: Dan Harris, Gretchen Rubin, Pema Chödrön. On top, my version of Epictetus. The walls were hung with photos of Lionel and the family. Lionel's left arm had once boasted a Māori sleeve tattoo.

The room looked like a parking-lot sale of medical equipment. Two wheelchairs. A Hoyer lift. Body slings draped over furniture. Pill cases. Tinctures and creams by the dozen. An incubator to warm socks. Everything money could buy.

Including me.

Next to Lionel's bed awaited an empty chair. It was an antique, with carved wooden arms, upholstered in trendy, urban-themed toile.

"Look who's here!" Layla sang.

There was no eye contact to be had from Lionel. Not with his wife, not with his nurse, certainly not with me.

"Adora Hazzard!" Layla said. "The one who wrote that book you like."

I'd been sprung on Lionel! I was angry and embarrassed. I recognized my impulse to blame and explain. I did neither.

Silence, but for a mechanical, rhythmic hum. On Lionel's legs were braces with paddles on the bottoms that stretched his feet from a right angle, towards his knees, and back again. Over and over.

"For his Achilles tendons," Layla explained, following my gaze. "So they don't tighten. He'll need them when he starts walking!"

She gave him a lively shake. I caught myself wincing.

Lionel pushed a button. The bed went flat, his gaze to the chandelier.

"Hi, Lionel," I said.

He flashed me a look of defiance.

I recognized the silent rage. The black anvil of depression. The inexhaustible self-pity. The mouth, grotesquely pinched from the violent and punishing thoughts ceaselessly circling, his only source of comfort.

It wasn't that Lionel couldn't bounce back. He didn't want to bounce back. To bounce back would be to forgive a world that had treated him so unfairly.

I, myself, had ended up there once. But unlike Lionel, I wasn't surrounded by family and support staff.

I'd been alone, friendless, in a West Hollywood apartment. In case there was any doubt about who was to blame, I'd Sharpied "TJ STEELE" on my thigh, laid out my wrist and cut deep.

The thing about having once crossed that line? Even if you don't succeed, you know it's always available. Even if you do bounce back, you find yourself checking your hip pocket to see if it's still there. It always is. Your little friend.

I looked down at handsome, wrecked Lionel. I was afraid for him. I was afraid for his boys. I was afraid for myself. I had a child now. I couldn't allow myself to get sucked into his self-poisoning vortex.

I stepped closer.

"Your wife told me what happened."

Another nurse entered carrying a tray. On it, exquisitely marbled steak cut into pieces and covered in creamy sauce. I smelled tarragon.

"I'll take that." Layla placed it on the side table and turned to me. "Last week we got diagnosed with exocrine pancreatic insufficiency. Lionel has to eat an all-protein diet. The hits just keep coming."

She stuck a fork in a piece of meat. "Hungry, babe?"

Lionel sucked his lips. Layla put the fork down and turned to me.

"Time to work your magic."

"I don't believe in magic," I said. "I believe in what works."

I sat in the empty chair. It hit my lower back right where you dream a chair might hit. Damn.

Lionel had responded to something I'd written in my Epictetus introduction. I proceeded slowly, hoping to tap a receptive vein.

"Things happened to you," I began. "As things do. But events are neutral. To the extent they make you suffer, that's on you."

"Puh-leeze," interjected Layla. "If anyone's to blame, it's the idiot with the camp chair. Fear not, we're suing him into oblivion."

I turned to her. "It's a stance grounded in ignorance."

A dismayed Layla turned to the nurse. Sylvia had clearly seen it all and was keeping her opinions to herself.

"Small-minded people blame others," I said to Lionel. "Average people blame themselves. The wise blame nobody."

"Don't worry, be happy?" Layla said. "Really? That's what you're selling."

"I'm talking to Lionel," I said, without looking back, and continued. "Acceptance isn't passive. It's active. Acceptance is an act of courage. It's not the end. It's the beginning."

Lionel started to speak but had cobwebs in his throat. He coughed them out.

"Look at me," he said.

"You fell. You messed up your body. Surgery caused a stroke. That's the past. It's over. But it's like you've woken up from a nightmare and are actively choosing to go back to sleep so you can keep living it. Who does that?"

Lionel coughed again and raised his bed. Sylvia rushed in with a cup and straw. Lionel hastily drank from it and turned his attention to me. We were eye to eye.

"I still am," he said. "Living the nightmare."

"You won't be climbing monkey bars anytime soon. But man, I look around. Think about all you still can do. Seneca has this quote that's totally clunky. I've tried to reword it but for the life of me I can't figure out a way—"

I was all over the place. Which is what happens when I get started on Stoicism. Fueled by enthusiasm, I talk faster and faster, bouncing between subjects, repeating myself. It's like running downhill. At some point, momentum takes over and stopping is impossible. All I can do is keep going and pray I've got a shred of dignity left when I reach the bottom.

"Seneca says, 'There's nothing you can be barred from that's so big it doesn't leave available something even bigger you can't be barred from.' Basically—"

"I get it," Lionel said.

There it was: my barely perceptible shift.

"That's what's so rad about acceptance," I said. "Once you truly accept all the shit that happened to you, you can get to work on everything that still is available. But even acceptance isn't enough. You have to love it. Nietzsche said, *Amor fati*. Love fate. You have to love what happened to you. I actually got that tattooed. When it truly clicks, no matter what the universe throws at you, you're like, Please, sir, I want some more. I'm not talking Wagyu beef and bearnaise, I'm talking the grand parade, the whole catastrophe, I'm talking life. You're like, Bring it on, motherfuckers. What else ya got?"

"Let's see it," Lionel said. "Your tattoo."

It was a level of intimacy I hadn't been expecting. I turned to Layla.

She'd taken so many horrified steps back she was practically plastered to the wall. Sylvia stood in a defensive crouch. (I later learned that every member of the household staff, Layla had stolen from the Mossad. Even the chef.)

I presented Lionel my left arm and turned it so my wrist was exposed. In a white tattoo, *AMOR FATI* neatly written over what (someone looking for it) could identify as a faint vertical slash.

Lionel took my wrist. There was a tenderness to his touch that made me miss a breath.

His eyes plumbed mine. "Did you . . . ?"

I didn't answer, preferring to savor the not unpleasant strangeness of the moment.

Lionel tightened his grip. He recognized a kindred soul.

I felt wide and well.

"I tried," I said, and gave him an impish shrug. "But what are you going to do?"

He broke into laughter. Something had begun. We both knew it.

Lionel: "I don't mean to laugh."

Me: "He said through laughter."

Lionel wove his fingers into mine.

I finally noticed Layla and Sylvia. They were holding hands, too. Layla's cheeks were streaked with tears.

"Let's hang out," I told Lionel.

The next day, Layla offered me a fellowship. When negotiating my salary, Layla asked me who she was stealing me from. (This was before I fully understood how much she liked to steal things.) When I told her nobody, she couldn't hide her disappointment. No doubt I left a small fortune on the table.

And so Lionel and I began our "bible study." Those first February days looking out on the mud, cinder block and steel were a challenge, Lionel truculent and defeatist. But I kept to the beat; each morning I brought in a new reading for discussion. As the days grew longer, so did our sessions. Soon, Lionel and I were letting our minds unfurl. There was no lesson plan. We chased our enthusiasms, tried on perspectives. One day it was a Montaigne essay. The next, John Locke. The day after, Richard Pryor videos.

We delighted in Rousseau, gerrymandered Nietzsche, dreamed of running off with the existentialists, bemoaned the unreadability of Kant yet plowed through regardless, aspired to Hume's conviviality, developed a parasocial relationship with Saint Augustine. But we'd always return to Stoicism and the big three: Marcus Aurelius, Seneca and Epictetus.

Meanwhile, the seeds that had traveled on the wind to the wintry garden floor of 6-20 East Seventy-Sixth Street were silently taking root. In the spring, they peeked to life and began fulfilling, with a terrifying single-mindedness, their destinies. On all sides, the trellis exploded with green, none of the shoots native, all determined to thrive.

Flowers uniquely bear fruit; birds uniquely build nests; humans uniquely reason.

With my guidance, Lionel used that reason to choose the contents of his character.

Over the next five years, Lionel worked out every day and regained 55 percent mobility in his right side. He defied his family and became a leading Democratic donor. This made Lionel Lockwood a favorite obsession of Fox News. Every morning, he wheeled up Fifth Avenue with the boys to drop them off at school, bodyguards in tow. Lionel always unfazed by the self-described "patriots" who'd periodically approach "just asking questions."

One day, a couple of years ago, it dawned on Lionel that the phantom limb pain had completely subsided. Much ado was made of turning the soundproof "screaming room" into a recording studio for the boys. They'd just discovered Daft Punk.

The family took a trip to Paris, their first time traveling since the accident. Layla arranged for the Louvre to open an hour early just for them.

While alone with the Venus de Milo, Lionel became overwhelmed by her limbless majesty. She was beautiful in her mutilation. So was he.

Lionel wept, his first tears since the accident. It was proof to Layla that his suffering was in the past. Layla's one job now was to keep it there.

When they returned to New York, Layla claimed Lionel had been cured at the Louvre. It was a bit of mythmaking on her part. I went along. Who would it hurt to let Layla believe the Venus de Milo had saved her husband's life? Lionel and I both knew the truth: philosophy had saved Lionel's life. With a major assist from Blanche's metaphor-generating rat wall.

I waved to Lionel and Blanche that I'd be right down.

In the back of the Lockwood Library, a grand staircase poured into a "parterre," a geometric vision of sculpted hedges, burbling fountains, arabesque gravel paths and classical marble statues.

While Blanche had turned the residence garden over to God's will, the parterre represented self-will. It bloomed with forced bulbs, espaliered trees and flats of color flown in from South America. Every Monday, when the Library was closed to the public, a battalion of gardeners moved in. Armed with architectural plans and measuring tape, they fanned into formation, dropped, and switched out the annuals. (Red, white and blue for the Fourth of July. Pastels for Easter. Halloween, forget about it.) The efficiency and finished product never failed to impress. But ultimately, it felt airless and safe. Me, I'm a God's-will girl.

Lionel was now upright in his standing frame, balancing on both feet. I joined him and Blanche on an expanse of unnaturally green grass. Beyond the high walls—diamond-latticed with ivy, natch—the city clamored. Sirens, squealing schoolchildren and ranchera music blasting from the resident taco truck.

"Here she is!" Lionel called as I approached. "I hear you're pulling a Thomas More without me. Your very own Utopia?"

"Don't be mad," Blanche said. She was in a standard-issue gardening hat and yesterday's black T-shirt. I recognized an identical bleach stain. "I told him about the man-haters on seven."

"I'm no man-hater!" I said, and looked around for witnesses.

Sylvia, in uniform, had moved Lionel's wheelchair out of the immediate vicinity. She stood behind it and pretended to be out of earshot.

"Where's my invitation?" Lionel asked. "Get lost in the mail?"

"You wouldn't want to join—"

Lionel fired back, "Why do you say that?"

"Because your concerns aren't the same as our concerns."

"Is that an assumption or a fact?" Lionel said, bobbing his weight from foot to foot.

"It's a solution to a problem that will never concern you."

"And what problem is that?"

"Women who divorce in their fifties have an eighty-five percent chance of dying single. While half of men get remarried within two years."

"What makes you think I won't die single?" Lionel said. "Where's your evidence?"

I finally got it. He was pulling the Socratic method on me.

"I'm putting you in a time-out."

"How long have y'all been outside?" rang a voice.

It was Layla, stepping out of the "gloriette," a large-scale, wrought-iron birdcage entwined in pink roses.

It had been modeled after one belonging to Marie Antoinette, as a wedding gift from Lionel's grandfather to his child bride. The gloriette concealed an elevator, which lowered to a tunnel under Seventy-Sixth Street and connected the Lockwood Library to the residence.

Layla wore a blousy, silk shirt with a pussy bow and . . . underpants. Yes, they were high-waisted. Yes, they were leather. Yes, they were buckled with a gold H. But they were underpants.

Ravi followed, presenting himself elegantly, as usual.

Layla had stolen Ravi from the Met. Unlike me, Ravi had proven to be hilariously recalcitrant. When referring to the extensive holdings of the Lockwood collection, he used the first-person singular. When it came to taste, his was binary. All things were either "tacky" or "kind of great." The distance he maintained from Layla as they approached indicated how he classified today's costume.

"Aww, baby," Layla said to Lionel. "You're getting pink." She dispatched Sylvia to the residence to fetch a hat and sunscreen.

"In the meantime," Layla said, turning to Blanche, "let's give Lionel yours."

Lionel blushed. "Really not necessary."

"Just until Sylvia returns." Layla lifted Blanche's hat off her head and placed it on her husband's.

Blanche: "You're welcome."

Lionel quickly switched subjects. "Adora was telling us about her project of colonizing a floor of the Ansonia so it's only her and other women."

Layla ran her eyes down my front. Another blue dress. This one with a shirt collar buttoned on the high side and sleeves rolled down because of the sun. Layla's eyes lingered on my hem. The dress had shrunk in the wash, rendering it too short for comfort. Instead of giving it away, I'd had the seamstress add six inches of blue denim.

"I'm not surprised," said Layla.

I flushed with embarrassment.

After five years, she still got to me. Layla Lockwood! Of all people! Just last week, she was shocked to learn Albany is the capital of New York.

"I'll show you where I want to put it," she said to Ravi, continuing their previous conversation. "Blanche, come, too. I want you to see."

They headed to the garden's epicenter. There, on a plinth, stood a statue of Fortuna, goddess of fortune.

Blindfolded, in one hand she held a ship's rudder. In the other, a cornucopia. Eight paths radiated out from the statue, instilling in her extra gravitas.

"Come here," said Lionel, after the others had moved away. "I need to apologize."

I stepped close. He weakly raised his right arm. I placed it across my shoulders.

"You're fine," I said.

"Teasing is the lowest form of speech. It's not the person I want to be."

He pulled me in.

That's what made my tears rise. Never the cruelty; only the kindness.

I leaned into Lionel, knowing his balance was tenuous. He leaned into me. We stood there pushing into each other, rassling, like brother and sister.

"Cut it out, you two!" scolded Layla. She, Ravi and Blanche were headed back. "It scares me when you do that."

"Sorry!" said Lionel.

Ravi had returned in some kind of huff. I snuck Blanche a quizzical look. She raised her eyebrows, confirming drama.

"Tell Ravi," Layla was saying to Lionel.

"Happy to tell Ravi," Lionel said. "What am I telling Ravi?"

"About the statue we bought in Paris," Layla said. "Boy With Apple."

"Boy With Apple!" Ravi threw up his hands, as if merely hearing the words was a debasement from which he might never recover.

"I haven't set eyes on it," Lionel said.

"I will certainly not put my Cavallini in storage for some tacky thing this woman bought off the street."

"This woman?!" said a galled Layla. "And who's saying it's tacky?"

"Boy With Apple?" Ravi said. "It sounds like a Hummel figure."

"Hardly!" said Layla. "It's dated 300 BC and from the school of Alexander of Antioch."

"Please!" cried Ravi. "Tell me another! According to whom?"

"The seller," Layla said.

Lionel jumped in. "How's this for a compromise? We keep Fortuna where she is. And design a new plinth for Boy With Apple."

He turned to Blanche.

"I'll design a plinth," she said with admirable indifference.

Ravi wasn't so easily placated. "Who's your mysterious seller?" he demanded of Layla. "You're not just taking their word for this balderdash?"

Layla took a dramatic pause and played her ace.

"Celine Montfort." For the benefit of Blanche and myself, Layla added, "She's from one of the oldest families in France. We met her in Paris. She's on the board of the Louvre."

Layla cocked her head for the win.

"Celine Montfort?" Ravi cried. "But why—"

WOOP-WOOP.

An alarm sounded. Not a police or ambulance siren. Something closer. It was difficult to discern which side of the wall it was coming from.

WOOP-WOOP.

We hung in silence, scanning one another's faces for clues.

"That's a test," Layla said with a wave. "Because of the Rosetta stone. Security is making us run through all the protocols."

WOOP-WOOP.

I located the source of the alarm: a nearby speaker disguised as a rock.

We all shrugged. Ravi picked right up.

"Why on earth would Celine Montfort be selling her family's priceless statuary?"

"Ask her yourself," Layla answered. "She's arriving tomorrow. With your new statue. I'm having a dinner party for her." She pointed to Blanche. "You're invited."

WOOP-WOOP.

"This is so annoying!" Layla said with a stomp of her platform heel. "We're in the middle of a meeting!"

Lionel, gently: "They probably don't know we're out here."

"Uh," said Layla, "I believe we're paying them to know we're out here."

WOOP-WOOP.

"The fuck?" Layla said, and took off towards the Library. No doubt, to start handing out one-way tickets back to Israel.

"How about we make sure it is a test?" Lionel said, looking mighty uneasy, exposed as he was in his frame. "I'm a bit of a standing duck here."

"*Code Red,*" came an automated voice. "*Code Red. Clear the area.*" Its calm tenor blended beautifully with our arcadian surroundings—to terrifying effect.

"Can we maybe find Sylvia?" asked Lionel. Poor guy, I'd never seen him so scared and helpless.

"I'll get you out of here," I said, forcing steadiness into my voice.

I draped Lionel's right arm over my shoulders. His fingers gripped me like talons.

"One, two—"

I dragged him out of his standing frame—

—and my knees buckled under his dead weight.

Lionel's hat flipped sideways, its stiff brim getting lodged between my face and his.

CRASH! Behind me, the standing frame toppled to the ground.

"I need help!" I yelled into the stupid hat, still able to hold Lionel upright, but I didn't know for how much longer.

"Someone! Help!"

Blanche and Ravi were at Lionel's wheelchair, struggling to push it—but it was Bentley-heavy, and could only be operated by Lionel's fingerprint.

"It's locked!" I yelled over the sirens. "Here, please!"

Blanche and Ravi rushed over.

"The elevator," I said.

In a flash, Blanche took Lionel's other side; Ravi lifted his legs into a seated position. We pointed our human sedan chair towards the elevator and ran—

—but made it three steps before tripping on a border and stumbling, me, Blanche, Ravi and a twisted, trembling Lionel.

Just then, Sylvia ambled out of the gloriette carrying a Tilley hat and La Mer sunscreen.

WOOP-WOOP.

"Code Red. Clear the area."

Sylvia dropped everything. In lightning speed, she hurdled over hedges, pitched Lionel over her shoulder like a duffel bag and ran him into the gloriette. The elevator doors closed behind them.

Lionel was safe.

I stood on the lawn, hands on knees, adrenaline still rampaging through my body.

"This, too, we get to experience," I huffed to Ravi and Blanche.

Ravi shook his head.

"Too soon," Blanche wheezed back.

WOOP-WOOP.

"Aaaah!" Through the sirens came a gut-piercing scream.

We swung to look.

It was Layla, near the top of the grand staircase, staring saucer-eyed at her phone. "Oh my God, oh my God."

She pivoted and wobbled back down as fast as her platform heels would take her. Halfway, she grabbed the cement rail with both hands and vaulted over—landing in the privet below. All we could see were the red soles of her kicking feet.

"What an odd thing to do," Ravi remarked, fingers stuck in ears.

"Guys?" said Blanche. "Did you just get a text?"

Ravi and I checked.

> Active threat: suspicious package found in lobby. Controlled detonation planned. Evacuate and avoid the parterre. Stay away from windows and doors. Do not go outside.

By the time I looked up—jaw dropped and mouth dry as a cave—black-clad security guards were cascading down the stairs, some holding shields, another barely able to control a German shepherd. Their practiced urgency confirmed this was no drill. Behind them, the windows of the Lockwood Library ominously darkened as the blackout shades lowered in lockdown protocol.

Barak, the head of security, was running right at us. "Go, go, go!" he barked, chopping his forearm.

"Really?" I was just standing there. (In my defense, it was all too weird!)

"Go, go!" Barak shouted, one hand on an earpiece. "Behind Goldy!"

In the southeast corner of the parterre loomed a bronze Rodin. Reaching it required navigating a maze with high hedge walls.

Blanche and Ravi chose the more direct route—through a garden room fashioned from precision-cut boxwoods, three feet in height. In the center, a reflection pool.

Blanche heaved one leg over the hedge, but the other one got tangled in the branches. "Stupid hunk of junk," she muttered as she used both hands to yank it out but lost her balance and toppled into the shallow pool.

The last thing I saw before I entered the maze was Ravi clambering over Blanche and running into the water, custom Jermyn Street shoes be damned.

Inside the maze it was ten degrees cooler, which served as a chilled washcloth for my jangled nerves. I took purposeful and measured strides along the path, one breath per step, my senses zinging to new heights of perception as my whole being dropped into new depths of calm.

Through the high leafy walls came considerable splashing, grunting and Blanche: "Hey, jerk!"

An image popped to mind, of a mixed bouquet being offered from on high; we could choose one stem. Ravi and Blanche had chosen "unbridled panic." I'd gone for "might as well enjoy."

I emerged to find Ravi (wet and trembling) and Blanche (wet and cursing) crouched behind the Rodin's craggy stone base. Barak, in runner's stance, motioned for me to hurry. I slid into the huddle.

Barak spoke into his lapel: "All persons accounted for and in safe positions."

"Are we?" asked a dubious Blanche.

In the distance, a voice called, “Fire in the hole in ten, nine . . .”

Ravi, eyes closed, turned a pinkie ring of 24 karat gold and rubies—one I’d never noticed before—while incanting a prayer to Shiva.

“It’s okay,” I said. “We’ll be okay.”

“. . . three, two, one! Fire in the hole! Fire in the hole! Fire in the hole!”

Then came the explosion.

More like a pop.

A momentary limbo as Ravi, Blanche and I scanned our individual realities and deemed ourselves alive, with limbs and senses intact.

The alarms and automated voice sputtered to a stop.

“All clear,” Barak informed us, and sprinted towards a cloud of smoke already dispersing in the breeze.

Ravi stood and gravely addressed Blanche. “Apologies for any lack of chivalry. But you must understand, I cannot die.” He carried himself off with a squish in each step.

“And I can?” Blanche said, dumping water from a clog. “What a little bitch.”

My phone, still in hand, vibrated.

> All clear: suspicious package has been safely detonated.
> No threat found. Normal operations can resume. Thank you
> for your cooperation.

Blanche and I crossed the parterre to where Ravi, Barak and security guards were gathered.

On a patch of scorched grass lay the blackened pieces of an aluminum briefcase.

“What just happened?!” Layla shrieked from afar. She’d freed herself from the hedge. Her pussy bow had come untied and was trailing behind.

She charged Barak, and looked like she was about to physically attack, when suddenly she got clotheslined by her pussy bow—the end had gotten caught on a rosebush.

"Agh," came a gurgling sound. Undeterred, Layla freed it with a yank and got in Barak's face.

"Will someone please tell me what just happened?"

"A suspicious package was found in the lobby," said Barak. "There was no note. X-ray indicated a metallic foreign body. Thermal imaging detected a heat signature. So we conducted a controlled explosion with low-order detonation."

"Where we were standing?!" she shrieked.

"It was in strict adherence to Render Safe Protocol," Barak mumbled. He could already taste the fresh orange juice from his mother's tree in the kibbutz.

"That's a wow," Layla said.

The German shepherd, meanwhile, was joyously licking the inside of the briefcase.

Which seemed odd.

On the gravel, something caught my eye.

It was shiny and white, and looked like—it was—

The heel of a burrito. Wrapped in foil. Filled with rice, beans and cheese.

A wave of realization almost knocked me off my feet. "Oh God."

"Guys!" Hannah called flatly as she made her way down the stairs. "My bad. There was a note. I just didn't see it."

As she approached our cluster, she held out an envelope. Please don't let it be for me. Please let it be for me. Please don't let it be for me. Please let it be for me.

On the envelope, in grandmotherly cursive, "*Adora.*"

Stunned eyes fixed on me as I opened it.

Inside was a thick, creamy card that smelled of fig. "DAVID IGNATIUS BEALE" was engraved at the top. Underneath, in cursive, "*I'm on the bench across Fifth.*"

"Who's sending you a briefcase?" asked Layla, her voice dripping with disdain.

I looked her straight in the eye.

"A man I met last night. At the ballet."

I reached into my pocket for a pen, struck out his message and wrote, "*Salumeria Rosi, 7pm tonight.*"

"The gentleman on the bench across the street," I instructed Hannah. "See that he gets this."

Meanwhile, joyous whoops from Blanche and Ravi.

"Thinking it's a bomb," Blanche said, "but it's really a burrito."

"And blowing it up!" Ravi added. "What is this? Italy?"

I joined in the laughter—how could I not? A handsome stranger had just tracked me down and asked me on a date.

How can I look less old? I have one hour.

This I texted to the coven as I raced across the park.

I returned home to find a bag hanging on my door. In it, spiky heels, black schmatta with a Prada label, pink razor, Korean firming mask, space-aged hair dryer, stick of blush in "orgasm" and a dye kit . . . for pubic hair.

"*Report back*," said the note in Minna's scrawl.

Face firmed, legs shaved and cheeks orgasmed, I put on the dress but couldn't reach the zipper. I was in the middle of drying my hair when Viv stepped into the mirror.

"No fair. You got a Dyson?"

"It's Minna's. And can you please with the tone? Remember, I'm taking you to Paris."

"Where are we even staying?"

"Seriously, you little brat?"

"Tessy is asking," she said. "When she looked up the address, all that came up was a falafel shop."

"You have your answer. Tell Tessy we're going to Paris and staying at a falafel shop."

"Rude."

"You can use this when I'm done," I told her.

Viv ran off with a squeal.

In my bedroom, Mr. Man was in my chair, curled up on a pair of dirty underwear that had overshot the hamper. He wasn't allowed on the furniture and he knew it. At getting caught, he looked afraid and ashamed. And really, is there anything cuter?

"Oh, Mr. Man! Do you consent to a kiss?"

"Where are you even going?" asked Viv in morbid fascination. How long she'd been watching, I didn't know.

"Dinner with a friend. Here, zip me up."

I turned my back to Viv. The dress, which had seemed basic, black and nothing much, transformed as it tightened around my hips, curved into my waist and finally closed in on my boobs. That last stretch required some muscle on Viv's part and produced quite the décolletage.

Viv beheld me in the mirror.

"Whoa, Mom," she said. "Body is bodying."

I headed out, passing Dante, the doorman on duty.

Once, after I'd learned the term "rizz," and was with Viv, I referred to a baby on the subway as having it. Viv almost fell over. "Mom! Babies can't have rizz." I asked if Mr. Man had it. "No," she said. "You're sick." A respite as Viv silently cycled through cute guys who had rizz. Then: "You know who does have it? Dante."

Dante wasn't the most classically handsome guy, and his hair was thinning, but he had an Italian accent, crooked nose and scarred eyebrow. His legend had reached as far as the private schools of the Upper East Side for having once shouted down an Uber driver who'd chased one of our teenage residents inside after the kid vomited in his Prius. Dante paid the $300 vomit fee himself and arranged for the boy to reimburse him on the down-low so his parents wouldn't find out.

As usual, Dante was deep in conversation with a married woman who'd stopped to linger. She was brazenly going nowhere, her elbows firmly on the counter, one heel kicked up.

"Yeah, she is," Dante catcalled as I passed.

Before I entered the restaurant, I stopped and took a moment.

He might not be here.

He might be gay.

He might be married.

He might ask me for money.

He might chew with his mouth open.

It's a thing Stoics do: meditate on worst-case scenarios. Which is not about working yourself into a neurotic doom loop. It's about preparing for things not to go your way. So when they inevitably don't, you can say, "I expected that."

Think of it as inoculation against emotional extremes. Because who needs those?

Thusly fortified, I entered Salumeria Rosi.

I hadn't realized the extent to which I'd built up David Ignatius Beale in my mind until I saw him standing at the corner booth.

He was even better than I'd imagined.

Lavender cashmere over white button-down. Great skin. Full lips.

"Adora." His deep voice speaking my name: it was already kind of over.

"First things first—" I said.

"You look lovely."

"What do you go by?"

"Friends call me Digby."

Digby. It was definitely over. What a great name.

Both waitress and waiter took a keen interest as I slid into the booth. Not the food-service kind of interest. The kind of interest that suggests gossip is brewing. I was a regular; never once had I entered in heels, little black dress and come-hither hair.

The waitress approached.

"Hi!" she chirped, pouring water from a glass bottle. "Can I start you off with a drink?"

"I'm not sure," Digby told her. "We haven't discussed our terms."

He turned to me with a raised brow. His hair. There was more of it than I remembered. It was as if he and it had entered into a nonaggression pact. He'd allow it to grow free if it stayed out of his eyes but for a few rakish strands. No way this man wasn't taken.

"I don't drink," I told him.

"And I was all set to get you drunk," he said, a chuckle in his voice.

"You'll need to do it the old-fashioned way."

"Alcohol is the old-fashioned way."

"No," I said. "That would be charm."

"I'll give you a minute!" The waitress left. As she passed her compatriot taking an order two tables over, she dropped her jaw.

"Alcoholic parents," I explained to Digby. "It's easier to make the decision not to drink, and never have to think about it again."

Digby picked up the menu. "What are we in the mood for?"

"I love the antipasti."

There were thirty to choose from.

"You throw out ideas," I said, "and I'll nix them."

"My favorite type of girl," he said, smiling to himself.

The waiter, who'd been watching, appeared. "Have we decided?"

"Take the reins," I told Digby.

"To start," he said, and checked with me. "Salami?"

"I don't eat meat," I said.

"Dolce gorgonzola," Digby continued to the waiter.

"My favorite," I commented.

"Fried artichokes?"

"Great here," I put in.

"Giant beans, sun-dried tomatoes and olives."

"You read my mind," I said. "See, I'm easy."

"Good to know," he said with a smirk.

Which was stupid. I can't believe I actually giggled.

"For your main?" asked the poker-faced waiter.

"All you," I said to Digby.

He ordered pasta with spring peas, and asked for the chef to surprise us with a veg polenta, suggesting mushroom.

The waiter scurried off, found the waitress and now dropped his jaw. She mouthed, *I know.*

Digby and I saw it all in the mirror. Them watching us. Us watching them. Us watching each other. Us watching ourselves.

"This feels ancient," Digby said.

Of us. He was already talking about us.

"How was the rest of the ballet?" I asked.

"Your dog walker. He's a good kid. But easily broken."

"Ah, Ziggy." I took a sip of water. "That's how you found out where I worked."

"It certainly wasn't going to happen from an internet search."

"I don't do social media," I said. "Eyes on the prize."

"What prize are we eyeing?" He threw me another stupid, stupid look.

"Secure joy."

The waiter loaded in several small plates. The gorgonzola came paired with candied walnuts and quince paste. The olives were giant and meaty, some red. Artichokes fried light as little pillows sat atop parmesan cream.

I felt pride of ownership that this was my neighborhood Italian. Screw those people who say the Upper West Side is a restaurant desert. Actually, I was one of those people. Screw me.

Digby and I heedlessly dove in.

"Tell me," he said. "What exactly is a philosopher?"

"That's the old-fashioned way."

He chose to let it sit.

"My friend Minna," I said. "She calls my job a 'real dick shrinker.'"

"I knew I liked you," Digby said. "Now I love you."

"Literally translated," I said, "philosophy is the love of knowledge. Philosophers use that love of knowledge to perceive reality clearly."

"And are you now?" he said. "Perceiving reality clearly?"

"Doing my best."

"What are you perceiving?"

"About you? You're asking a lot of questions, which serves to make me feel strangely relaxed. Obviously a diversionary tactic. But I'll indulge."

"And once you've perceived reality clearly," he said. "Then what?"

"I keep perceiving reality clearly."

"That's a hard dollar."

"True," I said. "But it allows me to roll with whatever life throws at me."

"Void of emotion."

"That's a common misconception about Stoicism. It's not Keep Calm and Carry On. It's Change Your Perception So You Never Have to Keep Calm and Carry On. Stoics are very passionate people. The key is to be correct in your passions."

It was happening. I was getting too excited, talking too fast and eating everything in sight.

"The four negative passions," I said, "are pain, fear, craving and pleasure. All are based on faulty perceptions of reality, and therefore can be avoided with reason and proper training. Now, the three positive emotions. There's joy, in the experience of what is truly good. Caution, towards the prospect of what is truly bad. And wishing, for what is truly good. Jesus, has your dick completely shrunk?"

"Size of a Tylenol," he said. "So pleasure is bad?"

"Self-control becomes the pleasure."

"Size of a baby carrot."

"Your turn," I said. "All I know about you is you go to the ballet alone and leave unattended briefcases in the most fortified building in Manhattan other than SDNY headquarters."

"Ah," he said. "The briefcase."

"Defend yourself, David Ignatius."

"I told you I'd pay for my ticket and I am a man of honor. After you pulled your Cinderella, I found out where you worked from your loose-lipped dog walker. Your currency of choice being the street burrito, I bought you one from the truck outside. When I arrived at the front desk, your colleague rang you. As we waited for you to pick up, I got to hear about the genius of Chris Martin and the backstory of the song 'Yellow.' You weren't answering, so I asked to leave said burrito with a note, but your colleague claimed the smell of takeout triggered her migraines. I went outside, where I had the bright idea to seal the burrito in my briefcase with a note. When I returned, your colleague wasn't there, so I set it and the note on her desk."

"Well, it's no more," I said. "Blown up. The burrito, too."

"Explaining your hunger. I've never seen a woman assassinate so much food."

I put my fork down and rested my chin in my hand. Digby said nothing.

"This," I said, "is me taking pleasure in the self-control."

His brows crossed. He'd seen my tattoo.

I dropped my hand so he couldn't look too closely.

"*Amor fati*," I said. "Love fate."

"That's kinda hot," he said.

"Fate is a cart driven by a donkey. And I'm the dog tied to the back with a rope."

"Less hot."

"There are two options," I continued. "I can struggle and fight, which would make no difference, anyway. Or take advantage of the slack and enjoy the journey."

Digby turned serious.

"I'm glad you found relief," he said.

"Me, too." My voice cracked as I said this.

"Ancient" was what he'd called it. Words were being spoken but it didn't matter which ones, or who spoke them. They'd been said before. They'd be said again. Nothing was at stake. Everything was at stake.

"I'm checking in," he said. "What would a philosopher do now?"

"The past is gone," I said. "So I'm not thinking about how this doesn't happen, me running into you at the ballet and ending up here. The future isn't guaranteed, so I'm not wondering what it will be like to kiss you and what you're planning to do to me. Or praying you have a place to go because I have a prying daughter at home. The present is all that's available, and right now I'm focused on riding this narcotic fizz into eternity."

Digby's finger shot up. "Check, please."

Digby stepped onto Amsterdam and hailed a cab.

"You still haven't told me what you do," I said.

"You're about to find out."

A taxi swerved to a stop. Digby leaned into the front window. "The Lowell Hotel." He opened the back door in footman fashion.

I hesitated.

"In town on business?" I asked.

"I am." His eyes flashed. The seriousness that had befallen him at the restaurant was still intact, but had edged into impatience. I found it sexier than the playful innuendo of earlier.

"Are we married?" I asked (even though the first thing I'd noticed was no ring).

"We are not."

In the window of the restaurant, the waitress and waiter stood shoulder to shoulder, openly staring.

As soon as I got in the cab, I did what I always do: mute Taxi TV. On the screen, as usual, *Jeopardy!*

"Not a Ken Jennings fan?" asked Digby.

"Major Ken Jennings fan. But more than I love Ken Jennings, I hate Taxi TV."

"Now I know."

As the taxi waited to turn onto Seventy-Fourth, Ziggy happened to cross in front with Mr. Man and Minna's pug, E. Jean. The pooches stopped to sniff their favorite patch of dried grass on the median between avenue and bike lane. Looming above, my Ansonia.

My heart hammered inside my chest. Excitement and fear: when you strip away the stories you tell yourself, they feel the same in the body. Fear you can re-label excitement. Excitement you can re-label fear.

When a woman decides to leave a marriage as late in life as I did, she's not leaving the marriage to find someone better. She's leaving the marriage because anything would be better than the marriage. "Anything" being that she'll most likely die alone.

Finding a man was never top of mind. It wasn't even on mind.

I'd just moved to New York when Minna invited me to a party thrown by a recently divorced friend, a man in his sixties.

The party was in Tribeca and full of show people, playwrights mainly, a few actors and directors. Our host, Ian, had written biographies of Twain and Eliot. His bestseller on the love lives of Byron and the Shelleys was the basis for the hit musical *Romantics,* directed by Minna.

It was a fun party. When things were winding down, Minna signaled it was time to leave.

"I should thank the host," I told her. "Which one is he?"

"You haven't met Ian?" Minna excitedly asked. "Go. Meet Ian."

She pointed him out.

Ian was a decade older than me. His thinning hair was gray and shoulder-length. Rosacea stained the right side of his nose. He hadn't even bothered to dress for his own party; he wore shorts and a T-shirt.

I did a thought experiment: if I were dating, this is the kind of man I'd get.

The prospect didn't appeal.

I introduced myself and thanked Ian for the lovely evening.

"You're the famous Stoic," he said, with Eton accent. "I had no idea you were at my party."

"I'm a friend of Minna's."

"Ah, Minna. Always delivering." Something occurred to him. "I associate you with New Haven."

"I just got divorced and moved to the Upper West Side."

"How are you?" he asked. "Doing okay?"

"More than okay."

"Fantastic. Me, too."

We shared a laugh that the only acceptable response to meeting a recent divorcee is a hearty "Congratulations."

"Let's meet for coffee," he said. "This week? I'd like to properly welcome you to my little island."

We exchanged numbers.

Before Minna and I left, I scanned Ian's loft afresh. It was book filled and surprisingly cozy. His teenage daughter, who had taken coats earlier, was now in her room playing Pink Floyd on acoustic guitar.

This makes sense, I thought. Ian and I have both written books.

We're both divorced. We'd keep our own apartments. Spend two or three nights a week together. Viv would have her longed-for sister. Augusts in Europe.

As for Ian's physical appearance, I could squint and get there.

Minna and I stepped onto the cobblestone street, a location used in movies for its fairy-tale quality. She checked behind her that nobody was within earshot.

"I'm so glad you met Ian," she said, hugging my arm.

Playing it cool, I said nothing.

"I was talking to his daughter," Minna said. "Guess who he's dating?"

Before I could—

"Demi Moore!" said Minna.

The reality of my situation locked into place: if single men were so rare that Demi Moore was swooping in from California to claim one this old and grizzled, my chances were officially zero.

Desire, even the desire to have love in your life, is a choice. I decided then and there to flip the switch. Eliminate the option. I never looked back.

Digby was studying me. He began to speak, but decided against.

"It's been a while," I said.

"Thank you for sharing that," he said. "How are you doing?"

He took my hand. The warmth of it. I was so starved for affection, it was all I needed. I could go home satisfied.

"I'm just thinking," I said.

"I understand."

I fought the urge to close my eyes and bathe in his touch.

Digby looked out his window so as to leave me in the privacy of my thoughts.

There was no way he could understand.

He understood.

A pair of uniformed doormen stood sentry at the Lowell and pulled open both doors at once. Digby and I breezed through without a kink in our strides.

"I feel like the Charlie girl," I said to Digby. "If you get the reference."

"Oh, I'm that old."

Ahead, the open elevator an invitation to glide right in. We obliged.

The desk clerks, both in their twenties, looked up and nodded hello with the cultivated blank expressions one expects of high-end establishments.

You got it right, kids, I wanted to say. Two old people about to have sex.

Digby pushed the button. I leaned back onto the mirrored wall. The elevator doors sealed us in.

Digby stood against the wall opposite, leaving a gulf between. Neither of us stepped closer. Neither of us broke eye contact as the floors ticked up. It boded hotly for the night ahead.

Digby's room was fussy: dark wood and damask. The curtains overornamented and so plentiful they could pay for college. The tartan carpet felt like stepping on a cloud. A spotlight shone on a delicate watercolor hanging above a love seat. Otherwise, the room was lamp-lit. Dim, flattering and allowing for dark corners.

"Let me." Digby slid off my jacket. He hung it in the closet, empty but for his camel hair from yesterday. Even the mundane felt momentous.

The bed was turned down on both sides with a point in the middle, as if halfway to a paper airplane. On one pillow, a palm-sized wooden crate. I picked it up and lifted off the top. Inside, artisan truffles, one a wee mouse, nose-up. A string of orange silk hung over the edge. Its tail.

My shins were pressed against the bed the way Mr. Man presses against people to mark them. I stepped back.

Digby had been studying me from across the room.

"Have a seat." He gestured to an armchair.

At this point, everything was foreplay. I submitted to his command.

Digby stood over me. "Your powers of perception verge on the terrifying."

"I try."

It's not enough to be happy. You have to be aware of it, and enjoy being happy. It's a subtle distinction, but it's the difference between living and being truly alive. In that moment, I made a point of immensely enjoying my happiness.

"When you said this doesn't happen," Digby began, "me and you meeting accidentally at the ballet—you were right. It doesn't."

He approached the coffee table and stepped between it and the love seat. He looked down, examining me. "It didn't."

Digby's tone, which, back at the restaurant had seemed all-business in a sexy way, I now understood was all-business in an all-business way.

He sat down, his legs slightly spread and feet solid on the ground.

"Yesterday," he said. "All day. I watched you from across the street. I followed you to Lincoln Center."

My spirits, moments ago so ebullient, turned to lead and crash-landed in my stomach.

Go slowly, I told myself. This is my only opportunity to hear the actual words being spoken. My one chance to assent to reality before it gets distorted by emotion.

"I didn't want to lose you," Digby said. "So I got in the standby line. Imagine my surprise when you approached me with your extra ticket."

"I'm imagining your surprise?"

"I'm sorry," he said.

Shame, disappointment, anger. They were all swirling within me and on the verge of creating a major weather event.

I looked down at my wrist. Love this, it reminded me. Love that this is happening.

"Continue," I said.

"Someone has stolen something that rightfully belongs to a client of mine. I've been tasked with getting it back."

Don't fight it. Love it.

Digby pulled open a slip of a drawer in the coffee table and removed an envelope. The same cream linen as the one he'd given me.

"I need you to deliver a letter for me," he said.

In the same penmanship, "*Layla Lockwood*."

It felt as if my skin might peel off my face.

Digby had written this before dinner and placed it in the drawer, certain he could lure me here. I burned with the knowledge that all along, it was Layla he wanted.

Not me.

"You're saying Layla stole something?" I threw in. For self-amusement if nothing else.

"I didn't say that."

"Why should I believe you?"

"Because you trust me."

I had no response. I couldn't begin to identify what I was feeling. I was pretty certain it wasn't trust.

"I need you to get this letter in front of Layla," Digby said. "Without being seen."

"You're asking me to compromise my ethics."

"I haven't tried to get any information out of you," he said. "For your sake. The less you know the better."

I knew more than he thought: the stolen object would have to be Boy With Apple. The statue that had already stirred so much controversy and would be arriving tomorrow.

"Once Layla receives this letter?" I said. "What happens then?"

"I will sit with her in the hope that common sense will prevail." Digby's fingers were crossed so loosely as to make him seem almost comically relaxed.

"If it doesn't?"

"That would be unfortunate for all concerned."

"And Lionel?" I asked.

"He knows nothing," Digby said. "I'd prefer it stays that way."

"And you get what you want," I said, recalling his words at the ballet.

"I do," he said, almost apologetically.

"How do you suppose I get this letter in front of Layla without being seen?"

The truth is, I already knew.

"You'll figure it out."

I turned the letter over. The back flap was tucked in.

"This is unsealed," I said.

"An indication of trust."

"So this was a job interview."

"MI5," he said. "When they recruit, they look for people with unplumbed passion and the stone-hearted ability to control it."

"So now we're with MI5!"

"I'm not," he said, with a fluidity that made me wonder if he was MI5 adjacent.

"What about—" I stopped myself.

"Tonight?" Digby said. "Us?"

My trembling lip confirmed he was correct.

"We both know what this is," he said.

"Tell me." Delusion was still very much on the table. I wanted to hear him speak the words.

He reached his hand to my face and cupped my chin.

"Not what you expected," he said. "And certainly not what I expected. A beginning."

This time I couldn't help but close my eyes. I opened them and came back woozy.

"Deliver the letter." He ran his thumb down my cheek. Rougher than I thought I liked. "And we'll pick this up tomorrow. The pleasure is in the self-control."

"You still haven't told me what it is you do."

"I make people whole," he said.

I wanted to be made whole.

I took the letter.

The next morning, the path across Central Park deposited me, for the thousandth time, onto Fifth Avenue. But I saw, for the first time, the bench across from it, dead center. The bench where Digby had spent hours waiting, watching.

I sat down.

Flapping in the wind, banners for "The Presence of Absence," the Library's exhibit of nineteenth-century Black portraiture. It was Ravi's first show and had proven a smash with critics, the public and A-listers alike. A line was forming even though we didn't open for half an hour. Uniformed schoolchildren poured out of a yellow bus and established a beachhead on the sandstone steps.

I am Digby.

My eyes on the employee door, I search for a trusted accomplice. Could it be her, the millennial in the loose-knit sweater vest hanging to her knees and holding an artisan coffee? Nope. Too conformist. Or the woman in bleached T-shirt and work pants? Nah, too ungovernable. Perhaps the man in bespoke finery and ruby pinkie ring? I know him from his picture in the newspaper, so no, too high-profile. Then:

a woman in her fifties, lost in thought, at an amused remove. Soft but strong. Ripe for challenge. Yes. Her.

The Lockwoods' plainclothes security guard stepped into frame nursing his coffee. I obliged him with our usual banter.

"Morning, Tony. Catch any crazies?"

"Whatever you're on," Tony answered, "I wish they made coffee that strong."

"Philosophy," I said. "It begins in wonder."

As I crossed Fifth, a spring gust caught the skirt of my dress and ushered me under the arched Gothic entry. Above me, a pair of winged gargoyles protected those who entered. Between the mythic creatures' clawed feet, each guarded an apple.

(Fun fact: New York is called the Big Apple because of the Lockwood Red, an apple bred by steel-baron-slash-amateur-orchardist Leo Lockwood, and strong-armed into every apple stand by Tammany Hall.)

I dumped my bag onto the belt and proceeded through the metal detector.

The schoolchildren had already drained the punch bowl of apple cider and were using the paper cups for hacky sack. Their teacher, who'd started the day pre-aggravated, was attempting to corral them.

"Y'all had better line up," she threatened, "or I am outta here!"

The kids paused to do the math, and continued their spirited marauding.

I headed straight for Command Central and found Hannah perched at her desk.

"Good morning!" I said. "Do you mind?" I pulled a Con Ed bill from my bag and moved past Hannah to the copy machine.

"Go ahead." After a pause, she added, "I honestly got the best sleep last night."

I punched in fifteen copies. This would buy me ample time to test a hypothesis.

I raised my hands over my head and stretched in half-moon pose, left, right, left, right.

"Have any dreams?" I asked Hannah.

"Actually, I don't dream."

"Why do you think that is?" Left, right. Left, right.

As Hannah droned on—something about her mother giving her too much Benadryl as a baby—I kept one eye on the surveillance monitors.

The grid was six across and five down. The images cycled through three times before starting over. Rudimentary math put the number of security cameras at ninety. In the words of Blanche, "Imagine it. Eat it." The Lockwoods don't do halfway!

I watched every inch of the Lockwood Library flash before me . . .

Except my swaying body.

As I'd postulated, the only place not being monitored was the monitor room itself. There was probably a metaphor in that . . . the mind's ability to perceive everything but the mind itself? Maybe!

I went to retrieve my copies and noticed on top a Xerox of a French passport.

The photo was of a man—white skin, cropped hair, no smile, impossibly high cheekbones—or was it a woman? I checked.

"CELINE MONTFORT."

My body tightened.

From the Louvre. The woman arriving today with the statue. Digby's statue.

"You left this." I casually passed the copy to Hannah.

"Can you say 'mommy brain'?" She added a raspberry sound.

I headed towards the double staircase. Between them, a landing and wall of soaring French doors that overlooked the parterre.

Today, its pleasing symmetry was marred by a crane that cut an ugly slash across the view plane. I paused to look.

In the garden below, a gaggle of jumpsuited art handlers stood on scaffolding surrounding the statue of Fortuna.

I watched as the men encased the blindfolded goddess's head in net. The crane moved in. Men secured the netting to a hook. Fortuna's head detached from her shoulders and floated skyward.

"This is madness," muttered a voice.

It was Ravi, at the other end of the landing, shaking his head, dudgeon higher than yesterday. "It makes no sense!"

I walked over and placed a sympathetic hand on Ravi's arm.

In response, a patronizing if amused look. "I have a feeling I'm in for some unsolicited advice."

(Minna often accused me of being a "tranquility bully." It was something I was working on. Not!)

"Anger is more likely to hurt you than to cure any perceived wrong," I said, paraphrasing Seneca, an absolute beast on the topic. "Anger sets out to destroy everything in its path. In a flash, it can cause even the most trivial affront to ignite a lifetime of regret. Sure, anger feels good in the moment, but nothing truly good ever comes from it, so—"

"Stop there," Ravi said. "As I see it, everything good comes from anger."

"Does it?"

"Off the top of my head? The civil rights movement, AIDS research, democracy itself. Anger is a spur to action. Without it, nothing in this world would get done."

"Or," I said, "one piece of marble is being replaced by another piece of marble. What's it to ya?"

"In a word," Ravi said, "everything."

His phone rang; he answered on the first ring. "Yes? Please. Print it out. I'll be right down."

He hung up. "Respectfully, Adora, I find your worldview as impoverished as you find mine hysterical. Luckily, there is berth for us both."

With a gentlemanly scrape, he was off.

I entered my office and turned on my computer. Immediately I typed in "Celine Montfort."

She had an extensive Wikipedia entry. I can't say it didn't give me a little stab.

> **Celine Montfort (born August 4, 1953) is a French cultural advocate and member emeritus of the Board of Directors of the Louvre Museum. She was appointed ambassador to Greece by Jacques Chirac (2000–2006). She is a founding member of the Art and Antiquities Recovery Council (2008).**
>
> ## EARLY LIFE AND EDUCATION
>
> **Montfort attended Le Rosey in Switzerland, and earned degrees from the University of Pennsylvania and Royal College of Art. She was employed by the Leo Castelli Gallery in New York from 1993–1997.**

PHILANTHROPIC AND ADVOCACY WORK

Through her deep ties to the diplomatic community, Montfort oversaw the return of eight works of art from the Getty Museum in Los Angeles to Greece, Egypt and Syria. This led her to form the Art and Antiquities Recovery Council (AARC), a multinational organization comprised of museum curators and experts dedicated to facilitating the return of looted or stolen artifacts from museums and private hands to their rightful owners or countries of origin.

I stopped reading.

Digby had said he was working to recover something that had been stolen. Celine Montfort had devoted her entire life, it would seem, to the return of stolen art. Perhaps they were working together?

I studied the lone accompanying photograph. In it, the woman from the passport stood beside her father and I. M. Pei at the opening of the pyramid entrance to the Louvre.

"*Et voilà!*" sang a familiar, muffled voice.

I swiveled to look out the window.

As if a tableau vivant, Celine Montfort sprang to life.

She was standing in the parterre with Layla, who was presenting the now-empty plinth à la Vanna White.

Layla's double-breasted suit might have bordered on good taste, but next to Celine Montfort, any woman would look clownish.

Sheathed in sleeveless silk, Celine stood as erect as a ballerina. Her white skin glowed as if from within. She wore her face minimally painted. Wrinkles radiated unapologetically from her green eyes. Her short hair was tousled to perfection. A gold necklace hung across her neck and dripped down her back.

Fortuna, now in four pieces, lay on a patchwork of moving blankets.

Celine and Layla chitchatted as art handlers came and went, transporting body parts.

The unmistakable rattle of ball-bearing-against-metal drew my attention. A gardener, shaking a can of spray paint. He aimed it at the scorched patch of grass from yesterday. The greens matched seamlessly.

Suddenly, Ravi came flying out, waving papers.

I cranked my window to better hear.

"My team has been working all night," Ravi announced, "checking every database. There is literally no known statue called Boy With Apple!"

"Bonjour to you, too," said Celine. She spoke perfect English but with the vaguely European accent of someone who didn't belong to one country as much as the entire continent.

"In 300 BC," Ravi said, "Eve held apples. Aphrodite held apples. Boys held shields and lutes."

"We'll be the exception that proves the rule," said a thoroughly unruffled Celine.

"That's right," added Layla with the defiance found in those standing behind a bully.

"Absolutely not," said Ravi. "I refuse to allow anything with unknown provenance into my statuary. You saw what those maniacs did to the Rosetta stone!"

(Reports were coming in that the bombing of the British Museum was the work of a terrorist group demanding the repatriation of stolen art from the world's biggest museums. If their demands weren't met, they'd continue their bombing spree.)

"Boy With Apple is hardly on the target list," Celine said with a smirk. "I give you my word." She scrunched her nose to mark the end of the conversation.

"He's holding an apple," Layla offered Ravi in baby voice. "Get it? It would go perfect."

Ravi bristled at both tone and grammar. He turned to Celine.

"One question."

"Bien sûr."

"Why?" Ravi asked, and went in for the kill. "I was honored to know and work with your father. Pierre Montfort cherished the family collection. And now his daughter is selling it off for parts?"

"What you might not know about my father," Celine returned, "is that he didn't pay his taxes. Which has left me chateau rich but cash poor."

"Uh," peeped Layla in sympathy-slash-horror.

Celine raised her chin in defiance. "I'm being forced to sell several hectares of the Montford estate to keep the taxman at bay." She paused to ward off tears. "I'm well aware of the disgrace this has brought on the family. I do not need you to remind me."

Ravi reddened.

Layla stroked her friend. "It's okay."

"Since you've taken such a personal interest," Celine continued, driven by what looked like—at least from afar—a perverse enjoyment at Ravi's mortification. "While clearing vines in preparation for the land auction, my gardeners came across Boy With Apple. Which tells me my father didn't much care for it if he stuck it off in a corner to be overrun by weeds. It never occurred to me to sell it. Until last week when I had the good fortune to meet Layla."

"At the Louvre," Layla added. "She was there before it opened."

"I introduced myself, we got to talking and hit it off."

"Aww," said Layla.

"How could we not?" Celine paused to share an affectionate smile with Layla. "Somehow, Boy With Apple came up. She just had to have it for the Lockwood Library. What can I say? The woman loves apples."

"On brand!" Layla said, and struck a pose.

"Considering my circumstances, I had no choice but to part with Boy With Apple. Which, like you, I considered nothing more than a curiosity. I now have your exhaustive research to prove it."

Ravi reflexively hid the papers behind his back.

"I will welcome Boy With Apple into my collection," he said.

Celine sighed. "Ah, vulnerability. It doesn't feel nearly as good as advertised."

"That popped my cherry," came a slow and boring voice. It was Hannah, joining them in the garden below. "Never seen a thousand-year-old body part walk by."

The moment I'd been waiting for!

I jumped up from my desk and flew down the stairs, feeling my dress pocket for Digby's letter. I went straight to Command Central, which was, of course, empty.

I pulled the mail cart out from under Hannah's desk, when—

"Dr. Hazzard?"

I spun around.

"Hannah!" What was she, a genie? How did she get back so soon?

"Can I help you with something?"

I opened the copy machine where I'd intentionally left my Con Ed bill, just in case.

"Mommy brain," I said, waving it for her benefit. "You and me both."

Hannah laughed. I didn't have it in me to do the raspberry.

Hannah pushed the mail cart under the desk and sat down. I stood there, Digby's letter burning a hole in my pocket.

"I was just in the gallery," I thought to say. "You won't believe— No, I can't."

"What?"

"We're not supposed to talk about celebrities."

"Wait," Hannah said. "Who?"

"The kids are going nuts. Someone with a song about the color yellow."

"Chris Martin!" Hannah gasped. "Back the truck up." She gaped longingly at the exhibit entrance.

"I won't tell," I whispered.

Hannah shot up and grooved across the lobby. Watching her go, I reached behind me for the mail cart, ran my hands along the array of letters with tops sliced open, and stuck Digby's in the middle.

"Oh my God!" came a laughing voice.

I whipped around.

It was Blanche, walking through the staff corridor with architectural plans. How much had she seen?

"Of course that girl loves Coldplay!"

"Prefers them to Radiohead," I added, and discreetly pushed the mail cart back under the desk.

"You're just making shit up."

"We literally had that conversation." I herded Blanche into the lobby. "She doesn't like Thom Yorke's lazy eye. She might be the only person on the planet who thinks Chris Martin is a good dancer."

"I bet she owns a doodle," Blanche said.

"And says the best part of the Super Bowl is the commercials. And considers herself uniquely transgressive for thinking *Succession* is a comedy."

"Socrates," Blanche said with a wink. "You're not dead yet."

I returned to my office. There, I sat down and kicked my feet on the desk.

Yeah, I can hang back and let my instincts dictate when to pounce. Yeah, I can conjure tall tales on the spot. Yeah, when Plan A doesn't work, Plan B will effortlessly present itself. Yeah, I can shit talk a co-worker just to fit in.

What else might I accomplish if only I decided to? Run a 10K? Knit a sweater? Get good at cartwheels? Crush the bar?

Put me in, coach.

It was just like sex.

Later that afternoon, a letter arrived via messenger. I inhaled fig and pulled out the flap.

> *That's my girl*
> *790 Madison Ave #1610*
> *5pm*
> *I will thank you.*

On the bottom, a hand-drawn heart with an arrow through it.

By 5:10 Digby and I were in a fluorescent-lit room sitting opposite each other on metal chairs with foldout desks. His-and-hers nurses tied us off. Digby and I couldn't take our eyes off each other. This was becoming a trend.

The nurse flicked my vein and I quickly looked away.

"Lights off or lights on?" Digby inquired from across the room.

"Lights on," I said.

"I can do lights on."

"All done!" announced the nurse. I hadn't felt the sting.

Digby and I rolled down our sleeves and exited to reception.

"You'll get the results in twenty-four to forty-eight hours," the girl at the desk informed us.

I must have looked stricken. Digby gave me a nod that he'd handle it.

Minutes later, he joined me in the hall. "Done and done."

As we waited for the elevator, my phone dinged. It was a secure link to a PDF; I held it up for Digby to see.

"SENSITIVE SEROLOGY TESTING. SYPHILIS, HIV, HSV, CHLAMYDIA, GONORRHEA: NEGATIVE."

Digby held up his phone and showed me the same.

We stepped into the elevator. I flung my arms around his neck. Our first kiss was a deep one, his taste unfamiliar. He took the lead, as if to say, This is me. I answered, I like you, this is me.

The doors opened to an unfazed Door Dasher.

Digby and I straightened and tipsily got ourselves the two blocks to the Lowell.

Even though it wasn't yet six P.M., Digby had prearranged turn-down service.

As he had done the night before, Digby helped me out of my jacket. On the coffee table, a Le Labo candle burned. It hadn't been there yesterday. From Viv, I knew Le Labo's shtick was their customizable labels. I picked up the candle to read what Digby had gotten inscribed.

"*I knew right away she was not like other girls.*"

It was a line from "Scarlet Begonias."

"You have good taste in Dead songs," I said.

"You're a noticer."

When I said that placing that letter in the mail cart was just like sex?

It was nothing like sex.

I had forgotten what sex was like.

The warm luxury of skin on skin. The human need for tender touch. Our two naked bodies searched urgently but with all the time in the world; we were almost unbearably serious, only to erupt in fits of laughter; sensations so foreign I was reduced to animal sounds, followed by expanses of immense silence.

With each round, I felt cleansed. Even the shame got washed away.

Digby and I talked constantly, hungrily, of everything and nothing.

How we wanted to be known! And how unafraid we were in the details.

We mythologized the night as it unfolded. We were both novel and marginalia.

Digby asked permission, then made me beg. He had me saying the words, and repeating the words until he was convinced, and I was, too.

"I want more."

—PART THREE—

THE UNTITLED ADORA HAZZARD PROJECT

Once, I had wanted.

Spring of 1998.

West Hollywood. A hot afternoon in April. I was twenty-nine years old. Lying in bed, napping off a sugar crash (black-and-white cookies from Greenblatt's . . . why, why?!) when the phone rang.

"Hold for Travis Burden," said the assistant.

I sprang up.

My agent calling me? When I hadn't called him? My galloping heart understood the implications before my cobwebby brain.

On the boxy TV, *General Hospital* had become Oprah interviewing someone at top volume. I pillaged my sheets and strewn *LA Times* for the goddamned remote.

"You're never going to believe it—" Travis got on and said.

I lunged at the TV and slapped buttons until Suze Orman went black.

"—I just hung up from Vince O'Quinn. He wants you as a guest writer on *Laugh Riot*."

My body and being shimmered. It was as if a giant magic wand had descended into my crappy apartment and tapped me on the head.

"He what?"

"I know," Travis said, his shock matching mine. "The last four shows of the season. They need a woman. O'Quinn said he met you at a party?"

"Like a month ago . . ." I walked my phone into the living room as far as the cord would permit.

"Whatever you did at that party, keep doing it. You start Monday. They're offering you minimum—"

"I accept!"

"Believe me, you already did. The idea being if you do well, they'll ask you back full-time next season."

"Oh God." My smile was so massive it engaged muscles I never knew existed.

"Congratulations," said Travis. "This is huge."

I stood there, roiling with excitement, not knowing what to do with myself. My living room wasn't big enough. My apartment wasn't big enough. Calling a friend wasn't big enough.

The only thing big enough was a drive along Mulholland.

I went to my boom box and ejected that day's cassette of *The Howard Stern Show*. (Back then, Howard was only broadcast live from the East Coast so I'd set my alarm for three A.M., hit "record," go back to sleep and play it later in the car.)

My keys were on the counter, right next to the Greenblatt's bag with two more black-and-white cookies, ones I'd been saving for later. (Why was I such a pig?!) I swiped both. On the way to the parking shed, I tossed the white bag into a garbage can.

I hopped into my Toyota Tercel, turned north onto Crescent Heights and began the climb up Laurel Canyon. It was rush hour, the city-to-valley traffic at its soul-destroying worst, frustration and rage visible through every windshield.

Not mine! I had nowhere to go and nothing to do but metabolize my fabulous turn of fortune.

Laugh Riot. The longest running and still red-hot sketch show. It launched movie stars. It spawned catch phrases. It swung elections.

And it had just anointed me.

The verdict was in: I had made it.

I waited to turn left onto Mulholland. Howard was berating Gary for his incompetence regarding a new CD player he couldn't get to work. Gary blamed Fred. Fred blamed Stuttering John. Stuttering John attempted to defend himself. This began a contest to see who did the best Stuttering John impression. Robin was the judge.

After two light cycles, I made the turn and drove into the sinking sun. The city rose to my left, the valley sprawled to my right. Both radiated a yellowish pink. They didn't call it magic hour for nothing!

I knew I wasn't crazy. I knew I'd made an impression on Vince O'Quinn.

It had happened at a barbecue in Altadena, thrown by a comedy writer friend. I'd spotted someone standing alone at the bottom of a sloping lawn, looking at a chicken coop. I'd never seen a backyard chicken coop and went to check it out. Only when I got there did I realize the person was Vince O'Quinn, head writer of *Laugh Riot.*

It was settled science that Vince O'Quinn was the funniest man alive.

Most people would be intimidated; I began talking.

It was my one innate talent, the gift of the gab. Without any forethought, I could launch into a story and spin it into tangent upon tangent. (All hilarious and interesting) but going nowhere and showing no signs of ending. Just as my listeners were experiencing peak fear that I'd never stop—I could see it their eyes, which only made me talk faster!—I'd pull everything together in a way so unexpected, that for one moment, even I loved myself.

I twisted past the thirsty red cliffs, lush greenery and gated drives, lovingly recalling every moment of that fateful conversation.

I'd begun by telling Vince O'Quinn about the Trojans game I'd gone to on my birthday. In the tunnel, a fan had collapsed in some kind of seizure. A passerby searched the guy's pockets and came out with an inhaler, which he stuck in the guy's mouth. When the Good Samaritan pressed on it, it turned out not to be an inhaler, but an air horn. This somehow led to the birthday message my mother had left on my voicemail. "Adora. I'll never forget the day you were born. I was gassed through the whole thing, and when I woke up, the nurse said, 'Congratulations, Mrs. Hazzard, you're the mother of a beautiful baby girl.' And I turned to your father and said, 'Ugh. Guess we'll have to keep trying for a boy!'" Seeing Vince's discomfort, I told him I was late for a meeting. OSA. Over Sharers Anonymous. The whole conversation, I sprinkled in references to me being fat, beating Vince O'Quinn to what he was already thinking.

What can I say? He was endeared.

My face started to cramp from smiling so hard. I figure-eighted my jaw as I passed Jack Nicholson's compound. It's where he lived with

Marlon Brando. It's where Roman Polanski had sex with that underaged girl. You could never see anything from the street. Just the gate.

My first job in LA, I was a production assistant. One day I was driving down Robertson to Culver City, a particularly nasty stretch of urban blight. Buckled sidewalks, topped trees, bail bond places, nail salons behind iron bars, auto repair shops with junked cars piled like pancakes. I stopped at the light on Pico. In the next car over . . . Jack Nicholson. I thought, Wait, isn't Jack Nicholson exempt from having to see all this shit along Robertson? Shouldn't he have a different route to Culver City? But no, there he was, flashing his trademark smile. LA, we're all in it together!

Sweat trickled down the back of my jumbo calves. I recoiled at the grotesque expanse of khaki spread across the seat. My disgusting thighs.

Why had I eaten those cookies?!

If I started work on Monday, that only gave me three days to lose weight. If I took two step classes a day and ate nothing but cabbage soup, I could lose six pounds. Not great. If the show only started a week later, I could lose twenty.

I blamed my mother. When I was in second grade, she stood up infront of my entire class and announced I was on a diet and could only eat cottage cheese and celery sticks. Under no circumstances were the other kids to share their food with me. "Not even the crusts. And she'll want 'em."

According to my therapist, this was the equivalent of my mother shooting heroin into my veins. Basically, she turned me into a food junkie. I was a total victim!

Last year, I dragged my mother into my therapist's office to confront her.

During the double session, I spoke with a quiver as I detailed my lifelong struggle with my weight. The self-hatred and yo-yo dieting that had me gaining and losing a hundred pounds in ten years.

My mother listened patiently. When I was done, she responded directly to my therapist: "Adora is trying to find someone to blame because she hasn't won her Oscar."

"My Oscar?" I said with a jerk.

"We all thought she'd have an Oscar by now," my mother explained to the therapist. "But she's stuck writing for television shows none of us have ever heard of."

My therapist recognized narcissism when she saw it, and this was God-tier. I half expected her to throw the Ali G hand sign and say, "Respect."

For some reason, the Tercel was heading downhill. Shit, I hadn't gotten into the left lane, and was now going north on Coldwater. I lurched into the first driveway and made a three-point turn into the voracious canyon traffic. My fellow drivers were not amused.

I found my way back to Mulholland and continued cruising west.

Not to say my mother wasn't right.

I'd arrived in Hollywood full of promise and certain of success. I was hilarious! Everyone said so! My first writing job was for a Nickelodeon show, and I got stuck in children's television for longer than I'd like to admit. When I finally did break into network, I always landed on shows that got cancelled after six episodes. Through no fault of mine. Shitty luck was all. Meanwhile, my writer friends—some much less talented than me—lapped me by getting on *Friends* and *Frasier.*

"To show those bastards."

According to my father, this is what Ernest Hemingway said when asked what drove him to write. I liked it so much I wrote it on a note card and pinned it to my bulletin board.

"I'm Tony Montana!" I screamed out the car window in my best Al Pacino. "You fuck with me, you fucking with the best."

I was a *Laugh Riot* writer, bastards!

It was beginning to sink in as I crossed the 405 where Mulholland started to get ugly—electrical substations, stucco schools with trailer annexes, a dispiriting seventies housing development. I pulled into an empty parking lot and turned around.

No matter what else happened, I would always be a *Laugh Riot* writer—

I hit the brakes. Oh God. Every year, *Laugh Riot* won the Emmy for variety show. That meant I would win an Emmy. Fuck.

I needed frozen yogurt. The place near my house had a zero-cal, sugar-free chocolate syrup. It made my farts smell like burnt rubber but I wasn't planning on seeing anyone that night.

As I dropped down into West Hollywood, Fiona Apple came into the studio. Howard told her that last night, in preparation for her interview, he'd jerked off to the "Criminal" video.

The space right in front of the yogurt shop was empty. Didn't mind if I did.

I entered to bright lights and a blast of frosty air.

And who was standing at the counter . . . but Allan Levin. The mulletted, earringed jerk.

Last fall, he'd hired me on his CBS sitcom.

I turned in my first script on a Friday. When I arrived at work on Monday, all the writers stared daggers at me. The writers' assistant, too. Turns out, they'd been called in over the weekend to do a page-one rewrite. Without me.

Allan called me into his office. He flung my first draft across his desk.

"I should fire you for this. But I won't. Instead, I want you to stand at the board and hold the pen all day while we break story. You're not allowed to speak, and you can only sit down for lunch. Pay attention and it will make you a better writer. I'm doing this because I believe in you."

I accepted; the humiliation of getting fired outweighed that of having to stand there wearing the dunce cap. A week later, the show got cancelled.

"Adora," Allan boomed in the confident voice of a man who stood six foot four.

With him was a potato-shaped guy. No doubt a comedy writer. Oh, this was going to be good.

"Hey, Allan," I said. "What are you working on these days?"

“Developing. Still on my DreamWorks deal.”

“Cool.”

“And what are you working on?” he asked, slightly singsong and emphasizing the word “you.”

Was he . . . mocking me?

“*Laugh Riot,*” I said with a shrug.

Allan and his friend spasmed at the news.

“Whoa,” said his friend.

“Yeah,” I continued. “Vince O’Quinn wants me to help out for the rest of the season. We met at a barbecue—”

“Are you okay?” Allan said. “Your voice is shaking.”

It was! I still hadn’t gotten the adrenaline out of my system.

“I ran here.”

Through the plate glass, my black Tercel. It had been the subject of many room jokes, because to save money I’d bought it off *The Recycler.* It had no air-conditioning and reeked of cat piss.

“You know what,” I said, “I just remembered something.”

I ran outside and fled to the adjacent RadioShack.

I went to the back and curled into myself, my body coursing with humiliation. Screw Allan Levin! I hated him, anyway. I reminded myself he was going through an ugly divorce and custody battle. That helped. After ten minutes of picturing Allan sobbing into the night missing his kids, I was calm enough to leave.

I peeked into the yogurt place to make sure Allan and his friend were gone. They were.

I wasn’t in the mood for yogurt anymore.

I drove home.

I parked my car and on my way up, passed the garbage cans. The Greenblatt’s bag was still on top. Nothing had touched it.

That night, I ate cookies for dinner and busted out my DVD box set of *Pride and Prejudice*. The good *Pride and Prejudice,* the one with Colin Firth.

Monday morning, I hadn't heard from Travis or anyone at *Laugh Riot*. I called WAC (my agency, Writers and Artists Collective) at nine when the switchboard opened. They transferred me, but I got Travis's voicemail. I left increasingly less composed messages until he finally got on the phone.

"You've got to stop calling."

"I'm sorry," I said. "I don't know where to go for work."

"The Warner's lot. It's Monday. Their day doesn't start until three."

"Oh, okay." I hadn't known.

Dressed in size-twelve khakis, white T-shirt and jean jacket tied around my waist—oh, and a girdle I'd bought at Macy's—I drove over the hill.

I was all nerves.

I pulled up to the Warner Brothers gate, told the guard my name and braced for the worst. When he handed over a drive-on—and numbered parking spot!—I crumpled onto my steering wheel, accidentally honking the horn.

"Sorry!" I said.

I followed the map to a nondescript office building of water-stained concrete, brown glass and forsaken tropical landscaping. Behind it, in the farthest parking space, a stanchion. On it was taped a piece of paper with my name in felt marker.

I walked across the parking lot. As I got closer to the entrance, the cars grew increasingly fancy.

And then, boom, boom, boom . . . the names.

"CLYDE CHAVEZ," black Lexus. "TJ STEELE," forest-green Range Rover. "MATTEO MATTHAMS," white Mercedes. "ANDY GALINSKI," red Audi. "ELIJAH STRICKLAND," gold convertible BMW.

I thought I'd barf.

Closest to the front, a Honda minivan. "VINCE O'QUINN."

How I adored that brilliant, down-to-earth man to whom I owed everything.

There was no guard at the front door, no nothing. I guess once you're in, you're in! My pass listed the office I was going to as "212." I climbed the carpeted stairs to the second floor. The hallway was eerily quiet. A man and a woman, deep in conversation, walked by. They registered mild curiosity but kept going.

I found 212, an inside office that shared a wall with the copy room.

I knocked. The door swung open.

"She's here!" cried Marla Valentine.

"Yay!" cheered Ann Rosenfeld.

Ann and Marla were actresses on *Laugh Riot*. Despite having been there forever, neither had broken out—no recurring characters, no feature films, not even a local commercial.

They looked older in person.

"Our woman writer!" Marla jumped up and enveloped me in her soft flesh.

I didn't think of myself as a woman writer. Comedy was comedy. I stiffly hugged her back.

"We've been harassing Vince," said Ann. No less excited to see me, she stayed seated out of necessity. Three desks had been crammed into an office designed for one.

"Here's your desk!" Marla said, of the empty one. On it, a vase of flowers. "Hope you like roses."

"From the place on Barham," Ann added. "Enjoy. Tomorrow this place will smell like a fish tank."

On the walls, a Milton Avery poster, kids' art and a cross-stitched quote by Betty Friedan. "NO WOMAN GETS AN ORGASM FROM SHINING THE KITCHEN FLOOR." The standard-issue couch was draped with a crocheted afghan. On the coffee table, a bowl of potpourri and box of panty liners.

Marla beckoned me inside. "Put your stuff down."

"It's like one of those sliding puzzles," Ann said, scooting her chair in and pulling mine out.

A force stopped me from entering.

"Let me go to the bathroom," I said, and shut the door.

I stood there in nothing short of panic, when there came a little voice.

"Who are you?"

Ten feet from where I stood, Andy Galinski. As fat and wonderstruck as in his movies.

"I'm a new writer," I said.

"What's your name?"

Before I could answer, a familiar Boston accent called from an open door. "Get her in here!" It had to be.

Elijah Strickland!

I followed Andy Galinski through an abandoned outer office into a cavernous corner one. It held five desks, beanbag chairs, a KISS pinball machine, basketball hoop, life-sized cutout of Anna Nicole Smith, a BowFlex machine and miles of leather sofas, with room to spare. It looked like a frat house, if every night a cleaning crew came to the frat house to vacuum, empty the trash and restock it with Red Vines.

Elijah Strickland, Matteo Matthams, Andy Galinski, Clyde Chavez and TJ Steele. The murderers' row of comedy. Their movies dominated the box office. They were right in front of me, crashed on the furniture, limbs akimbo, looking at me with archaeological interest.

"O'Quinn met her a party," Elijah Strickland said.

"Right," drawled TJ Steele in his inimitable way. "That story about the air horn."

"That was you?" sneered Matteo Matthams. His brand was sarcasm.

TJ Steele looked up from his *Maxim*. "O'Quinn said you were funny." His eyes were an icy blue that didn't read nearly so striking on TV. He continued thumbing through his magazine.

"How long are you here?" Andy Galinski asked.

"The rest of the season."

"Goody!" Andy Galinski gave his body a little shimmy. It was no act: he did have the personality of a six-year-old. I wondered if there were other challenges, as well.

"I hope you can take a joke," said Matteo Matthams.

"I'll laugh at anything," I said. "If you're funny."

"Ooh," said Elijah Strickland. "We got a live one!"

"The last one couldn't," Matteo Matthams said.

"Where'd they put you?" asked Andy Galinski.

"Down there," I said vaguely.

"Where comedy goes to die," said Matteo Matthams.

"Comedy goes in," Elijah Strickland said. "And outrage comes out."

"The magic box," I said.

It wasn't funny and it didn't make sense. But it was mean-spirited and vaguely sexual. And with it, I was in.

Next came the best weeks of my life, headier than anything I could have dreamed, and I lived to dream. I effectively became one of the guys, their office my office. I never saw the inside of the magic box again.

Here was a typical week at *Laugh Riot*. . . .

Mondays and Tuesdays were spent doing everything but writing.

George Clooney swung by to shoot hoops. A matinee of *Something About Mary* had to be seen at Mann's Chinese. A Nike representative dropped in with order forms for free shoes. "Give her one, too," Elijah instructed the woman. I marked down a pair of Air Jordans. "You can do better than that," Elijah said. He grabbed my form and mischievously ordered me more stuff before handing it back to the Nike woman. Matthew Perry wanted us to hang out in his dressing room after a run-through. That was cool. Even cooler? Me rolling into the *Friends* soundstage with the guys, just as the *Friends* writers were trudging out. Scripts in hand, they looked beaten down as they headed back to the office for a long night of rewrites. "What are you doing here?" asked one, who'd been on Allan Levin's show and witnessed my humiliation. I answered, "I'm on *Laugh Riot*."

Laugh Riot was a bubble, a moneyed bubble, the envy of all Hollywood. We had a private chef who prepared lunch and dinner, a car detailer who came to the lot, a masseuse who roamed the halls to give neck massages.

Me and the guys, though, we were a bubble within the bubble.

We'd procrastinate by inventing new things we wanted delivered, only to watch them magically materialize. It was a friction-free environment. If we deemed the chef's food gross, eager PAs made steak runs to The Palm.

Once, we were in line at Pink's Hot Dogs and Matteo said, "I did the math. I have enough money that I should never have to wait more than fifteen minutes for anything." Indeed, at the three-minute mark, the manager spotted us and hustled us to the front of the line.

I told the guys about the hot syrup that made your farts smell, and soon, a container of it appeared. The guys dared Andy to eat the whole thing, and tossed hundred-dollar bills into an empty Charles Chips tin until there were so many Andy couldn't refuse. He gulped it down and started farting so badly he was quickly banished. He literally cried as he pounded on the door, "Guys, let me in. Please! I promise I won't fart anymore!"

Out the mirrored-window walls, we had a perfect vantage point of the parking lot for the building next door, which happened to be the studio casting department. Gorgeous, skinny girls, scenes in hand, prepared and paced before going in for that life-changing audition. When a critical mass formed, Elijah, Matteo and Andy would make fumbling excuses for having somewhere to be.

"Do what you have to do," I said, never judging.

TJ didn't partake. He was married, with a daughter back home in Canada. Neither did Clyde, being gay. This left TJ, Clyde and I awkwardly alone. We used the time to nap, one to a couch.

Elijah, Matteo and Andy would eventually return, slightly shamefaced, and the antics would fire back up in overdrive.

Bets on basketball. Demands for burgers from Apple Pan. Crank calls to fellow celebrities. Matteo once called into my answering machine and changed my outgoing message to one in his world-famous sneer: "Adora isn't picking up because she knows it's you. Don't leave a message." For a second I was worried this might hurt my career—what if someone was calling with a job?—but I quickly remembered this was a job.

I was a writer on *Laugh Riot*.

Tuesday nights.

We had no choice but to pull all-nighters, as sketches were due Wednesday morning.

I'd never written a sketch in my life and had no ideas for any, but nobody seemed to notice. I'd sit at the keyboard, transcribing what the guys said and formatting it into sketches. Most of which were based on their breakout characters, and basically wrote themselves.

The only original sketch that made it to air one week was spear-headed by Matteo. It was inspired by the woman writer who'd quit. (She was a low-grade obsession of the guys. Sometimes it felt as if my main purpose was to listen, with fresh ears, to their granular dissection of her buzzkill face.) The sketch was called "I Have a Problem with That." I wrote it up and handed out copies for the guys to proof.

"Andy!" said Matteo. "Go to the magic box and get Ann and Marla. Tell them we wrote them a sketch and want to hear it read."

Andy did. Moments later, Marla and Ann appeared.

"Yo," they said all cool, but their excitement ricocheted off the walls.

We handed them the sketch and watched as their expressions morphed from elation . . . to puzzlement . . . to disgust.

Elijah was the first to bust out laughing.

On their way out, Marla muttered, "Childish pricks."

Ann's parting words: "This place smells like jizz." It was my idea to add that line to the sketch.

When "I Have a Problem with That" got chosen for air, Marla and Ann refused their casting assignments. Matteo and Andy happily played the easily outraged women themselves, donning crooked wigs, smeared lipstick and farcically large brassieres.

I'm not saying it couldn't get rough. But comedy is rough.

Rape jokes were de rigueur. Homophobia, anti-Semitism and racism abounded. But it was all in good fun and fell well within the accepted stereotypes. I didn't mind, and I was a woman. Clyde Chavez didn't mind, and he was Black and gay. And Elijah, he'd always refer to himself as "Boston's biggest Jew boy."

The other woman writer couldn't take the heat.

I could.

Tuesday nights were when Vince O'Quinn would make his rare appearance. He'd slip in, take a seat, listen and—without having to be read in—toss off one-liners, pitch cuts, give us outs and slip away.

Vince O'Quinn: the elusive legend.

Wednesday at five P.M. was when shit got real.

This was the table reading, where a hundred people would pile into a conference room built for thirty to watch the actors read the week's sketches. Vince and the guest host would have already culled the submissions to forty. Afterwards the writers would learn, based on laughs and the whims of Vince, which ten sketches would make it to air.

This was the ultimate currency at *Laugh Riot*: how many sketches a writer got on. It determined your place in the hierarchy, your salary, your future.

An invitation to a table reading was the golden ticket for studio execs, agents and rando celebrities, much harder to score than show tickets. Those table readings were ground zero of cool.

Thursdays and Fridays. The festivities moved from the offices to the stage for rehearsal and blocking. But this was actors only. The writers would mill around the offices until they got the call to come to stage to watch their sketch being rehearsed.

The first Thursday, I was wandering the empty offices when Russell the PA told me I was wanted onstage—even though I hadn't written a sketch.

On my way out, I ran into Vince. "The jesters are requesting an audience," he said with an affectionate shrug. I went straight to the stage and never left.

Friday nights were show nights and the after-party, which lasted until four A.M.

Weekends should have been for sleeping and seeing my friends.

Instead, the guys and I would pile into Elijah's convertible and hit Century City for a movie. Once, the Padres sent a limo for their series against the Mariners. Clyde, famously from Orange County, threw out the opening pitch. Wherever we went, heads turned, catchphrases were shouted, autographs were asked for. And of course envious looks were aimed at me.

I was thrilled. But also disconcerted. Do I smile to the fans and expose my own gooney excitement? Do I not smile and appear rude? Do I avoid eye contact and lessen my enjoyment? Do I make eye contact and risk getting trapped in conversation? (This had happened at the Century City mall and the guys kept walking. After a panic-filled fifteen minutes, I finally found them.) Soon, though, I metabolized all the attention. It felt as natural as breathing.

Monday it would start all over again.

It was the Monday of the final show of the season. Heather Locklear was the guest host.

I'd been on *Laugh Riot* for three weeks and had yet to pitch a sketch idea. The thought occurred to me, What if I don't get asked back? But no, I reassured myself. My presence solved a huge headache for Vince; he finally had a woman writer who couldn't be offended. ("Talk about a magic box!" Matteo once said after I contributed to a brutal joke run about PMS.) Plus, I'd made myself indispensable to the guys by typing up their sketches.

To play it doubly, triply safe, that Sunday I decided to eschew Bowie at the Universal Amphitheatre to stay home and try to come up with sketch ideas.

And I did! I came up with one. I thought it was good? I had no idea.

I was too nervous to pitch it to the guys so I decided to run it by Vince. He, after all, had a soft spot for me. I drove to the lot and loitered for hours in the hallway until he emerged from his office.

"Hey, Vince. I wanted to pitch you a sketch idea."

"Ah," he said in his even way, "the day has finally arrived."

For a nauseating moment I realized it hadn't gone unnoticed that I'd written nothing.

"It's called 'Virgins on Their Wedding Night,'" I said, plowing ahead.

Vince waved to someone over my shoulder. "Come here."

It was the guys, arriving from a day at Magic Mountain.

"There's this thing called work," Vince told them. "I want you to witness what it looks like."

I now had the five biggest comedy stars in the world looking at me.

"It's called 'Virgins on Their Wedding Night,'" I stammered. "The idea is they—the virgins—have saved themselves for marriage, but when they get into bed on their wedding night, she, the bride—she knows every sex position in the book."

The response was immediate and positive.

"Heather playing the wife," Vince said. "Who's the husband?"

"I was thinking Andy," I said.

"I'll ball Heather Locklear," he said. "No problem there! Maybe this time she'll let me go au naturel!"

Vince gave me a nod. "Go off and write."

Everyone scattered except for TJ.

"Hey," he said. "Maybe we can write it together."

"Yeah, sure!"

"We can work at my place—" TJ stopped when Russell the PA approached with lunch from Koo Koo Roo.

"Hey, Russell," TJ said.

(His name wasn't Russell. It was a joke because we always associated him with the rustle of takeout bags.)

I waited for Russell to pass.

"I'd love to," I told TJ, voice lowered.

"Cool." Without naming a time, TJ walked away.

The next day, Tuesday, the guys' manager called to say Pauly Shore was on the lot and wanted to stop by. When he arrived, the guys acted all honored and asked him to do a ten-minute set. Pauly Shore sweatily obliged. The minute he walked out he was mercilessly roasted.

That evening, full of resentment, we got around to the task of writing. Me at the keyboard, while the guys freestyled sketch ideas for their recurring characters. The only mention of my Virgins sketch was when the guys fantasized about sexual acts they wanted to perform on Heather Locklear.

Anytime it came up, TJ looked at me from across the room. Without saying it, he was telling me to wait, we were still writing it together.

I'd never had a real boyfriend. Fat, funny girls didn't. I had drunk guys having sex with me and making me promise not to tell anyone. I had guys I was in love with use me as their emotional support dog between girlfriends. But a guy I liked who liked me back, and wanted to hang out with me and have sex because he thought I was pretty? Never.

I knew better than to even dream of dating one of the guys. That was reserved for models and aspiring actresses.

But TJ was different. Since that first day, the way he held my gaze for one extra second. He'd done it again at the concession stand at *Something About Mary*. And once, when it was just the two of us in Elijah's back seat on a drive to Malibu. Our legs touched and he didn't pull his away. I didn't know what it meant, if anything. But maybe? Maybe it was something?

Tuesday, nine P.M.

We'd sent Russell over the hill to get sushi from Matsuhisa, but it was taking too long so we hit the Smoke House instead. There, we sat in a red circular booth and ordered martinis and prime rib.

"Just like the Rat Pack," said Elijah, stretching his arms across the banquette.

"If Shirley MacLaine had a fat ass," I quipped.

I tensed, hoping for even mild reassurance. None came.

Dinner ended and the check was magically taken care of. Russell had been in the lobby the whole time, waiting to pay with the *Laugh Riot* Amex.

"I've got to get something at home," TJ said, getting up.

He locked his blue eyes onto mine. We had a plan.

I returned to the office with the guys, changed from girdle to regular underwear and slipped out.

I knew TJ lived in a bungalow on Curson, from when we'd swing by to get him for weekend excursions.

But I'd never seen the inside.

I knocked; TJ opened the door.

In the living room, the only furniture was a brass standing lamp with the tags still hanging from it and the same leather couch and coffee table we had in the office. Clothes were strewn in the direction of an open suitcase. A vase of dead flowers lay sideways on the shiny beige carpet.

"I know," TJ said. "My roommate's a serial killer."

"It's great!" I said, too loudly.

"I don't know what I'm doing," he said. "My wife doesn't want to raise our kid in LA so I just rent and . . ." He trailed off. He didn't want to talk about his wife any more than I wanted to hear about her.

"Shall we?" I said.

TJ pushed empty Chinese cartons to one side of the couch and we sat.

I was crazy with nerves. But once we got to work and my ideas for the sketch poured out, the nerves vanished.

A new TJ emerged, a serious and hard worker. This made sense. You don't go from a farm in South Eastern Ontario to *Laugh Riot* by accident. He must have spent years toiling in clubs, perfecting every word of every joke.

He confessed that whenever he got around Andy, Elijah and Matteo—the ones with the runaway movie careers—he felt pressured to act like he was too cool to care about the work.

Sitting alone, we were both free to shed the pretense. Time flew as we popped with ideas, cracked each other up and moved around words.

At one point TJ looked over and said, "You're really good at this, aren't you?"

"You are, too," I quickly added.

The silence grew.

I'd been holding in my pee for three hours and the pain was beginning to stab.

"Do you have a bathroom?" I asked.

He gestured down the hall. I got up and passed one bedroom devoid of furniture and another with nothing but a mattress on the floor. Through that was a bathroom.

And it was filthy! Toilet stained brown, sink caked with toothpaste, bathtub heaped with trash and dirty (I mean dirty) jockey shorts on the floor. No toilet paper.

I came out and had to ask, "Has that ever been cleaned?"

"I've been meaning to," TJ said. "I bought all the stuff. But I don't know what I'm doing." He pointed to a Thrifty bag in the corner.

My heart melted. TJ couldn't walk through a food court without people asking for his autograph. And he didn't know how to clean a bathroom?

"Wait there," I said. "Five minutes."

I grabbed the cleaning supplies, shut the door and got scrubbing.

I'd imagined it would take five minutes. I opened the door an hour later.

TJ was out in the living room, talking on the phone to what sounded like his daughter. When he saw me, he quickly wrapped up.

"Come see," I said.

TJ stood there and beheld the sparkling bathroom. "This is insane. . . ."

"Your clothes are in the wash," I proudly added.

TJ couldn't wipe the smile off his face. "I can't believe you just cleaned my bathroom."

Put that way, I didn't like how it sounded.

"Let's keep going!" I said.

We returned to the sofa.

"Where were we?" I said, my energy growing manic.

"Hey," said TJ, laughing. "Not so fast. You must be tired."

What I was, was confused. What had I just done? And why?

"Not at all!" I said.

But TJ wouldn't stop marveling. Those blue eyes saw it all: my desire, my shame at my desire, my helplessness that I could hide neither.

He leaned in and kissed me.

I kissed him back. I reached for his head. His hair was fine and silky soft. I sucked in my stomach as his hand reached under my shirt. I thought I'd pass out from all the new sensations.

"Get this goddamned thing off," he said.

I unhooked my bra.

Eyes shut, he squeezed my breasts with both hands and let out a moan. We kissed ravenously.

My hand reached into his pants.

"We can't fuck," he said, coming up for air. "It would be cheating on my wife."

"Oh," I said, trying to block out the images of used condoms I'd just scraped off the side of his bathtub. "Of course."

TJ unzipped his pants and laid back.

I gave him a blow job, and swallowed.

When I joined him back on the couch, he looked over at me.

"What can't you do?" he asked, and closed his eyes.

Half an hour later, the buzzer on the washing machine jolted TJ awake.

"It's getting late," he said. "We're pretty much done with the sketch, right?"

We weren't.

"I'll go back and write it up," I said.

I drove over the hill. It was past two in the morning.

I was ecstatic over what had happened, but also freaked out that the guys would see that TJ and I were unaccounted for, and put two and two together.

They didn't.

I sat at the empty desk in the outer office and wrote up "Virgins on Their Wedding Night."

Jawbreakers pelted me on the head.

"Adora!" Andy howled from the big office. "Where are you? We need help!"

I closed the door with my foot and furiously typed, TJ's voice, "What can't you do?" a constant, joyous loop.

I finished the sketch at four A.M. I typed our names at the top: Steele and Hazzard. It had a nice ring.

All I could do now was hope it got picked to read at the table tomorrow. I went to the PA's office to turn it in. When I got there, Matteo and Elijah were reading a sketch Marla and Ann had just submitted.

It was called "Fair World." In it, Heather Locklear walks into a bar in a hot pink bikini and men ignore her in favor of Marla and Ann, who are outspoken and intelligent.

"Get it?" Matteo said. "Because it's a *fair world*."

On my way out, I ran into Vince.

"How's the writing?" he asked.

"Great! Just turned it in."

"Congratulations." He stuck his hand out. "On having your first sketch in the show."

"You haven't read it."

"I don't need to. You're in."

I drove home and slept for eight hours.

The next day, I gave myself ample time to get to the lot, but there was a crash on the 101. Traffic was stopped and the clock ticking. In growing panic, I began to whimper.

"Please, God. You can do anything to me. Just don't make me late."

God heard me. Traffic cleared. I arrived at the office just before five.

Ann and Marla were in the stairwell rehearsing "Fair World." Pens in hand, they were repeating every line, marking which words to hit for maximum comic effect. Thank God they didn't notice me pass or they'd have seen me in full-body cringe.

I went straight to the guys' office but it was empty. I dropped my bag and noticed, in the Charles Chips tin, a bunch of hundred-dollar bills.

Clyde came out of the bathroom.

"What's the bet?" I asked.

He mumbled something—

—which I couldn't hear because it was suddenly drowned out by the iconic opening of "Welcome to the Jungle."

It was the assistant director, walking through the halls with a boom box. This was the signal to gather for the table reading.

That day, the season twenty-five finale, the conference room was more packed than I'd ever seen it. The jabber was deafening. People talked politics, movies, restaurants—

"Hazzard!" someone called.

My agent, Travis! Of course he'd finagled himself an invitation.

There was no way I could reach him across the packed room, so I waved. He pointed to me, flashed a thumbs-up and posed as an Emmy statue.

The table was huge, but real estate scarce. Seats were reserved for Vince, the guest host, the cast and those writers whose sketches had made it into the packet.

The writers whose hadn't sat against the wall with the department heads, execs and guests. Until today, that was me.

I scanned the room for TJ.

On the far side of the table, in their usual spots, sat Elijah, Matteo, Andy and Clyde. Elijah had just gotten a Palm Pilot and everyone was energetically admiring it.

But where was TJ?

"Looking for someone?" came his Canadian drawl.

He was opposite the guys, patting the empty chair beside him.

The seat he had saved for me, apart from the others. I just about died.

I looked over to make sure Travis had been watching. He had.

The desk chairs around the table were crammed so tightly that in order to get in, I had to pull mine out, sit and scoot in.

"How you doing?" TJ's eyes glimmered with memories of last night. He wore the same clothes as yesterday: jeans and blue T-shirt under an unbuttoned plaid flannel. Shoot, I'd forgotten to advance his laundry before I left.

"Fine," I said. "You?"

"I'm excited for your sketch, I'll tell you that much."

"Our sketch," I corrected.

The AD called on everyone to settle.

Sketch packets, sharpened pencils and bottles of water had been laid out at every seat. I flipped through and found "Virgins on Their Wedding Night." The placement of the sketches within the packet was highly political and the source of much jockeying.

"We're number five," TJ whispered. "Right where we want to be."

"Fantastic," I whispered back.

Vince O'Quinn introduced Heather Locklear to raucous cheers and applause.

The table reading began. I was completely wired. There was no way I could concentrate. Even the sketches TJ was in, I barely understood the meaning of the words. When other people laughed, I laughed. Where other people made check marks in the margin, I made check marks in the margin.

I could only think ahead to TJ's and my sketch. I knew Andy would sell it. Vince already liked it. Travis would witness it kill. He'd go back to WAC and tell everyone their B-list, intermittent earner was now a bona fide star.

Finally, Vince spoke the words: "'Virgins on Their Wedding Night.' Written by TJ Steele and *Laugh Riot*'s own Adora Hazzard, of the Connecticut Hazzards. Welcome to the table, Adora."

There was an enthusiastic round of applause, even a whistle. Probably just Travis. Still, it was enough for Heather Locklear to give me a surprised and encouraging smile.

If things couldn't get more perfect . . .

I felt TJ's hand on my knee.

At first, I startled, then realized nobody else could see. To them, it looked like TJ had that hand in his lap.

I nodded at him. To anyone looking, it would come off as a wish of good luck between writing partners. Only TJ and I knew the deeper truth.

With that simple gesture, every question I'd forbidden myself to ask was answered. Yes, TJ and I were more than writing partners. Yes, he'd tell the guys. Yes, it would be tough to navigate because of his wife and daughter.

I longed to squeeze his hand back, to mark this moment of us having our first sketch read. But both my arms were above the table. The seats were so tightly jammed that squeezing TJ's hand would require me pushing my chair back, and that would be conspicuous and weird and—

"This place is gorgeous!" exclaimed Heather Locklear.

The sketch had begun.

I expected TJ to remove his hand. But he kept it on my knee. I was so disoriented by the electricity that I had no idea how the sketch was playing.

I heard laughter, but forgot to mark it—this was not good.

I just had to wait until TJ needed his hands to turn the page.

"Mrs. Barton," Andy asked Heather Locklear, "what was that?"

The whole room, following along, turned to page two. TJ as well. But with his one hand above the table.

The other hand still rested on my knee. . . .

And was now moving to the more sensitive flesh of my inner thigh.

I was turned on. And angry. My whole life had been leading up to this sketch. I needed to be present for it.

I glared at TJ.

His face was blank and gave no indication of what was happening under the table.

I looked around and saw a sea of eyes volleying between Heather Locklear and Andy. Nobody was looking at me. Nobody had any clue what TJ was doing.

I pulled my leg away, but TJ's hand had gained purchase on my jiggly thigh. His fingers walked up the inside of my leg. I squeezed my legs together. He clawed his fingertips past the elastic of my underwear.

My breathing stopped.

This wasn't happening. Not here. Not now. Not in front of everyone. Not when my first sketch was being read at the table—

I felt the chill of a wedding ring against my hot, wet flesh.

I went limp and allowed him to slide his straightened, sideways hand inside me.

TJ removed his hand and discreetly wiped it on his jeans.

It was over.

I had one purpose: not to pass out and embarrass myself in front of everyone.

Laughter echoed with each joke, but all I saw were white spots skating around. Through the laughter, I could make out strange hyena howls.

I focused my eyes on the source. Across the table, Elijah and Matteo were out of control, twisting in their chairs, laughing at the jokes, but past the jokes, too.

They were laughing at me.

I found Clyde, whose tormented face confirmed what I already knew.

I was the bet.

Thunderous applause. Career-making applause.

I scanned the room for someone who had witnessed what TJ had done; all the looks that came my way were of genuine happiness. For the nice girl who'd finally achieved her dreams. Travis shot her with an air pistol.

TJ didn't look at me for the rest of the table reading.

The next two hours: sketches were read.

A final round of applause.

People rose. I rose.

I thanked those who showered me with congratulations.

Travis found me.

"You are awesome," he said. "I just spoke with O'Quinn. He told me to call business affairs. They're making you an offer for next season. 'Virgins on Their Wedding Night'? I'm going to put the arm on them for a feature deal. We've got to get started on your transition to the big screen. And I mean, yesterday."

I put one foot in front of the other.

In the hallway, Elijah, Matteo, Andy, Clyde and TJ were up ahead joking around with Mark McGwire. I didn't have the energy or thought process available to turn around and walk the other way.

Clyde saw me coming and averted his eyes.

"Here she is," proclaimed Elijah. "The man of the hour."

He raised his hand to high-five me. So did Matteo, Andy and Mark McGwire. Not TJ. In his shirt pocket, the roll of hundreds.

I walked through their gauntlet, and have often wondered if I high-fived them back.

I made it to 212. There, Marla was openly crying. Ann was bitterly consoling her. "Fair World" had bombed. Elijah and Matteo had tanked it.

"I hate this place," Marla said.

"It hates you," said Ann.

I wanted to blurt out and tell them what had just happened. What

TJ had done. But I didn't dare. They'd want to make a huge deal. Or God forbid, march me into Vince's office to tell him.

I staggered through Thursday and Friday. My body quivered, even in my sleep. I drove to the lot. I waved to the guards at the gate. The cast and staff had migrated to the stage, which meant the offices were mercifully empty. The jesters made no demands for my audience.

I spent the days behind the closed door of 212.

The fun parts of getting a sketch on, the parts I'd so looked forward to—choosing wardrobe, consulting on set design, opining on hair and makeup—I never got called down for. I'd put TJ's name first on the sketch; the department heads probably directed their questions at him.

Russell knocked on my door and said I was wanted onstage for rehearsal.

Writers usually watched from the floor. I watched "Virgins on Their Wedding Night" from behind glass in the control booth. The director asked if I had any notes. I told him I didn't.

On my way out, I passed the craft service table. They'd just put out hot finger food. I was loading some into a paper bowl when, in the hushed shadows, TJ and an AD walked towards me.

"We good?" TJ asked as he passed by.

I couldn't speak.

Good enough for TJ. He kept going and didn't look back. I waited until they turned a corner, then fled, scattering pigs in a blanket on the concrete floor.

My mother had flown in from Connecticut to see the show with her manicurist, Gina, and Gina's fourteen-year-old son. I'd gotten them tickets. Even before what had happened with TJ, I tried to prevent my mother from coming. She insisted, and I'd read her the riot act about not bothering me until the after-party.

On show night, my mother, Gina and Jimmy watched from the bleachers. Me, from across the lot, alone, off the live feed in the writers' offices.

The year-end party was always the biggest, and thrown on a soundstage. I sleepwalked over to put in an appearance. For my mother. That's what I told myself.

But *Laugh Riot* was the only life I had. Somehow I felt more locked in than ever. It was as if my whole existence pre *Laugh Riot* had been erased by the glamour and exhilaration of the last four weeks. There was no finding my way back to it.

I'd never seen my mother more at peace than at the after-party, perfectly at home among celebrities, absorbing the glow of her impressed manicurist.

Outkast played. I watched alone in a corner nursing a can of Diet Coke.

In the crowd, but also standing alone: a mousy woman who looked out of place, and she knew it. Bad perm, blue eye shadow, dowdy glasses. On her hip she bounced a toddler. When her arm got tired, she shifted the little girl to the other side. That's when I saw the child's piercing blue eyes. TJ's wife. And daughter.

TJ was across the stage with Elijah, Clyde, Andy and Matteo, all gathered around Vince. I watched as they told him a story he was finding hard to believe. Vince scowled.

The guys hopped up and down, insisting it was true.

I knew it was about me. Even before TJ made the gesture with his hand, flattening it out, sliding it up. This left the guys in stitches and Vince shaking his head with paternalistic fondness.

No part of me wanted to run over and yell at them to stop.

I went home and stayed there. I ate what I had in my pantry, even when it got down to fermented soy sauce and moth-infested brown rice. The TV at the foot of my bed was always on. But mostly I ended up staring at the unpainted bureau on which it sat. When I'd moved to LA, I bought the cheapest one I could find. It was held together by staples. I had visions of sponging it pink and white like I'd seen at Shabby Chic. Its knobs, depending how you looked at them, could form a peace sign, the hazard symbol, or a face with no mouth.

At some point, the phone rang. I rolled onto my side and answered.

"Hello?" My voice had dropped two octaves. I hadn't spoken for a week.

"Look." It was Travis, from his car. "There's no good way to say this. I just got off the phone with *Laugh Riot*. They're not picking you up for next year."

"What?" I said, pushing myself to sitting.

"These are the calls you hate to make as an agent. They looked at their budget and—"

"That's what they said?"

"—they just don't have the money. I asked if they could find some at scale or be open to developing—"

"It's not true," I managed to sputter.

"Like I tell all my clients, a job isn't an entitlement. It's a privilege."

"Who did you speak to?"

"O'Quinn."

Vince. He had seen how special I was.

"Is that all he said?" I asked, voice rising.

After a confused pause, Travis said, "I told you. It's a budget issue. I really worked him. He's doing a bunch of writer deals. If one falls apart, he promised to give me a call—"

"Did-he-tell-you-what-happened?!"

"Adora, this sucks. I know."

"It's because he raped me!"

"Whoa— What? Who raped you?"

I could identify the telltale rustle of being taken off speaker.

"TJ! He raped me with the side of his hand!" My mouth was producing a copious amount of saliva; it cascaded down my chin and onto my T-shirt.

"He raped you with what?" Travis asked in nervous laughter.

"His hand!"

"When did this happen?"

"At the table reading."

"The one I was at?"

"Elijah Strickland, Matteo Matthams, Andy Galinski, Clyde Chavez. They paid him to stick his hand up me. They bragged about it to Vince. I saw them. And now he's firing me."

"That's not what's happening," my agent said. "It's the budget."

I let out a wail.

"Look," said Travis. "This is not what I was expecting when I called. And I don't really understand what you're saying."

"Ask TJ," I said, pacing back and forth. "Ask Clyde Chavez. Ask all of them."

"Let me make some calls," said Travis, "and try to get to the bottom of what happened."

"I told you what happened!"

"You gotta calm down," he said.

I could only sob.

"Are you okay? Do you need help?" I heard Travis whisper, "Keep it out front." He must have pulled in to the valet. For lunch. It was one o'clock.

I threw the phone against the wall. I went to pick it up. Travis was gone.

I walked to Greenblatt's and got a turkey sandwich, latkes, potato salad, waffle fries, black-and-white cookies and a big thing of pickles. I brought it all home and grimly stuffed myself on the couch.

The five o'clock news had just started when my phone rang.

"First off," Travis said, "TJ Steele is a scumbag."

"He is?"

"Jesus, what a sack of shit."

"He is. Right?" Optimism surged through my veins and lifted me to my feet. "I was just sitting there. I did nothing wrong."

"Look, I'm trying to keep the circle small."

"Thank you."

"For your sake."

"Good. I don't want people to know."

"Actually," he said. "Who else have you told?"

"Nobody. Just you. I wouldn't have even brought it up to you, except—"

"Great," he said. "Let's keep it that way. I spoke to my mentor. He's been around since the seventies. Without naming names, I explained what happened. And I'm working something out."

"Really?" The shock of someone being on my side had me pacing in circles. "Thank you! It was so crazy. I was just sitting there. I didn't ask for this to happen—"

"You're preaching to the choir."

"I know," I said. "Thank you."

"I'm still in the middle of it. But come in tomorrow."

My first thought: if I'd known I had to go into WAC tomorrow, I wouldn't have stuffed my face.

"Three o'clock," he said. "See you then. Just know—I feel really fucking shitty."

I tried to apologize, but he'd already hung up.

WAC was then, as it is now, the white-hot power center of Hollywood. Even the lifers rubbernecked whenever a visitor was escorted to the conference room.

That day, the visitor was me.

With each movie poster I passed—the latest from Mel Gibson, Johnny Depp, Will Smith—my confidence grew. I had the big guns behind me now. They would take care of me. All I wanted was to move on, and WAC would make sure I did.

I pictured something like this. . . . TJ would be let go, citing family obligations in Canada. I would return to *Laugh Riot* as a full-time writer. The guys, who'd have been reprimanded, would avoid me at first. It would be awkward. Until one of them made a joke about it, we'd crack up and everything would snap back into place.

The assistant, an icy blonde with shiny flat hair and giant engagement ring, opened the door to the conference room. Travis was there, and a man in a suit.

"Here she is!" said Travis, playing bongos on the table.

"Can I get you something to drink?" asked the assistant.

On a sideboard, a station of soft drinks.

"Diet Coke," I said. "I can get it myself." I turned to the men. "Do you want anything?"

"You sit down," Travis said.

I did, across from Travis, who resumed ranting to his suited colleague about a bad call at last night's Lakers game.

It had rained that morning and wiped away the smog. Out the window, the mansions dotting the hills popped to life in 3D, like berries asking to be plucked.

The assistant placed a tumbler of iced Diet Coke in front of me and removed herself.

When the door clicked shut, Travis introduced the man in the suit as an outside attorney.

"Oh!" I said. "But I don't want to sue."

"I know," said Travis. "And everyone totally appreciates that."

"Great," I said.

"So. After our talk, I spent all yesterday trying to get to the bottom of what happened."

I was confused. I'd told him what happened.

"Everyone's going to have their own opinion," Travis continued. "Nobody's here to litigate what will never be agreed upon. We're here to resolve."

"Right," I said.

My stomach turned. It was perfume. Even though the assistant had left, her scent lingered. It was so strong, I considered the possibility it was worn by one of the men.

"You didn't speak to anyone else about this last night?" asked Travis.

"No. And I wouldn't have even told you, but—"

"Good. It's in nobody's interest to turn this into a docudrama."

"I totally agree," I said.

"Let me start out," said Travis, "by telling you something you already know. TJ Steele isn't going anywhere."

I did not know that.

"Nobody likes what he did. But they're never going to fire him. We had shitty luck that boys will be boys right when networks are tightening their belts. If that's a pun, I apologize."

Travis looked at the lawyer to share a bonding chuckle. The lawyer wouldn't partake. He was in the process of assessing me. Rather brazenly.

"My point is," Travis continued, "we shouldn't have to pay for TJ's bullshit. They should pay."

"Oh, okay!" I hadn't realized how dry my mouth had gotten. I took a sip of Diet Coke. My glass had sweat all over the conference table.

I started to stand.

"Wait—" Travis practically yelped. "Where are you going?"

"Sorry!" I said. "Just getting one of these."

In the center of the table was a caddy of leather WAC coasters. I grabbed one, and set my glass on it. The condensation I wiped away with the front of my T-shirt.

Travis placed his hand on a brown accordion file, the same color as the table. It was so well camouflaged I hadn't noticed it.

"Here's what we've come up with." Travis unwound the string and removed white pages backed by sky blue.

A contract.

That particular shade of blue always brought a smile to my face, and today was no exception. What was it for? I had no idea.

"You're about to find out how much *Laugh Riot* values you," Travis said.

Anticipation had me moving my hips. I forced myself to remain still.

A movie deal for "Virgins on Their Wedding Night"? Travis said he wanted to fast-track my feature career. This would be insane. Making the leap so soon.

Travis flipped to page two and scanned the document. He pulled an envelope from between the last page and blue backing.

"Here's the deal," he said. "You keep doing what you're doing, which is writing great comedy."

"Amazing," I said.

"And not go around blabbing about TJ."

"Yeah," I said. "Sure."

Travis had one eye on the attorney as he spoke to me. "This is not a 'sure'-type situation. We're moving into the land of black and white."

"Sorry," I said.

"Which is what you want to do, anyway," Travis said to me, "if I'm hearing correctly? Not talk about it."

"Yes." I punched the word to prove my comfort with black and white. "I mean, no. Yes. No, I don't want to talk about it."

"In exchange," Travis said, "they're going to give you this."

He passed over the envelope. In it, a check from "Wandering Rocks, LLC" with no address. It was made out to me.

For $250,000.

I'd been living on $30,000 a year. A thousand a month for rent, fifteen hundred for expenses.

My father ran a nonprofit theater in Connecticut. My mother was a hammy actress who the directors were compelled to cast. I'd never seen anything close to $250,000.

No doubt my eyes went boing.

"Even better?" Travis said. "I'm not commissioning it."

I had to suck in the corners of my mouth to prevent a Cheshire cat grin.

"You have the *Laugh Riot* credit." Travis was talking fast now. "So we got what we needed. It doesn't matter if it was four shows or four thousand. *Laugh Riot* is a notoriously horrible place to work. Nobody's going to think twice about why you left."

"Great," I said.

"There are a million comedy camps I can get you in with," Travis said. "We represent Chuck Lorre, Steve Levitan, all the big show-runners."

My head frolicked with visions of choosing between *Just Shoot Me!* and *Dharma & Greg*.

"It's literally a matter of me picking up the phone."

The lawyer, though. He was focused on me as if trying to . . . communicate something?

I looked around the room. My eyes caught another shock of sky blue peeking out from the file folder. A copy of the contract? Or perhaps a different one?

On impulse, I heard myself say: "What if I say no?"

Travis: "Heh?"

And audible in-breath from the attorney.

"If I say no," I repeated, an inexplicable calm having descended. "What happens?"

"What exactly would you be saying no to?" Travis carefully asked.

I didn't know myself. But I sensed something shifting. Something opening up.

"You're not thinking about reporting this?" asked Travis. "That's not what you want, is it? Because that's an entirely different ball of wax. It means the check goes away, and—"

"The amount," I said. "What happens if I say no to the amount."

"Oh."

Travis turned to the lawyer. They had planned for this. It was Travis's call.

"I have been authorized. . . ." Travis pulled out the second contract and emitted a sigh of death. Tucked in the back of this contract was another envelope.

In it, a check. This one for $350,000.

For a flash, I felt like I was really good at something.

Silence, as loaded as any I'd ever experienced.

"May I?" I pointed to the contract.

"It's just what we've been saying." Travis passed it over. "Plus a bunch of legalese. I asked them to dumb it down. For my sake. But you know, lawyers."

He made a "this guy" gesture to the man on his left.

"I need to concentrate," I said.

This Nondisclosure Agreement ("Agreement") is entered into as of May 21, 1998, by and between Laugh Riot LLC ("Company") and you, Adora Hazzard ("Recipient"), collectively referred to as the "Released Parties."

NOW, THEREFORE, in consideration of the mutual covenants and agreements contained herein, you, Adora Hazzard, agree as follows:

1. Settlement Payment

The Company will pay you the amount of $350,000 (the "Settlement Payment") on the day of execution of this Agreement. This payment is a full and final settlement of any and all claims you may have against the Company or any of its representatives related to an alleged workplace incident involving Tomas Stelinski (hereinafter referred to as "TJ Steele").

2. Confidentiality

a. Confidential Information: For the purposes of this Agreement, "Confidential Information" includes any and all details regarding the alleged workplace incident, the settlement payment, and the terms and existence of this Agreement.

b. Nondisclosure: You agree not to disclose any Confidential Information to any third party, including but not limited to friends, family, or future children.

c. Medical Exception: In the event that you require medical or psychiatric treatment related to the alleged workplace incident, you will obtain a confidentiality agreement from a licensed practitioner and present it to the Company's representative for written approval.

3. **Warranties**

You warrant that as of the date of this Agreement, you have not disclosed any Confidential Information to any person other than your representative at Writers and Artists Collective.

4. **Non-Disparagement**

You agree not to make any statements, written or verbal, or cause or encourage others to make any statements that defame, disparage, or in any way criticize the personal or business reputation, practices, or conduct of the Company or TJ Steele. Similarly, you will not use the alleged workplace incident or this Agreement as inspiration for future artistic endeavors.

5. **Parting Explanation**

You agree that if asked about the circumstances of your departure from the Company, you will represent that the decision to part ways was made voluntarily by you. Furthermore, you agree to limit your response to one of the following statements or similarly vague language:

—"It didn't work out."

—"It wasn't for me."

You shall not make any additional statements, written or verbal, that suggest or imply that your departure was involuntary or the result of any dispute, misconduct, or agreement.

6. **No Admission of Liability**

This Agreement does not constitute an admission of liability or wrongdoing by the Company or TJ Steele. Released Parties acknowledge that the Settlement Payment is made solely to avoid the expense and inconvenience of the litigation process.

7. **Communication Protocol**

a. No Direct Communication: You shall not communicate directly with TJ Steele or anyone at the Company regarding any matters covered by this Agreement. To do so will be considered a breach of confidentiality.

b. Communication Through Legal Counsel: All communication regarding this Agreement shall be conducted through the law office of Idelson, Bradstock, Toll and Miller. (See Appendix A.)

8. **Liquidated Damages**

In the event that you breach the confidentiality provisions of this Agreement, you agree to pay the Company liquidated damages in the amount of $1,000,000. The Released Parties acknowledge that this amount is a reasonable estimate of the damages that the Company would incur as a result of such a breach and is not a penalty.

9. **Perpetuity**

The terms of this agreement are in perpetuity.

10. **Reporting of Payment**

You agree to report the Settlement Payment to the Internal Revenue Service and the Writers Guild of America as a script payment for the "Untitled Adora Hazzard Project." Any tax liabilities or guild dues arising from this payment are your sole responsibility. For clarity, there is no "Untitled Adora Hazzard Project."

It was followed by signature pages and an appendix.

In no particular order, here's how I felt after I finished reading it: important, excited, powerful, at peace.

"Do you need us to walk you through it?" asked Travis.

Oh, and relief. Relief being the biggie.

"It didn't work out," I uttered, trying it on for size.

"You like that?" Travis said. "I put that in to make it easier for you."

"The people are great," I said, now looking between Travis and the attorney. "But it wasn't for me."

Even without a contract, I would never tell my mother. As for friends, in the weeks since it happened, I didn't have the slightest impulse to pick up the phone to tell anyone. My future children? Who were they?

"A million dollars," I said, staring at the amount I'd have to pay if I ever did talk. "That is the land of black and white."

"Boilerplate," Travis said with a wave of the hand.

"Are you in therapy?" It was the first time the lawyer had spoken.

Something occurred to me. "There's nothing in here that says how they can talk about me."

"Yeah," Travis said. "We went back and forth. But it would mean getting Strickland, Matthams, Chavez and Galinski involved."

"No!" I'd already adjusted to the idea that this whole thing was boxed up and buried. "I don't want that."

"Basically," Travis said, "you're great. Everyone knows you're great. Believe me when I say TJ Steele has been scared straight. Vince feels like shit. Trust me, this will be a blip."

Did I mention I'd never seen so much money?

I signed the contract.

Travis told me to get a list of shows together, ones I wanted to work on. To think big.

"When hiring season starts," he said, "we'll have to beat away the offers."

What to say about the next few months? They started off okay.

Something I learned? There are a lot of hours in the day when you're waiting for hiring season to roll around.

My downstairs neighbor got *Variety* and the *Hollywood Reporter* delivered. He never woke up before noon, so every morning I'd sneak down and scour both trades to see which pilots had buzz and which shows had gotten renewed. I'd refine my list accordingly. The list Travis asked for, to have ready when the time came. But that was weeks off.

I went to the gym until I stopped going to the gym. I went to movies by myself, and then didn't. Driving to my first party, I decided I wasn't feeling it and turned around. I saw one of my favorite people, an assistant from my Nickelodeon days, at Borders. Instead of bounding up, I slinked out before she could see me.

I told myself this limbo was temporary. That once I got on a show, things would return to normal.

I volunteered serving lunch at an old folks' home. I quit after I became repulsed by how much the old people wanted their coffee. They lived in constant fear they might not get it. When I'd come around to pour powdered lemonade from a plastic pitcher, they'd cover their paper cups with age-spotted hands and beseech, "Not if it means I don't get coffee."

The networks finally announced their schedules. Hiring season was afoot.

Travis didn't call.

I called him.

And called him.

He was never available.

His assistant would periodically call back at odd hours, gambling that I wouldn't be home to answer. I always was. When I did pick up, she'd say, "Shoot, I lost him in a canyon."

The last time she did this, I got verbally abusive.

"I'm telling you this to help you," she said. "He's not your agent anymore."

Something else I learned? Friends are a house of cards. The minute you stop calling them, the whole thing collapses. My phone stopped ringing completely.

It makes you wonder if anyone liked you in the first place.

Or, if maybe they'd heard something.

I took to bed. I hated my body, its repulsive fat, my face.

I made noises akin to Tibetan throat singing. Sometimes, I channeled Nancy Kerrigan and wailed, "Why? Why me?" And discovered that abandoning yourself to self-pity can feel pretty damn good. When that wasn't enough, I'd repeat into my drool-cold pillow, "It didn't work out. It wasn't for me."

El Niño struck. My apartment leaked. I put down pots. In my bedroom, the ceiling had been painted over so many times the water couldn't break through the layers. I watched with fascination as the paint stretched and sagged but wouldn't break. It grew to the size of a cat.

One day, I stood on my bed to give it a bounce. The water inside was warm.

The phone rang.

Normally, I wouldn't have picked it up, but the image of a warm watercat in my ceiling had made me momentarily forget who I was.

"Adora," said a man's voice. He told me his name but it meant nothing. "The attorney."

My throat closed.

"The one you can talk to."

I said nothing.

"I'm calling because you haven't cashed your check."

It was true. I hadn't.

"And I wanted to see—"

I slammed down the phone and drove to the bank.

I handed the teller the endorsed check and a deposit slip. There weren't enough boxes for all the zeroes.

"Whoa," she remarked. "What do you do?"

I had no idea what to say. Or what she would say. Or what I would say. Or what she would say.

"I'm a TV writer," were the words that came out. I held my breath.

"I'm in the wrong line of work," she said, and blew her bangs off her forehead.

I drove to yogurt.

I was the only customer other than two people sitting at a table. When I went to the counter, they lowered their voices. It was so blatant I turned to look.

Marla and Ann.

"Hi!" I said with genuine warmth, surprising myself and them.

Marla returned a rueful look.

"Wazzup," said Ann, her voice injected with poison.

I pressed both palms against the sneeze guard to prevent my whole body from flying apart. I ordered my usual. Large vanilla with rainbow sprinkles.

Behind me, I sensed they'd gotten up to leave.

"I don't know what you heard—" I blurted before I realized it could cost me a million dollars.

"That you went to TJ's house," Marla said flatly, "cleaned his bathroom and blew him. And when you didn't get asked back, you demanded a settlement. Thanks to you, they'll never hire another woman writer."

"Cheers." Ann touched her yogurt to mine. "Hope it works out."

They left.

I was hollow, about to implode. I got in my car. I made it home on muscle memory.

My parking space was blocked by a maroon Jaguar. It was my landlord. He stood outside with a roofer.

"Oh, hi," I said. "My apartment's been leaking."

I remember thinking, This is good. This is me living life. This is me existing in the matrix of the day-to-day.

"For how long?" asked my landlord.

"I don't know, weeks."

"You're telling me this now?"

"Yeah. Sorry."

"Sorry?!" he erupted. "You just turned a hundred-dollar problem into a thousand-dollar problem!"

"I-I didn't want to bother you."

"Bother me!" he said, his hostility unrelenting. "Wake me up at four in the morning when my building is leaking! Call me the minute it starts! Weeks?! Jesus! What kind of moron are you?!"

I was too stunned to answer.

I ran up the stairs to my landing.

A box had been delivered while I was out. How could this be, I remember thinking, when there's no me? The box was so big it blocked the doorway.

The return address read, "PORTLAND, OR." I figured it had been misdelivered, that it was meant for my downstairs neighbor. But the name read, "ADORA HAZZARD."

I hated Adora Hazzard. I hated her fat. I hated her face. I hated her voice. I hated her personality. I hated her more than I hated the old people and their coffee.

I kicked the box inside. I got a box cutter and opened it.

Inside, lying across the top, the order form from Nike. The one I'd filled out, and Elijah Strickland had swiped from me so he could fill out the rest. I lifted it from the box. On top was the pair of Air Jordans I'd ordered. Beneath those, the box was packed with sports bras, size XXXL. A hundred of them—it was circled on the form.

I'd had no clue the box would be there. I didn't know I'd be standing in my living room holding a box cutter after running into Marla and Ann. And getting yelled at by my landlord. But there was a natural next step. All I needed to do was take it.

Feeling nothing, I went to my desk and found a Sharpie in my pen cup. I took it, and sat down. On my left thigh, the scene of the crime, I wrote, "TJ STEELE."

I picked up the box cutter, slid open the blade and touched its corner to the inside of my wrist. Just that, and my eyelids went heavy with gratitude for the relief to come. I added force, piercing skin. It only stung. I pushed hard, until none of the blade showed. I pulled until it hit something hard. There was plenty of blood.

I looked up. The index card pinned to my bulletin board.

"SHOW THOSE BASTARDS."

Thanks, Ernest Hemingway. Thanks, Dad.

You kind of have to laugh.

I did.

The roofer found me.

The doctors glued me up. They made me call my therapist, who called my mother in Connecticut. (My father had died the year before.)

When I walked through the door of my childhood home, my mother greeted me.

"Poor thing," she said. "It's okay. There'll be other fellas."

I had no idea what my therapist told her.

My mother gave me a hug. "I always pictured you with Timothy Hutton, anyway."

She really loved *Ordinary People.*

JANUARY OF 1999

I first came across Stoicism in *The New York Times.* I'd been living with my mother for six months, and happened upon their weekly philosophy column. It laid out Stoicism's first principle: events are neutral.

Events in and of themselves don't contain emotion. Yet we go through life as if events and our emotional reactions are inextricably twinned. Our car breaks down? Of course we're upset! Someone else got the job we wanted? Of course we're jealous!

Stoicism tells us it's not a two-step process (event + emotional reaction). But a three-step process (event + *our judgment of the event* + emotional reaction). What we're having the emotional freakout about is not the event itself, but *what we tell ourselves about the event.*

A universe of possibility exists in this middle step. What if we tell ourselves that we'll fix our car and life goes on? Or that the job could have been a washout, and now we're available for the next, better opportunity?

Change the judgment to change the emotion.

It all struck me as obvious and reasonable. Refreshingly, thrillingly, doably obvious and reasonable. The promise of Stoicism was a tranquil mind, abiding good cheer and secure joy. Added bonus: you could start this minute. Added, added bonus: you didn't need anybody else to do it.

I felt something lift.

My gateway book was William Irvine's *A Guide to the Good Life.* (Which I still have, and cherish; by now the whole thing is underlined, highlighted and starred in a dozen different inks.) From there, I went straight to the source: Seneca, Marcus Aurelius and Epictetus.

The leap from TV writing to philosophy might seem improbable. But I'd always been an enthusiast. Sudden, all-consuming passions were nothing new. Whether it be learning guitar, the *Titanic,* and copying the dictionary (when I was a teen) or tarot, dog rescue and Sondheim (when I got older).

Stoicism was another in a long line.

Hours passed as minutes whenever I transcribed quotations, journaled, or dove deep into a text.

I couldn't get over how modern Stoicism felt. Not just ahead of its time, but ahead of our time, too! I rued the hours I'd wasted in therapy blathering about my terrible childhood while a nice lady nodded sympathetically and checked her watch. Sure, I got some insight. But insight is the booby prize. What good is insight if it traps you in victimhood? In Stoicism, there are no victims. It's all you.

Especially jazzifying/horrifying was the realization that I'd never given a single thought to my personal character. And I was raised Catholic! But my main takeaway from catechism was that Jesus performed magic tricks, nuns hated kids, and never, ever tell the truth in confession. Now, I understood with jarring clarity that my character—or lack of it—was to blame for my past suffering.

Heraclites: *Character is fate.*

Of course I wanted to talk about it! By talk about it, I mean dig my fingers into someone's arms and trap them in an endless conversation.

But the only person around was my mother, and she didn't want to hear it. I'd gotten a job at Kinko's—to have something to do—and my coworkers weren't fans of my verbal fire hose. "Did you know AA's Serenity Prayer came from Epictetus? Do you realize cognitive behavioral therapy is literally just Stoicism? You know Aristotle? Who invented logic, the scientific method and the classification of species? That Aristotle? Well, I'm listening to this great course and he breaks down what makes a thing a thing—"

This is why I applied to grad school. It was my $350,000 solution to finding people who didn't run the other way when they saw me coming.

What happened next was: philosophy saved me.

First off, there's no more thralling nor romantic environment than the philosophy department of a bucolic, historic campus. Classes were held in a brick colonial building, the oldest at Yale, the seminar rooms smelling importantly of books and cigarettes, the wooden tables polished over generations of tweed elbows. I'd look out the window at the ancient elms and think, Nature and a curious mind, who needs more?

Thoreau (who had reached the same conclusion): *My thanksgiving is perpetual.*

Nobody studies philosophy for money or status. When students meet you, all they want to know is what you're passionate about. You tell them what you're into; they tell you what they're into. Have they read this book? No, have you read that book? There's so much to share you have no choice but to go grab coffee. You're distilled down to your enthusiasms. Everything else falls away. I was home.

At first, I was self-conscious about being the oldest student in the department. Until one day, purely by accident, I let slip in seminar that I'd been a comedy writer in Hollywood. All eyes turned to me. I panicked, expecting a barrage of questions about what shows I'd worked on and why I left. Nobody cared. To them, my age and abandoned career were further validation that philosophy was the coolest pursuit in the world.

I muscled through the required courses in metaphysics, logic and epistemology. But when it came to moral philosophy? Cue music: I could have danced all night.

I adored learning about the personal lives of the philosophers and tracking the progression of collective thought throughout history. How every breakthrough idea had been a radical response to a previously entrenched belief system. It felt like church and I was dedicating myself to those secretly responsible for how we live now. Without Rousseau there'd be no democracy. Without Nietzsche, no Picasso.

Without Kant, no Einstein. That philosophy is seen as irrelevant only strengthened my devotion and resolve.

I spent an hour each morning on Stoicism itself, poring over the foundational texts. And attempting to define my personal philosophy of life. I finally boiled it down to . . .

VIRTUE = HAPPINESS

I set about concerning myself only with virtue. Or—in less churchy terms—my character. Everything else, I decided to let the universe handle. Without trying, I lost thirty pounds and kept it off.

Philosophy: it works for weight loss!

One night, I was wasting time on the internet—yes, philosophers are humans, too—and ended up on my IMDb page. It listed my Nickelodeon credits, my lame sitcom credits . . . but not *Laugh Riot.*

It used to be there. I'd seen it with my own eyes.

Laugh Riot must have contacted IMDb and had me erased.

I felt myself detach from my body. The girl I had once been—the one I'd left back in LA—she was now sitting at the computer.

I watched her initial disorientation at not believing her eyes. Her dawning realization that someone from afar had taken time out of their day to find a new way to hurt her. The body blows of humiliation as the shameful images flashed before her: the can of Comet, the blow job, the cold wedding ring, the high-fiving in the hallway, "What can't you do?"

She wasn't a person, but a palimpsest. Layers of suffering and delusion bleeding faintly into the next, never erased. Being born but not wanted. Put on diets at age eight. Crying alone in her room during school dances. Lured to Hollywood by foolish hopes and baited bounties. A joke to famous men.

And she was separate from me.

Me, Adora Hazzard, the student of philosophy?

I saw the missing *Laugh Riot* credit and thought: Oh.

It was official. My old operating system had been replaced with a new one.

I sat there in amazement that I felt nothing.

Next came a flood of joy that I felt nothing.

(Fully aware of that irony,) I found an all-night tattoo parlor and had *AMOR FATI* written across my scar.

SPRING OF 2003

I was four years in, slow rolling my PhD. I'd landed a job at Choate, teaching philosophy to tenth graders.

From the outside, my life must have appeared small and cosseted, ferrying between Connecticut campuses, but inside I felt vast.

Nothing is more invigorating than watching fifteen-year-olds play Lifeboat. (Warning to movie stars everywhere: you're always the first to be thrown overboard.) Or helping them work through Singer's Drowning Child. (Warning to drowning children everywhere: you're SOL if the passerby is late to take the SAT.) Or gaming out the Trolley Problem. (Warning to fat men everywhere: enjoy life while you can and keep off bridges.) The history teacher next door would come over to scold us for our raucousness; finally he just switched rooms.

One day, I was walking down the university path when I spotted a familiar man approaching. Horn-rimmed glasses, crumpled seersucker, Danish school bag, sweetness radiating.

"Oh, hi!" I said to this man I couldn't place, but for some reason seeing him had set off a frisson.

When he looked up and met my enlivened stare, the man reacted in puzzlement.

"Hi . . ." he said.

We were now locked into small talk.

"What have you been up to?" I asked, casting out a line. Was he a professor? A student? A friend of a friend?

"Teaching," he said. "The usual."

"Right!" I said. "Me, too."

So, he was a professor. Definitely not in the philosophy department. I stood there, at a rare loss for words.

". . . I think you might know me from TV?" he bashfully said.

My hand flew to my mouth.

Hal Weymouth. The economist. He'd been a member of the Clinton administration, and had stayed on for Bush until Yale nabbed him. And yes, I did know him from TV.

"CNN! I am so embarrassed!"

"Don't be." He was a kind soul, I felt it immediately.

"Adora Hazzard. Not on CNN. Philosophy. Taking forever to get my PhD— Oh! I've always wanted to ask an economist—"

That look was forming on his face, the one people got when they experienced my brand of enthusiasm for the first time. When men in particular got that look, I'd immediately try to act more shrinking. But not with Hal. His inquisitive and receiving eyes freed me to be my full self.

"Adam Smith," I said. "The Scottish philosopher?"

"I'm familiar with Adam Smith," he said, in the understatement of the year.

"I've always wanted to find an economist to ask, is Adam Smith good or bad? Because I kind of love him. But something tells me I'm wrong, and if so, I'd like to be set straight."

Hal marks this as the moment he determined to make me his wife.

We slept together that first night, after—okay, and during—a debate on whether Adam Smith's *Theory of Moral Sentiments* and *Wealth of Nations* present opposing views on human nature. I thought yes. Hal, the expert, and a great kisser—who knew, behind the seersucker?—convinced me otherwise.

I woke up the next morning and had that same experience of stepping outside myself and seeing the person I once was: the fat adolescent no boy tried to kiss, the young woman who gave herself away, the adult who'd reflexively recoil at a man's touch. Yet there I was! Rolling around this gentle stranger's mattress, enjoying my nakedness. Enjoying my enjoyment.

I did this, I thought. Sure, it was Hal. But mainly, it was me.

The best thing about Hal and me? We played no games. We were nerds in love. Our minds clicked and our bodies followed. We devoured each other, never without gratitude.

A week in, lying in bed, Hal brushed my hair out of my face. "How did I get so lucky?"

I almost told him everything . . . TJ Steele, my NDA, the suicide attempt. Largely out of curiosity. I'd always wondered if it would make me feel any differently if I talked about what had happened.

But I didn't want to feel differently! I wanted to keep feeling exactly how I felt in that moment. I didn't want to risk Hal seeing me as damaged goods. I didn't want him feeling sorry for me. I didn't want sex with me to become sex with a victim.

I said nothing.

Anyway, I'd signed the NDA.

Hal and I jumped into the deep end. We moved into his apartment and got married at the courthouse.

I loved Hal for his absentmindedness, his quirky passions (Joni Mitchell, the Red Sox, his collection of vintage campaign buttons). Plus, it's pretty irresistible when Bill Clinton comes to town and, to a packed lecture hall, refers to your man as a "real national treasure." Hal loved me for my unapologetic braininess, my witchy ability to anticipate his every need and the pleasure I took in keeping a humming household.

While we lived modestly, Hal's reputation provided free access to a starry existence. Invitations to the Aspen Ideas Festival in the summer, Davos in January. Our third Christmas together we spent with a bunch of other bewildered overachievers and their plus-ones who'd been handpicked by Paul Allen to cruise the Antarctic Peninsula on his yacht. Paul Allen never showed up. We were all convinced it was a murder mystery.

Perhaps the truest expression of Hal's character was he wore it as a badge that I taught tenth-grade philosophy.

Indeed, those Mondays, Wednesdays and Fridays in Wallingford anchored my existence. People think you teach for the kids, but the secret is, you teach for yourself. I loved being forced to articulate and defend my beliefs. I loved being an example of what sheer fun it can be to live a life of the mind.

Every day, before class, I'd start out by writing an Epictetus quote on the whiteboard.

Epictetus was born into slavery in 55 AD. His master was Nero's secretary(!), who was so impressed by Epictetus's intellect that he freed him to study philosophy. Epictetus became a beloved teacher.

None of his writing survives, only notes taken by his students that had been compiled over the years. What makes Epictetus so special is his ability to distill giant concepts into little, mind-blowing soul-snacks that make you want to jump out of your chair and change your life.

At least, this is how I experienced Epictetus.

See, all the available translations were formal and stilted. They created separation between him and the reader. I knew in my heart Epictetus wanted to meet simple people where they lived, as all his metaphors are of nature or household objects.

(Bear with me. I promise this is going somewhere!)

So, as part of my Stoic practice, I'd lay out the dozen available translations of Epictetus and synthesize them into my own. I made mine more conversational, and organized them in a way that made sense to me. It was a work in progress, my little Epictetus chapbook.

I'd go to the copy shop to print it out and have it bound. Every day I'd revisit it, add to it and revise it. When it became too marked up, I'd edit my master document and have a new one printed up.

I'd refer to this chapbook for the passages I'd write on the whiteboard at the beginning of class. Some days, the students would ignore it. Other days, we'd talk of nothing but. At the end of each semester, I'd set out a stack of chapbooks for the kids who wanted one. All did.

SUMMER OF 2009

It was after I became pregnant with Viv and had taken a year off from teaching that I received a call out of the blue.

"I'm looking for Adora Hazzard," said the brusque voice.

"This is she."

"First off," she said, "were you born with that name or did you make it up?"

"Born with it."

"Congratulations, it's fabulous."

She introduced herself as a theater director from New York. Her name was Minna. She said she was in possession of a tenth-generation Xerox of my "Happiness Handbook."

From what she could trace, a Choate mother had come across it one summer while searching for her son's stash. She liked it so much she gave it to her sister-in-law, who gave it to her shrink, who made copies for his patients(!), one of whom was Minna's hairdresser.

"Why haven't you published this?" asked Minna. "It's brilliant."

"It's not mine to publish. I'm not a real translator. I don't know Greek."

"Who cares?"

"It would feel fraudulent. It's just a compilation of my favorite quotes and ideas. I couldn't put my name on the same cover as Epictetus."

Minna responded with a *pfft*. "Would a man say that?"

I persisted. "All I did was dumb stuff down."

"Which is the single biggest key to success in the world of ideas. Do I have your permission to give this to a book agent?"

"Sure, I guess."

"Good. Pretend you're going under general anesthesia. I'll count you down. Five, four, three, two, one. Now you're awake. Great news! The agent loves it. She sent it to a New Age editor. The editor has made you an offer. What's your email?"

By the end of the day I had an agent and $5,000 advance.

Hal had been at a conference in Mexico City. When he returned home that night, I greeted him with flutes of champagne.

"What's this?" He had the same sweet, puzzled look as that first day on the path.

"You're married to a soon-to-be-published author!" And the whole crazy story came tumbling out.

"Who is this person in New York?" Hal asked. "Why is she doing this?"

"I don't know! She just really likes the book."

"What's the publisher?" he said, flipping through his mail.

"Some New Age company."

"And you accepted their first offer?"

"It's what they pay translators," I said. "My agent said so."

"You have an agent now?"

"Anna something. I can check."

"It seems low," Hal said. "But New Age books aren't my thing. Maybe that is what they pay."

His confusion was now my confusion.

"What?" he asked.

"Aren't you happy for me?"

"I just got off a plane. It's a lot to process. If you're happy, of course I'm happy."

He tossed the junk mail into recycling and headed upstairs. I went to the living room and sat in my chair.

I reminded myself: nothing bad had happened. Hal had reacted differently than I'd expected, that's all. It only injures me if I allow it to injure me. Assume good intent. He's jet-lagged, he just walked through the door. He's still smarting from not getting that job in the Obama administration. His questions were perfectly reasonable. He was looking out for me, as husbands do.

What had actually happened was I'd let something out of my control (another person's reaction) disrupt my tranquility. That was on me. I'd allowed a taste of success to get me overly excited, boastful and insensitive. But every situation is an opportunity to work on one of the four virtues. Tomorrow, I would recommit to temperance.

The next day, I stood in the bathroom and waited for Hal to get out of the shower. He'd gone in without saying good morning.

"Are we good?" I asked.

"We're fine," he said, toweling off. "I guess I'm a little hurt. I'm surprised you didn't ask my opinion. I've written books."

"You're right. I'm sorry."

The Happiness Handbook was published to zero fanfare. Honestly, I was relieved.

SPRING OF 2014

A TED Talk on Stoicism given by one of the big tech bros went viral.

Stoicism was hot!

The Happiness Handbook got swept into this latest self-help craze. My publisher ordered a reprint of 1,500 copies. Those vaporized. A third printing of 10,000. A fourth of 50,000. On the HBO show *Hard Knocks*, a wide-receivers coach opened every team meeting by reading from *The Happiness Handbook*. One week, I actually hit the bestseller list after an actress on *Cougar Town* included it in her "What's in My Bag." There I was, in *Us Weekly*, spilling out with face-blotting tissue, quartz eye roller and travel sage.

But these signals from the outside world that people were reading my book were rare. The strangest thing about my success is it didn't change my day-to-day life. My name was rarely mentioned in relation to *The Happiness Handbook*. (Although I did write a bomb introduction.) I had no speaking engagements, no press inquiries, no nothing. Twice a year, I'd get a royalty check that reminded me I'd even written it in the first place.

I was right where I wanted to be: mother to growing and bubbly Viv, and wife to Hal, who was increasingly down in the dumps. His hits on CNN had dried up in favor of the woman who'd gotten the job he'd been expecting in the Obama administration. The glamorous invitations had slowed to a trickle. This left Hal spending more time at home.

It was an adjustment, having Hal around the house needing cheering.

Epictetus says to think of ourselves as actors in a play. We can't choose our roles, and they can be switched at any time without warning. Once we're recast, our job isn't to question or complain, but to accept and shine. If my role in the marriage had changed, I was determined to play to the cheap seats.

SPRING OF 2016

I got swept up in Bernie mania. I loved his message of dignity for all Americans, and agreed that the country needed a radical redistribution of wealth. Hal considered Bernie's policies pie-in-the-sky promises that would bankrupt the treasury. I didn't care. It felt right, dismantling the structures that kept people in poverty. I'd happily pay higher taxes for the cause.

Meanwhile, on the Republican side, Donald Trump was the best show on TV. I couldn't get enough. Every time he came on, he revealed himself to be a bigger, more entertaining clown.

"Trump! Trump! Trump!" I took to chanting anytime he said something ridiculous on the debate stage.

Other than for Bernie to win the nomination, my other wish for primary season was that Trump didn't drop out too soon.

I got one wish.

Hillary was the nominee. I was disappointed; I found her entitled and shrill. I'd never thought of myself as a feminist, and the whole first-woman-president thing didn't resonate. Growing up, I'd associated feminism with angry women who burned their bras instead of wearing them. I felt that as a country, we'd moved past all that. There were already plenty of women CEOs, astronauts, senators—and now the Democratic nominee for president.

But the voters had decided. Hillary it was!

Trump was coming to the Hartford convention center for a rally. I wanted to go as pure entertainment.

One of my favorite quotes is from Voltaire. When asked if he would like to attend an orgy for the second time, Voltaire replied, "The first time, a philosopher. The second time, a pervert."

In other words, anything once.

The day of the Trump rally, Viv came down with a fever. I was crushed. I begged Hal to go and report back.

He returned a shell of the man who'd walked out the door.

"So?!" I said. "How was it?"

"Trump is the worst."

"No detail too small," I said. "Hit me."

"I got there at four because it was supposed to start at five. The line was massive, all the way down Columbus, past State Street. All these people had been waiting in the sun, some since eight in the morning. Turns out, Trump wasn't letting people in. Intentionally. Just so he could say he had the longest line."

"What an asshole," I said. "Were people pissed?"

"Not in the slightest. It was as if they were all quietly resigned to being treated badly. They finally started letting people in and security took forever. When Trump went on, most everyone was still outside."

"Did you get in?"

"No," Hal said. "I spent my time walking up and down the line, taking everyone in. Taking them seriously."

"Ugh."

"The thing about them?" he said. "They're good people."

"How can you say that?"

"I was the one there. Do you want to hear this or not?"

"Sorry," I said. "Go on."

"They're not evil or stupid. They're just beaten down. And Trump gives them hope."

It seemed like a smart place to end the conversation.

FALL OF 2016

As the days marched towards November 8, something deep within me started to stir. I didn't just grow to like Hillary. I grew to love Hillary. I had no idea where it was coming from. My eyes would well up anytime she came on TV.

Hal, on the other hand. He'd walk away shaking his head.

At first I ignored it. My feelings for Hillary were so new I wouldn't know how to defend them. Nor did I want to.

Finally, I couldn't take Hal's grumblings.

"Is it personal?" I asked. "Is there something about her I should know?"

Hal's chapter with the Clintons was before I knew him. His friends—our friends—many were from his days at the White House. They made it sound like Camelot. Hillary was rarely mentioned.

"I hate Trump more than you do," said Hal.

"So? What's the problem?"

"I wish there was another choice."

"Why? Did Hillary do something to you?"

"I just . . ." he said. "There's something about her I don't like."

Hal and I had never argued about politics before. We were completely aligned. In '08 we'd flown to Las Vegas and knocked on doors for Obama. We got upgraded to a suite at Caesars Palace that had a mirrored ceiling, a sunken gold tub and greasy handprints on the windows overlooking the Strip. We had the best sex of our lives adding to those greasy handprints.

I let it go.

NOVEMBER 8, 2016

That morning before school, with Viv at the counter, I reminded Hal that our polling place had changed from the elementary school to a church.

"Good," Hal said. "I'm going to write in Willie Nelson."

"You can't be serious," I said, buttering toast.

He pointed to his shirt. On it, a WILLIE NELSON FOR PRESIDENT button from his collection.

I was unamused. "Trump is a million times worse than Hillary! What about 'grab 'em by the pussy'?"

Hal shot me an angry look and indicated Viv, who at that time was seven.

"Please!" I said. "Thanks to Trump, she's heard worse."

"That's because you're always blasting MSNBC."

"What about 'all Mexicans are rapists'?" I said, waving the butter knife. "What about mocking the disabled *Times* reporter and the Gold Star family? What about the contractors he ripped off?"

"You can stop pointing a knife at me."

"Jesus." I put down the knife.

"Why are we even talking about this?" Hal said. "Voting should be private. And if you remember, you wanted Bernie."

Driving Viv to school, I began to cry. Viv spoke up from the back seat.

"I know why Dad doesn't like Hillary. It's that she's a woman."

Viv must have heard it at school. Still, what does a mother do with that information?

You thank God the election will be over tonight. That Trump will take his place as a footnote in history and your family can return to life as you knew it.

You make cupcakes and decorate them red, white and blue. You and your daughter wear white to watch the returns. Our first woman president. You're a weepy wreck.

You tell your husband that out of consideration to him, you and your daughter will watch in the living room with the door closed.

He storms out with a slam that rattles the windows. Where he goes, you don't care. You're relieved you can enjoy this historic moment outside his glowering presence.

Things go terribly wrong.

Hillary loses Ohio.

She loses Florida.

There's no math to get her to 270.

Trump is our next president.

Moments later, your husband enters chanting, "Trump, Trump, Trump."

You're horrified. Your daughter runs upstairs to her room.

"What's going on around here?" your husband says. "It's a joke!"

"Nothing will ever be funny again," you say to the floor, through tears.

"Thanks for letting me know."

Your husband hasn't moved from the doorway. You cover your face. He sighs and enters the room. You sense a softening of his energy. He gives you time to look at him. You can't.

"No wonder you left comedy," your husband finally says. "You can't take a joke."

His words are so exquisitely cruel they could have been engineered to hurt you. You can't hold it against him. You've never told him the truth.

You accept that it was a joke. Your joke, in fact.

Stoicism helps. There are some amazing quotes that apply.

Marcus Aurelius: *Be forgiving with others but hard on yourself.*

Something has changed, though. You find you don't want to be touched by the person who made that joke, the person who wouldn't vote for Hillary. You avoid the subject until one day you can't.

"We never fuck anymore," your husband says.

You invoke perimenopause. It's biology's fault. A woman's sex drive changes over time. He pretends to buy it. So do you.

"This is insane," you both say after sex one afternoon. The sex, when you have it, is still great.

You're two smart people who love each other. You're both Democrats. You line up on 98 percent of the issues. It's beneath you to let politics come between you. There are far-right Republicans married to lefties. Look at James Carville and Mary Matalin. Look at George and Kellyanne Conway. Your husband reminds you he didn't vote for Trump. When you point out he didn't vote for Hillary, either, you both laugh. You make a promise: no talk of politics. And shake on it.

It's tense, though. There's no denying it. There are things you both want to say but can't.

Brittleness has entered the chat. You both feel misunderstood by the other. You spend more time in different rooms, finding comfort in your laptops. You send your husband a link about how female apes reach menopause and will try to kill a male ape who attempts to have sex. Your husband answers with a link to a George Saunders piece in *The New Yorker.* George Saunders, whose writing you love, went to a Trump rally and empathized with the voters, too.

Your Seneca translation hits the list. Its cover is similar to Epictetus. So now you're . . . a brand? You get an advance for Marcus Aurelius. This gives you reason to spend more time at the library.

OCTOBER OF 2017

#MeToo erupts. It becomes not a question of which women have been sexually assaulted, but which women haven't been sexually assaulted.

Powerful men fall in astonishing succession. It's a crazy few weeks to be alive, more eventful than OJ.

You're in your daughter's room making slime together when there's a cry.

"Oh no!" It's your husband.

You rush downstairs. He's pacing with his open laptop.

"Don't tell me," he says. "They got TJ Steele!"

It's a collision of realities you never saw coming. The name TJ Steele in your husband's mouth.

Your first response is surprise that your husband even knows who TJ Steele is. TJ Steele never broke out. He left *Laugh Riot* soon after you. He tried and failed with a sitcom. He seemed to be nothing more than a favorite if infrequent guest of late-night talk show hosts.

You could tell your husband then. But too much time has passed. He'd use it against you that you'd kept this part of yourself secret for so long. And you wouldn't blame him.

You say nothing.

You are curious, though. That night, you settle in with the proverbial popcorn to read the *LA Times* article. You know you're not mentioned because you would have heard about it. The article states that "Steele has been involved in a handful of settlements dating back to the 1990s." His grown daughter puts out an emotional and confused statement condemning him.

Twitter is aflame with women recounting their own experiences with TJ Steele. You expect to binge on schadenfreude deep into the night. But within half an hour you lose interest and find yourself going down a rabbit hole about a feud between two celebrities you've never heard of.

That's when you really know Stoicism works.

TJ Steele is so irrelevant you get no enjoyment from his downfall.

SEPTEMBER OF 2018

The Brett Kavanaugh confirmation hearings. Christine Blasey Ford testifies before Congress. For some reason, this is the one that undoes you. More than Hillary, more than Harvey Weinstein, more than TJ Steele.

You sit at the foot of the bed and watch. You are shaken by this woman's strength. It's unfathomable to you, her courage and integrity, her dedication to justice. Her decision to speak.

Your husband passes through and shakes his head.

"What about 'believe women'?" you ask. This time you are looking for a fight.

"Of course I'm not going to believe all women," he says. "Just like I'm not going to believe all men. I am not a member of the mob. I have a brain in my head. I thought you did, too."

SUMMER OF 2020

You take to the streets.

"Say his name," says the man with the megaphone.

"George Floyd," you shout.

When your husband hears you brought his daughter to the march without asking, he accuses you of exposing her to COVID and tear gas.

"We were outside and masked," you say. "And there was no tear gas."

He shakes his head and mimes washing his hands. Of you?

The New York Times runs an op-ed by the woman who got your husband's job in the Obama administration. It's about the economic policies of Bill Clinton, and points out that "America's first Black president" gutted welfare and criminalized the poor. Your husband's name is invoked as the architect.

It's unfair and hurtful.

He cancels your subscription.

His students, who adore him, want to show their support. You throw the surprise party at your house.

Weeks later, your husband enters the room. You're at your computer reading a Style piece in the *Times* on the return of polka dots.

He's incredulous. "You're siding with *The New York Times* over your own husband?"

There's so much that wants to come tumbling out of you. Words of explanation and empathy, apology and advice, criticism and confession, humor and hope.

But you can't know for certain it won't lead to a fight.

You sit there in silence, the tension and your nausea building.

"This won't end well," your husband says.

Every time you turn on the car after your husband has driven it, the radio is set to the station that plays Adam Corolla on perpetual repeat. You switch it back to NPR.

Your husband records *Bill Maher* and watches it religiously. He calls you in for choice bits. You say you're not interested in anything Bill Maher has to say. The term "cold as stone" in reference to you frequents your husband's lexicon. The book deal resurfaces as the moment that marked the beginning of the end.

"The end of the marriage?" you say. "Is that what you want?"

"All I know is I refuse to live out my days with a woman who hates me."

"I don't hate you!"

"Here's what you hate me for." He counts on his fingers. "You hate me for being a man. You hate me for being white. You hate me because I voted for Trump. Wait! I didn't vote for Trump! So that's a real head-scratcher. You hate me for making one bad joke, your joke, for which I've apologized."

You have no response because he's right. He's done nothing wrong. And you hate him.

You don't hate him!

You love him. He's a good man, the best man, the father of your child. You have a life together, the only life you know. The only life you want. The whole point is to grow old together.

You go to a couples therapist.

She gives you a simple homework assignment. To look into each other's eyes for five minutes without speaking. Neither of you make the time.

"Why do you think that is?" asks the therapist.

Your husband looks over, expecting you to answer.

"If he wants sex so badly," you say, "shouldn't he be the one to initiate it?"

"That's your job," your husband says. "You're the one who hates sex."

The therapist points out that while your husband frequently cries during the sessions, the only time she's ever seen you cry was when you talked about Hillary Clinton losing the election.

"What is it about that, do you think, that makes you so emotional?"

Something trembles inside. You go quiet. They wait for you to speak. You know these words will change the course of your life. You speak them slowly.

"It was the first time I understood how much this country hated women. It was the first time I understood how much I hated women. It was the first time I understood how much I hated myself."

"Aha!" your husband says. He has his smoking gun.

Pretty soon there's no marriage left to save. One day, stemming from a misunderstanding about emptying the dishwasher, your husband threatens to contact a divorce lawyer. You hand him the number you'd gotten from a friend.

A week later, you get a call from a florist in Boston about a missing apartment number for a delivery to a woman named Claire. Your husband has just returned from Boston. You don't mind. You want your husband to feel good about himself. You can no longer serve that purpose.

Mediation happens in record speed. You're generous with each other. If there is ill will, you keep it to yourselves. The mediator keeps expecting you to announce you've called off the divorce.

But now that you've both smelled the barn, you can't wait to start fresh.

Your husband takes an offer from Tufts and claims he's always wanted to live in Boston. You say nothing.

You have to move out of faculty housing. You can go anywhere. With Viv's urging, you choose New York. (Thanks, *Gossip Girl.*)

Your husband drives you and your daughter to the apartment you just bought. A little place in the legendary Ansonia.

You hug goodbye with the car still running.

You hand each other letters you've written. (Neither of you knew the other was writing one.) In your letter to him, you list the happy times and promise him you're still a family, that you'll take care of him if he gets sick. His to you is more succinct and that's why it guts you.

"*Thank you*," it reads.

You reconnect with your old friend Emily Ann, who you know from grad school. She taught law and has since returned to private practice in New York. Minna welcomes you into her artsy whirl. One night at dinner, you tell them about your husband on election night chanting, "Trump, Trump, Trump."

"I would have divorced him on the spot," Minna says.

You make a note to yourself: stick with these women.

You're genuinely happy when your ex-husband remarries within the year. He isn't a bad guy. You've never thought that. You will never think that.

He's the father of your child. The love of your life. The brilliant, sweet man you dreamed of growing old with.

Maybe you are cold.

You still start every day with your Stoic practice, by writing out your philosophy of life.

VIRTUE = HAPPINESS

One morning, after you've been living in New York for a year, you realize you've gotten it wrong.

It's not happiness you're after. Happiness is a subset of what you're feeling now. The thing that's bigger. From now on, you start each day by writing the words . . .

VIRTUE = FREEDOM

Freedom from tension. Freedom from being misunderstood. Freedom from self-pity. Freedom from fear. Freedom from shame. Freedom from helplessness. Freedom from obsession.

Freedom from desire.

Until now.

—PART FOUR—

THE EVIL GENIE

Resist the temptation . . ." read a discontented Lorenzo.

It was the next day, after my epic night with Digby. The boys and I were back in the third-floor sitting room, hacking our way through Seneca's *Letters from a Stoic*. Letter Five, one I knew would hold little relevance to the incurious youths.

". . . to give your attention to those who crave it."

Crave. Hearing the word was all it took for my mind to flash pornographically to images of me and Digby.

It was as if a dye pack had been released in my bloodstream, instantly breaching the blood-brain barrier, and now my every organ was colored by sex.

Or something.

My knack for metaphors had taken a hit.

"Especially," Lorenzo continued, "to those who dress and lead lifestyles calculated to invoke envy."

"I'd like to pause," I said.

Lorenzo's eyes hit the ceiling and remained there. Lucien picked at the crewelwork on a throw pillow.

"Hey," I told him. "Let's not."

"We get it," Lucien groaned. "Don't want nice clothes."

"Seneca goes on. Listen to what he says next. Lucien, you take over."

"Avoid all misguided means of self-advertisement," Lucien began, "such as shabby attire, long hair, an unkempt beard, sleeping on the ground, and an aversion to silverware."

The boys cracked smiles.

"Back then," I said, hitching a ride on their curiosity, "philosophers had a bad rap for believing they were superior to everyone else. 'The pride of the philosopher,' it was called. But philosophers didn't show off in the usual Roman way. If you were a super-rich Roman, you know how you'd show off?"

Now I really had their attention.

"You'd wear gold-embroidered robes, oil yourself in perfume and stroll the Forum with a boy on your arm who was waxed and made up to look like a girl."

"Ew!" said Lorenzo.

"Philosophers," I continued, "made equally grand but opposite gestures. Socrates walked around in smelly robes. Diogenes the Cynic ate dog food with his hands and slept in a bathtub in the town square, naked."

Me, on the edge of the bed, naked as Digby is on his knees, glasses off, my feet on his shoulders. I'll demand that exact thing tonight. But if I demand it, Digby might refuse. His strong grip on my wrists, pinning me to the bed—

"Are we done?" asked Lorenzo.

"No." I recrossed my legs. "Seneca is saying that while it's important to uphold the strictest values on the inside, outwardly you should be able to pass for the rabble—"

Ding!

The elevator doors parted and presented Celine Montford. Lionel trailed in his high-tech wheelchair, the seat of which was raised to put him at eye level.

"Sorry!" said Lionel, seeing we were mid-lesson. "I'm just giving Celine a house tour."

"That's okay!" Lorenzo and his twin sprang to their feet and hopped on waiting skateboards.

"Hey, you little heathens!" I said.

Lucien, over this shoulder: "May we please be excused?"

"Not until you tell me what Seneca wants you to pass for."

"Rabble!" Lorenzo said. He and his brother whooshed down the spiral ramp.

"What's rabble?" I called over the banister.

"I don't knoooow!" floated up a squeaky voice.

Celine Montfort stepped in, appraising me with the amused eye of an apex predator. "And who is this?"

My heartbeat quickened at my proximity to Digby's woman of interest.

"The in-house philosopher," I said.

Lionel introduced us and added, "Celine was just telling me about her father, Pierre. It's the most fascinating story."

"I'd love to hear," I said.

"He was a curator at the Louvre," Celine began, by rote. "In 1940, on the eve of the Nazi invasion, he helped smuggle out the Mona Lisa using scenery trucks from the Paris Opera. They hid it in our chateau until the end of the war."

"That's you?" I'd learned about the remarkable events in Art History 101.

"My father," Celine said. "He lived by his epitaph, *Je préfère mourir de passion que d'ennui.*"

"Gérard Depardieu played him in the movie," Lionel added.

"And now," I said to Celine, "you're continuing on in his tradition."

"Oh?" she said with a start. Astonishment at being interrogated by the help.

"Boy With Apple?" I said.

"I am here to deliver a gift from my family to theirs."

"Next," said Lionel, continuing the tour, "is my wife's closet-slash-office."

Celine's body followed, but she hadn't taken her eyes off me.

"Literally," Lionel said. "Layla loves her closet so much she moved her desk in."

I went to help him by turning the doorknob—

—but someone on the other side had beaten me to it.

The door swung open. Standing there, Layla . . .

And Digby.

This whole time, he'd been on the other side of the door? No wonder I'd been going so animal-mad! I must have smelled him.

Playing our parts, Digby and I avoided eye contact.

"Hello!" chirped Layla.

If she was at all unsettled by the sight of us, she didn't show it. Her sailor pants, striped tank and jaunty yellow neckerchief made it seem as if she would, at any moment, break out in tap.

Layla gave Lionel a peck.

"Baby, this is David Beale. We're meeting about the school auction."

A lie.

I'd always wondered how talented an actress Layla was. I had my answer: get that woman a Tony!

"Mr. Beale, this is my husband, Lionel."

How would Digby possibly stay composed? Fresh from his high-stakes sit-down with Layla, face-to-face with Celine. The exalted and elusive Lionel Lockwood thrown into the mix. And me, keeper of his secrets, holder of his heart.

I fixed my gaze on Lionel who weakly raised his right hand. In my periphery, Digby took it.

"Thank you for all you do," he said.

"And this," Layla continued, "is Celine Montfort. From Paree."

Digby: "*Enchanté*. If we still say that."

"Some do," answered Celine. Her droll tone belied her busy brain, which appeared to be firing at a thousand calculations per second.

Celine turned to Layla and gave the slightest questioning smile. Layla pretended not to see, and moved on.

"This," said Layla to Digby, "is the boys' tutor."

The moment had arrived. Me and Digby.

Our eyes met.

I'd seen Digby naked. Without his glasses. Seen the face he made when he came.

"Adora Hazzard," I said.

Digby responded, "My pleasure."

When it came to acting, Layla had nothing on us.

Digby and I shook hands, neither breaking character. I'd never been into role-playing. But now, my mind bloomed with its possibilities. Digby gave my hand an extra squeeze. It shot currents.

"I'll show you out," Layla told Digby. He followed her to the open elevator.

I watched him step in. Oh, how I ached for a turn or some kind of lagniappe. Neither came. The doors closed.

"*Comme c'est très français!*" announced Celine. "A strange man emerges from a closet with another man's wife and nobody thinks to comment."

"I love the woman," Lionel said. "But all I have to hear are the words 'school auction' and as long as I don't have to go, Layla can meet with anyone she likes." He turned to me. "What's that Marcus Aurelius quote?"

There were many to choose from.

"Don't be overheard complaining about life at the court," I said. "Not even by yourself."

"Very impressive," remarked Celine, eyeing me with fresh curiosity.

Ding! The elevator had delivered Digby and Layla to the first floor. I looked over the railing. Below, Layla and Digby shook hands and parted ways.

"You can put a quarter in this one," Lionel was telling Celine. "Come on, Adora. Give us another."

"Love," I said turning, "is friendship gone mad."

"Where's that from?" asked Lionel.

I held up the Seneca still in my hand. "Letter Nine."

"First time she's pulled that one out," Lionel boasted to Celine.

"First time I've had to," I said.

"Don't we love Adora?"

It's not something one says out loud, so I contented myself with the thought: we kind of do.

I crossed Seventy-Sixth Street and returned to the Lockwood Library, half expecting a message from Digby on my desk. But no. How would he get in touch? I hadn't given him my cell. Whatever the gesture, it would be grand and unexpected. Written in the sky? Pizza delivery with our next assignation scrawled on the inside of the lid? Or something more traditional? Spring daffodils—

Rriinng-rriinng. Rriinng-rriinng.

A room-shaking jangle jolted me from my reverie. The house phone. Wall-mounted, rotary and yellowing, every office had one, but I'd never heard them ring. I'd always assumed they were kept as a wink to the past.

Rriinng-rriinng. Rriinng-rriinng.

Oh, Digby.

I got up and answered.

"How'd you swing this?" I purred, rolling my back against the wall.

"*Désolée de décevoir,*" returned a familiar voice. "*Ce n'est que moi.*"

"I'm sorry—" I said. "This is—"

"I'm aware," said Celine Montford. "Do you mind coming over? I'd like to have a word."

In moments, and without a second thought, I was floating down the grand staircase of the Lockwood Library. I made the turn towards the lobby and saw Tony, the security guard, chatting amiably with Hannah.

I skidded to a stop. What if they saw me heading over to the residence? Would it raise a red flag? Could it expose Digby?

I then realized: on the inside, I was Digby's girl. On the outside, I was still the family philosopher popping over to the residence.

I swanned down the stairs with a friendly nod to my coworkers. Hannah and Tony barely registered my presence.

Ah, the invisibility of the middle-aged woman. I'd read countless pieces on the indignity of it. My hot take on turning invisible? Finally! No more being the object of men's scrutiny and the inevitable insecurity, self-hatred and insanity that goes with it. Please, ignore me. Go size up and lust after (or reject!) someone younger. I've got a coven to run.

I continued to the basement, as the underground tunnel was the quickest route between Lockwood Library and residence.

The hallway was sheathed in red: painted cinder-block walls, rubber floors, even the pipes along the ceiling. "Lockwood Red," Farrow & Ball, named after the legendary apple.

A picture window stretched the length of the corridor. Through it one could survey Ravi's domain, a cavernous space two stories deep. It housed the extensive Lockwood collection. Snaking along the ceiling was a motorized rack from which hung priceless works of art. With the push of a button, old masters and modern silkscreens, rich tapestries and rare photographs would whizz along a track, just like at the dry cleaners. For this it was dubbed "the Laundry."

Something was off, though.

The Laundry was usually crawling with Ravi's team of white-gloved archivists and art restorers, painstakingly at work under blinding white lights.

It was only four o'clock and the place was empty, lights off.

Through the window I could make out, in the center of the room, wooden crates. I stepped to the glass and cupped my hands around my eyes.

Four crates. Plastered with labels, plastic customs pouches and the stamped words "*MANIPULER AVEC SOIN.*"

Boy With Apple.

In four pieces, just like Fortuna, whose plinth he had come to usurp.

Just then, a muffled *clank*.

The lights blazed on.

I jumped back. Then tiptoed close enough to see what was going on. . . .

The freight elevator opened. From its maw appeared two men pushing a wooden dolly. Teetering on it, something the size of a dishwasher. It was protected by moving blankets sloppily secured with packing tape.

Following was Ravi, speaking with a woman I didn't recognize.

Who was she? Digby would ask.

I crept closer.

The woman was dark-haired, dressed in all black: trench, wool trousers and impractical stiletto boots. Long hair worn loose, a claw clip attached to her lapel. In her hand swung a bottle of tequila tied in red ribbon.

She stopped mid-sentence as she beheld Ravi's fiefdom.

What was going on? Digby would want to know.

I'd say: *Ravi had sent his team home early because he needed the Laundry empty for this woman, who was seeing it for the first time, and was in possession of a piece of equipment Ravi needed. She'd come hastily, as a friend would, and wouldn't accept payment, thus the bottle of tequila.*

Damn, you're good, Digby would say.

You don't know the half of it. And I'd show him.

As much as I wanted to keep watching, Celine was waiting. I made haste through the tunnel under Seventy-Sixth Street.

In the residence basement, I rang for the glass elevator, and ascended into the afternoon sun. As I rose, I kept abreast of a British flag being raised by a staff member.

Ah, yes, tonight's dinner party. Lockwood protocol.

Wait, Digby would ask laughingly. *What*?

One of Layla's many affectations, I'd explain. *She flies the flags of whomever comes to dine. She'd gotten the idea when she and Lionel were invited to a state dinner.*

Already flapping were the flags of France (Celine), India (Ravi) and of course the Lockwood family crest—

Oh God, I'd have to tell Digby about the family crest Layla designed!

It's divided into quadrants: a red apple for the Lockwood family, the Venus de Milo for Lionel, a California poppy for Layla's birth state, and for the boys . . . a pair of gaming controllers.

Digby and I would break out laughing—

The elevator opened.

Waiting for me in the door of the guest suite, wearing silk robe and wet hair, Celine Montfort.

"Ooh," she said, all wide-eyed and girlfriendy. "Someone's got it bad."

I froze. Had she seen right through me?

I reminded myself: a rapid heartbeat is a fear response.

What is fear?

Fear is the mistaken belief I can't handle an event in the future.

Celine is about to say some words to me. There is nothing about that I can't handle.

It was my first time on the second floor of the residence, home to the gym, laundry and utility rooms and notorious "screaming room."

The guest suite was luxuriously appointed and wallpapered with a mural of ibises peacefully existing in wetlands. On it hung clusters of gilded, mismatched mirrors.

My first step inside felt like sinking into quicksand. It was only the carpet; its shags were cashmere and as thick as licorice.

The silk robe poured loosely down Celine's pale body and tied askew. One white leg emerged from a slit so high it would appear she was naked underneath.

"Shall I come back?" I asked.

"Here's what I'm wondering." Celine circled around and shut the door behind me. "How does the nanny figure in?"

Marcus Aurelius, the Roman emperor who found himself in wickets much stickier than this: *You always have the option of saying nothing.*

So I did, as Celine towel-dried her short hair with rough abandon.

"It's a rhetorical question," she said when finished. Her hair was now spiking in every direction. "I don't expect an answer. Not an honest one, anyway. Take a seat?"

"I'll stand."

Celine bent over, gave the towel a twist and came up turbaned. She looked into a mirror and tucked in a few errant strands.

"Nascent love," she said despairingly. "I'd have thought it was so distant in my past that I couldn't recognize it if I saw it. But I did today. When David Beale stepped out of that closet. You were dripping with it."

I felt my face catch fire.

"There it is again," she said, off my many reflections. "The betraying blush."

I pulled a breath into my churning stomach.

"Let's play a game," she said, turning. "You like those. What do we know about your David Beale?"

Only then did it fully strike me. I didn't know anything—not where he was from—not what he did for a living—not why he'd chosen me—

"I thought so," said Celine. "Now I'll go. I know that David Beale was able to penetrate ludicrous layers of security to come into contact with arguably the most protected man in America. And how did he swing it?"

"I don't understand the point of this conversation. Nor do I appreciate its tenor. Therefore I will excuse myself."

"By seducing the nanny."

My muscles locked. I stood there, unable to move.

Celine opened the closet. A sparkly, champagne dress hung from a silk hanger. "Zip me up?"

Her back to me, Celine dropped her robe, revealing a sinewy body and whisper of lacy underwear.

"What a day," she bemoaned, pulling the dress over her head. "I arrive in New York for what should be a straightforward art deal with my new bestie Layla Lockwood. While I'm being given a house tour, what happens? She pops out of a closet with a man I've never seen. Ten minutes later, she's standing right where you are telling me our deal is off!"

Celine moved closer.

"What conclusion would you draw? I'll tell you mine. That David Beale must have said something in that meeting to give Layla cold feet. I wonder what it was?"

"I have no idea." Fear had found its way into my voice. "I'm the help, remember? Your art deal has nothing to do with me."

"Yet here you are. Running when I call. Zipping up my dress."

I had done so without even realizing it.

Celine sauntered into the bathroom.

I scurried after. "That was me being polite—"

"Here's a trick," she said, "if you ever have trouble putting in earrings." She reached for a pair of emerald studs in a cut-glass dish. "First, close the drain. There's nothing worse than being late for dinner because housekeeping is fishing your diamonds out of a P-trap."

She pumped a drop of hand soap onto her finger, dipped the post into it and pushed it through her ear.

"*Et voilà*. Slides right in."

"Good to know," I said.

"The people David Beale are working for. They don't want my deal with Layla to happen. They should be made aware that the alternative will be many times worse."

"If this is a message," I said. "I suggest you deliver it yourself."

"I can see why you're a Lockwood family favorite. They will be so disappointed to find out you opened the door to let in the serpent."

My fear had crossed over into panic. "What do you want from me?"

"Ah," Celine said. "We have arrived."

She sprayed perfume into the air and stepped into its invisible cloud.

"Tomorrow, David Beale will inform Layla Lockwood that his client has changed their mind and that our deal, the one between me and Layla, is to proceed as planned."

"You want me to do that?!" I said, abandoning any pretense of calm. "How possibly—"

"I have faith."

"I know nothing about this! I promise you. Whatever you want from Digby, ask him yourself."

"I would ask Digby . . ." she said, putting a wicked spin on the name.

Crap! Had I just called him Digby—when she'd been calling him David?

"But," she continued, "I hold no sway."

"And I do?!"

"Oh, I saw his face. He's got it as bad as you." She booped me on the nose and sashayed out of the bathroom.

Was I being blackmailed? Get Digby to call off his deal . . . or I lose my job?

I rushed out. Celine sat on the bed, wiggling into a pair of strappy heels.

"You can't put me in this position," I said. "There's no way I'll be able to do what you're asking."

"Try money," Celine said. "Tell Mr. Beale that once my deal with

Layla goes through, I will personally compensate him for his inconvenience. I promise many zeros."

She checked her watch.

"You should be off," she said. "You have a job of work ahead of you. And I am expected in the garden for cocktails. In a bid to impress, Layla has invited Victoria Beckham for dinner. Yay, me."

Walking the streets of New York, you figure a minute per block. The thirteen blocks to the Lowell Hotel, I made in five.

"Welcome back," said the front desk attendant. "Mr. Beale is expecting you."

Digby's door was cracked. On the knob, he'd hung the DO NOT DISTURB sign. I entered without knocking.

"Here she is." Digby stood at the bed, all smiles, lighting the candle from last night. "Lady Philosophy paying a visit to my cell."

"What have you gotten me into?" My voice quivered with rage.

Digby dipped his chin and looked over his glasses. He certainly hadn't been expecting this. On the coffee table, a sweaty bucket of white wine.

"Tell me who you are," I demanded.

"After last night," Digby quipped, "you know better than anyone."

"Cut the pillow talk."

Digby blew out the candle and sighed, as if settling in for a tedious but necessary course correction.

"I was asked to handle a delicate situation with discretion."

"That had no content," I said. "You just told me nothing!"

A knock on the door. From behind, "Food delivery."

"Don't make me scream," I said.

This amused Digby. He opened the door to a bellman holding a neatly stapled paper bag. The aroma of orange blossom and saffron entered the room.

Motherfucker. Last night, I'd told Digby about a Tunisian restaurant in Queens I wanted to take him to. He'd said he preferred to spend his time with me "more productively."

He peeled off a few bills for the bellman and closed the door.

"All I can divulge," he said, "is that I'm involved in a precarious negotiation with many moving parts. The scope is international. Western civilization is on the table."

Suddenly I realized: this guy is a bullshit artist. I'd fallen for a total bullshit artist.

"I know all about Boy With Apple," I said.

"Is that what they're calling it?" Digby opened the paper bag. "In the mood for *chakchouka?*"

"Celine Montfort connected me to you."

Digby put down the bag. "How?"

"I have no idea." I didn't dare tell him the truth. That she'd seen I was as crazed as a dog in heat.

"You spoke with Celine? About me?"

"She summoned me to her room and asked me to give you a message."

His aplomb flipped off, as if by switch. "What's the message?"

"Who are you?"

"This is serious," he said. "Tell me the message."

"You have no idea who you're up against."

"My problem is," he said, "I do. What's the message?"

He wasn't the only one capable of flipping a switch. "I'm not going to tell you."

"You really are uncorruptible." He smiled with pride of ownership.

"Hardly!" I said with a guffaw. "One night of hot sex—"

"It was pretty hot."

"—and I'm being blackmailed by a thirty-pound Frenchwoman!"

"This is about money?" Digby brightened. "Let's talk money." He motioned me to sit down.

"You're gross. This could cost me my job."

"I'll get you another job."

"I love that family."

"So I'll speak to them." He stepped towards me. "Smooth things over."

"Stay away from me."

He stopped and spoke measuredly. "Tell me the message. And then you may go."

"I can go now."

"You're really doing this, aren't you?"

"Drawing the ethical line I should have drawn my first night in this hotel room? I absolutely am! And thank God. It's the first time I've felt like myself since the moment I met you."

"And who is that?" Digby asked. "Last time I checked, you outsourced your sense of self to three-thousand-year-old white men."

"Keep the ignorance coming," I said. "It actually helps."

"And what has it gotten you? A tidy little life you've convinced yourself is fulfilling?"

I suddenly got it: "You despise me."

Digby growled in frustration. "Fuck!"

"If this is how you wring information out of people, you'd better go back to spy camp."

"I knew better!" He shoved his palms into his cheeks and pulled.

"That makes two of us."

Digby went to the window and parted the privacy veil. He was angry and thinking, concentrating and calculating.

In the distance, the midtown skyline, its office windows glowing to life against the deepening dusk. Nearer, on the brownstone roofs directly across, a coil of corroded wire, a busted deck chair, folded beer cans.

Digby turned; he had arrived at a decision.

"I will tell you who I am. And what I have come here to do. In exchange, you will have to join me."

"Join you?" I said with a scoff. "Where?"

"In the arena."

This time I actually laughed. "The arena?! That's what you're calling your black market art deal?"

"Are you in or are you out?"

"Out!" I cried. "How can you ask such a thing?"

"It's time for you to step up, Adora." My name, spoken in that voice, with those lips. I wished he hadn't. "It's time to stop being afraid."

"Me?" I said. "Afraid?"

"It's time for you to become the person you're destined to be. It's not losing your job you're afraid of. Or money. That's playing small. What you're afraid of is playing big. Show the world who you are, Adora. You're ready. Take up space. Do it for yourself. Do it for Viv—"

"Speak her name again and I will literally vomit on this carpet."

"Okay, okay." He scratched his fingers through his hair.

I yearned to touch that hair. So deeply I felt it in my stomach.

"You told me you loved me," I said, my voice bitter and small.

He'd said it while he was on top of me, pausing to look deep into my eyes. His exact words, "I fucking love you." Of course they didn't count. I braced myself for ridicule.

"I've never cared for that word," he said.

There it was, the dagger.

"It's imprecise," he added.

With the pain came understanding. I'd been holding out hope that Celine was right: that Digby did have it as bad as I did. Now, that hope vanished.

"What a world-class asshole you turned out to be."

The framed watercolor over the settee caught my eye. I'd taken it for a splashy bouquet of flowers. All along, it had been an abstract.

"I meant," Digby said. "You and me, Adora, we're not like the others. We're not tethered to space and time."

He grabbed my wrist. It was what I'd been craving. Violence. His rough touch. His skin on mine.

He raised my wrist to my eyes.

"Love fate. You had it burned into your flesh. You want to know who I am? I am fate."

I tried to pull away, but his grip tightened. He pushed me. The bureau dug into my back. I tried to twist free. A wooden box fell, spilling a rainbow of pyramid-shaped tea bags across the carpet.

"Love fate?" Digby said. "Love me."

The bed. It was right there, promising another night of abandon. Orgasms and stillness, room service and showers, tenderness and YouTube videos. Loving Digby, and loving myself; they were one and the same.

Digby's eyes flashed to the bed, too.

His grip flinched. I jerked my arm free. I shoved him hard, sending him stumbling back.

"You are such a man," I said.

And I left.

"Fuck me!" I screamed when I got in the elevator, and not in the sexy way.

I was neither wide nor well.

Had I just made a bad situation worse?

The Stoic seeks the most useful perspective in all circumstances. These were my own words, written in one of my introductions.

C'mon, boys, don't fail me now!

I cycled though some greatest hits.

Marcus Aurelius: *The cucumber is bitter. Throw it away. There are briars in the road. Go around. That is enough. Do not ask, Why were they put there?*

It provided little succor.

Seneca: *Nothing is heavy if we take it lightly.*

I was too hopped up.

I swooshed out of the Lowell to be received by a gold-adorned doorman. Buttons, fringed epaulettes, whistle around his neck.

"Taxi?" he asked.

"Please."

No sooner had the doorman blown his whistle than the cell phone in my pocket vibrated. I checked the caller ID.

Lowell Hotel

Seneca: *When in doubt, do nothing.*

I sent it to voicemail.

Over my shoulder, in the dim lobby, the elevator lights worked their way up and stopped on Digby's floor.

I got an idea and turned to the doorman. "Lockwood Library."

He shut me in the cab and bent into the passenger window.

"Lockwood Library," he instructed the driver.

We pulled away.

In the mirror, Digby was now on the sidewalk questioning the doorman, who pointed to my taxi. Digby tipped him. The doorman put him in a cab.

After we were out of view, I told the driver, "Change of plans. Take me to the Ansonia, Broadway and Seventy-Third."

He took the first left. I turned and watched Digby's cab whoosh uptown towards the Lockwood Library.

The sign on Hannah's desk: *The first rule of holes: when you find yourself in a hole, stop digging.*

What mattered above all was I not take impulsive action out of fear and anger.

Seneca: *The greatest remedy for anger is delay.*

I needed to calm down and remember that this, too, shall pass.

Seneca: *We suffer more in imagination than in reality.*

Nothing bad had actually happened other than me being on the humiliating end of a couple of ugly conversations. All my negative emotions were the result of conjecture.

Jane Austen: *Time will explain.*

Celine could be bluffing. This whole thing could go away without the Lockwoods ever learning my part in it. And if things did go spectacularly to hell?

Marcus Aurelius: *Treat what happens as wholly neutral, not novel or hard to deal with, but familiar and easily handled.*

I closed my eyes and experienced the weight of my body on the cushioned taxi seat. I ran my hands across the black pleather, my fingers finding a curled edge of electrical tape.

I am safe.

I have a roof over my head.

I have women down the hall who'd do anything for me.

I am healthy.

My daughter is healthy.

I reached for my phone to text Viv, to tell her I was on my way. She'd already beaten me to it.

We're out of oat milk

????

Girl where are u

Let's make this (with link to TikTok)

Pipipi but he's with ryder and he always calls me after he rips bong

Whoops that was for tessy

Love you mama

Don't make me hate you

Can u stop at Fairway

Where are u grrrrr

Plzzz queen

I texted her back.

Meet me at Fairway in 15.

Can u go? Fairway is bad for my mental health

Bring bags.

Fifteen minutes later, Viv and I wended our way through the narrow, smelly and understocked aisles that brought out the worst in all ye who enter here.

In my pocket, my phone kept buzzing. Digby. He wouldn't stop calling.

"Viv?" I asked as I scooped oily sun-dried tomatoes into a container. "How do you block someone?"

"You go to Contacts and do Block Caller." She said this without looking up from her phone.

I reraised the subject while unloading the cart at the register. "What happens when they call? After you block them?"

"Nothing. They're blocked."

"Can they tell they're blocked?"

"Like eventually," she said. "Why?"

"It's for a metaphor I'm working on."

Viv looked dubious.

"Will you be needing bags today?" asked the cashier.

I realized, at the same time as Viv, that she'd come empty-handed.

"Don't yell!" she said.

I turned to the cashier. "Paper. Single bag only." Then, to Viv, "Put one hand on the bottom. Which will require you putting away your phone for a full five minutes."

Viv complied, but only after an eye roll so extravagant it could have thrown out her back.

We crossed Seventy-Fourth and fell behind a deliveryman who, too, was entering the Ansonia.

"Mom!" said Viv. "It's the flowers you like."

Up ahead, on the mail desk, the deliveryman had placed a flamboyantly large vase of peonies.

Last night—I'd told Digby they were my favorite flower.

So. Digby knew where I lived. That didn't take long. It would only be a matter of time before he showed up in person.

I do-si-do'd to the other side of Viv so when she passed she'd be looking at me and not the flowers.

Up ahead, on the left, the alcove with circular velvet sofas. I pictured Digby in his camel hair coat, one eye on the display of Babe Ruth memorabilia, the other eye peeled. There'd be no way to avoid him on our way to the elevators.

"I have an idea!" I said as we passed the mail desk.

"What?" said Viv.

Over her shoulder, I could see the card inside the cellophane. On it: "ADORA HAZZARD."

We passed the alcove. To my immense relief, Digby wasn't there. Yet.

The only available elevator was the dog elevator. (Another of the Ansonia's quirks is our dedicated dog elevator.) One of Viv's many aversions was using the dog elevator when we didn't have the dog.

"Get in," I ordered, leaving no opening for sass.

"That's your big idea?" said Viv. "Taking the dog elevator?"

"Let's take this party to Connecticut."

"This isn't a party."

"To visit Grandma. We haven't seen her in forever." I stepped out on seven. "It will be nice. Mr. Man loves the country. Emily Ann is out of town. We can take her car."

I turned. Viv had set the grocery bag between her feet and was texting.

"Seriously?" I said. "All I asked was five minutes."

Viv quickly grabbed the bag.

Riiip. The handles tore off. The bag dropped to the floor, spilling groceries everywhere.

"And," I said, "you're leaving your phone at home."

I called my mother from the car to tell her we were on our way.

"Oh, wonderful!" she'd replied. "Lucky me."

Viv and I arrived at eight to find Phyllis in bed for the night, Vaseline-faced and watching television. Her hair in the same boyish cut she'd had forever; I'd always suspected she went to the same guy as the nuns. Her cat, Dolly, was tucked in at her side.

Mr. Man, sniffing feline, frantically led the charge.

"Here he comes!" Phyllis said, and muted the TV. "Oh no, you're not getting my cat."

Mr. Man spotted Dolly on the bed and sat down.

"He knows he's not allowed on the furniture," I said.

Mr. Man gave a whimper and gazed forlornly at the cat.

"I love that little mutt," Phyllis said. "He has such low self-esteem."

"Hello, Mom." I leaned over and gave her a kiss.

"Hi, Grammy," said Viv from the doorway.

Phyllis assessed her with deep pleasure. "Don't I have the most beautiful granddaughter?" She reached for the remote. "You don't mind. I was in the middle of something."

"We'll stay out of your way," I said. "We brought stuff to make."

"I love that you came to visit me," Phyllis said. "Close the door."

On our way out, she unmuted the TV. It was a Barbra Streisand concert video.

"Start dinner," I told Viv.

I found the first-generation air mattresses in the garage and lugged them into what was once my bedroom.

It was small, my childhood home. The day I left for college, I literally passed California Closets on their way in. Down came my vision boards, David Bowie posters and friend collages. Up went white melamine. Even over the window I'd spent my youth gazing out and thinking my illogical thoughts, wanting my misguided wants, dreaming my destructive dreams. The view was now blocked by hanging knit and silk separates.

"Phone," said Viv when I returned to the kitchen. "I need to see the recipe."

I handed over mine. "Only while we cook. And fire up some music."

Viv impishly booted up a song. The opening riff of the Clash's "Should I Stay or Should I Go." Next came a dreamy, girlish boy-voice.

"Hey, girl, I'm waiting on ya. I'm waiting on ya. C'mon and let me sneak you out."

I let out a Beatlemania scream. One Direction! The album Viv and I had listened to in the car more than any other, back in New Haven when I'd drive her to school.

"My favorite song!" I said, dredging the tofu in flour.

When the second song started, I realized no, that was my favorite. As was the third. And the fourth.

"Is it a known thing?" I asked Viv. "That this is a perfect record? Like every single song."

"You know what that's called?" Viv said. "No skips."

"I'm going to do the thing," I said as one song ended.

Viv and I used to play a game where we'd call out what member of One Direction sang which line.

"Niall!" I said when the singing started. "Zayn!" at the next voice. "Liam!"

Then came the bridge. "*Would he say he's in l-o-v-e?*"

"Zayn!"

"Mom," gasped Viv. "That's clearly Harry."

"It's Zayn."

"You're embarrassing yourself."

"I'll prove it." I grabbed my phone.

On the screen, a stack of missed calls.

Lowell Hotel

Lowell Hotel

Lowell Hotel

"*Un momento por favor.*" I popped over to voicemail and made my way down the list, sweeping each message into the trash. "Later for you," I muttered. "Later for you. Later for you."

Lowell Hotel

Lowell Hotel

Ravi Bhardwaj

"That's odd," I said.

Ravi never called me. But he had today. At 6:12. Two hours after I'd seen him in the Laundry with the crates and that woman. . . .

I raised the phone to my ear.

Viv cleared her throat.

"Yes?" I said.

"Today at school, we learned about Gandhi. You know who Gandhi is, don't you?"

"Of course." I lowered my phone.

"Gandhi used to meet with the public, and one day there was this mother who brought her son. They wait for hours. When they finally get to see Gandhi, the mother says, 'Please tell my little boy to stop eating so much candy.' Gandhi won't. He tells them to come back in two weeks. The mother and her son leave. Two weeks later, they come back and wait in line. When they get to the front, Gandhi immediately recognizes them and says, 'Little boy! Stop eating so much candy!' The mother is confused. She asks Gandhi, 'Why didn't you tell him that two weeks ago?' Gandhi says, 'In order for me to ask him to stop eating candy, I needed to stop eating candy my-self.'"

Viv pointed to the phone in my hand.

"Point taken." I placed it face down on the counter.

Viv began opening cupboard drawers. "She never has anything sweet."

"Pro tip?" I said. "And it's a dangerous one. No matter how bare these cupboards may seem, there's always what you need for snicker-doodles. Butter, eggs, flour, sugar, cinnamon, vanilla, baking soda. Cream of tartar, which will still be good. Even if the expiration date is late eighties."

Viv went to work gathering ingredients.

My phone was still glowing against the counter. I casually flipped it over. The transcript of Ravi's voicemail was right there.

> "Adora, I'm afraid it's Ravi. Ha ha. I have an ethical dilemma. Ha ha. Call me. Ha ha. Please don't."

That was weird. Ethical dilemma? It couldn't be too serious if he was laughing about it. And Ravi wasn't one to laugh. Perhaps he'd tied one on at cocktail hour with Victoria Beckham. I flipped the phone back over.

Viv and I spent the next hour eating Marry Me Tofu, making snickerdoodles and negotiating what to watch when we got into bed.

Before we hit the sack, I popped into Phyllis's room.

"We're going to sleep," I said.

"Where's Viv? I want to tell her something."

Viv had been standing in the hallway. I made room for her in the door.

"Once," Phyllis said, "I was at a dinner party and Barbra Streisand was there. Everyone was treating her like a normal person. But not me. I told her I loved her, and that I considered her one of the great beauties, even with her nose."

"That's wonderful, Grandma."

Phyllis stared off in full Norma Desmond. "Barbra liked me. I could tell."

"I'm sure you made her feel really good about herself," I said.

"I did," my mother said. "Didn't I?"

"It's what they say," I added. "People don't remember you for what you did, but for how you made them feel."

"That's right." Phyllis smiled and unmuted the television.

I shut the door and turned to Viv.

"And you accuse me of having no sense of humor."

"Girl."

Full of giggles, Viv and I commando crawled onto the air mattresses and settled in. She had just cued up *Fatal Attraction* when the oven timer beeped.

I was too exhausted.

"Could you get that?" I said. "Please?"

"But I turned on the movie."

"C'mon."

"I don't know how," Viv said. "I'll burn myself."

"Just get an oven mitt, take the cookies out, transfer them to a cooling rack, turn off the oven and . . ." I got up with a "*grrrr.*"

I dragged my weary bones to the kitchen. My phone was still on the counter. My connection to Digby. My stomach tightened.

"Nope," I said, and began to transfer the cookies. "Not doing that."

I employed a trick I picked up from the Stoics.

When a situation causes you distress, imagine a friend coming to you and telling you the same thing had happened to her.

Would you panic? Would you feel like vomiting? Would you lose all bearings? Of course not. You'd listen and feel sympathy. It would have no physical effect on you and afterwards you'd continue on with your day. According to the Stoics, this is the proper response to your own situation.

In my case: a secretive man had acted secretively. A member of the French aristocracy possessed poor character. An older woman had feelings for a man who didn't reciprocate.

To the extent that any of it came as a shock or caused me emotional distress, that was on me.

When I returned to the bedroom, Viv was asleep. Michael Douglas hadn't even met Glenn Close at the book party.

I carefully lowered myself onto the mattress and nestled into Viv. The warmth of her body. I could never not need it. The Stoics make a strong case. But none of them were mothers.

"You're no skips," I whispered. "You're the balm, baby. Nothing beats you."

"I'm glad we did this, Mama," she answered sleepily.

I was awoken by the sun slicing through hanging palazzo pants and moiré silk shells. I felt as if I'd died and heaven was an Eileen Fisher sample sale.

Viv snoring delicately, I tiptoed into the living room, put on my running shoes and drove fifteen minutes to the nature preserve I knew so well.

The loamy floor was rich and springy. Baby birds shrieked in the trees above. The morning air still clung to its nighttime chill. I greedily breathed in the bracing dampness, a power wash for the lungs, blood and mind.

As much as I love Central Park, it ain't nature.

I arrived back at the house, feeling refreshed and even-keeled.

I found Phyllis sponging down the already clean sink. She was all made up and wearing a satin tunic over velvet leggings.

"Don't you look nice," I said.

Viv was slumped at the counter.

"Viv was just telling me," Phyllis said, "that she doesn't have a fella."

"She woke me up," Viv grumbled.

"And I told her she's too pretty to be a wallflower."

"I'm sure Viv doesn't know what that is."

"I do now," Viv said.

Phyllis went on, "I was telling her about the time I looked through my datebook—"

"And you saw you went out on a date every night for a whole year," I said. "We know."

Phyllis gave me a blank look, as if this was completely irrelevant information. "And every night for the whole year I'd gone out on a date. A different fella every night."

"You were very popular," I said.

"I could have chosen anyone. But I chose your father. Not because he was the richest or the most successful. But because he made me laugh."

"And got you pregnant," I said.

"That, too!"

I went to throw away my coffee cup. In the trash sat all dozen snickerdoodles. "How did these get here?"

"I didn't know what those were," answered my mother.

"Cookies, obviously. That Viv and I made."

"I don't want cookies in the house. And neither should you."

I looked to Viv. She was doing a slow burn.

"I'm off to lunch!" Phyllis announced. "Saturdays I go to Taka Sushi."

"We like Japanese," I said. "Wait for us. We'll all go."

"Oh," Phyllis said.

"What?"

"It might be hard to get three seats together at the sushi bar."

"Not at eleven. Or we'll sit at a table." I gave Viv's shoulder a tap. "Get your shoes on."

"Ouch!" she said, recoiling.

"Then I can't talk to Haruto," Phyllis said, wringing her hands together. "I love to see what he's making. He always saves me a yellowtail collar."

"Okay, Lady Macbeth," I said. "It seems like you'd rather go alone."

"It's best," Phyllis said.

"Wow," I said. "Fine."

I turned to Viv. "I guess we'll just have to . . . teach you how to drive!"

More than wanting to listen to celebrity blind-item podcasts, more than wanting to try the new cold foam flavor at Starbucks, more than wanting to go thrifting with Olivia Rodrigo, Viv wanted to learn to drive.

With the enthusiasm of being asked to do the dishes, Viv pushed herself up.

When I got to the car, Viv was in the passenger seat sulking theatrically.

Having a teenage daughter is like Choose Your Own Adventure, a constant set of junctures in the road. She's in a mood? How do you respond? Do you snap? Do you sympathize? I chose my go-to: ignore.

"You know where we're going to teach you to drive?" I said. "A place that's bound to be empty. The Catholic church parking lot, am I right?"

"It's Saturday."

"What do you want to listen to? Viv's choice."

"Nothing."

We drove in silence past the mall where Phyllis's Mini was parked. You could tell it was her Mini because it was squeaky clean and decked out in racing stripes and checkered mirrors. Also, the license plate read, "MY MINI."

"Goodbye, Mother," I said. "Enjoy your yellowtail collar."

I pulled into the church lot, empty as predicted, and parked under the shade of a spruce.

A teenage boy emerged from the side door of the church. He lugged a plastic bin and was dressed in low-riding black jeans and Def Leppard T-shirt. His hair was dyed jet black.

"Look!" I said to Viv. "A juvie."

"You don't know that."

"A church juvie," I said. "When I was a kid and we'd go to confession? The priest would give us the usual Hail Marys. But the kids who confessed really bad things, they had to do chores around the church. Watch. He's changing the sign."

The kid used a key to open the glass-encased sign. The current one read:

GOD'S GARDEN:
LETTUCE PRAY. SQUASH GOSSIP.
TURNIP FOR CHURCH.

"Credit where credit is due," I said.

No reaction from Viv.

"We ready?" I said. "Let's switch."

Viv wasn't moving.

"What is it?" I gently asked, and waited.

"I know she's your mother and everything, but I hate that woman.

She's never come into the city for my birthday or grandparents day. She has more pictures of her stupid car than she has of me. She's never once asked me about myself. She just makes me sit there and listen to her boring stories over and over."

The heaviness of Viv's words filled the car.

I blew out a sad sigh. "You're absolutely right."

"Was she always like this?"

I thought about it. "When people get older, they become more like themselves. So yes, this is what she was like. But no, she wasn't always this bad."

"It makes me really sad," Viv said.

"I know, baby. Me, too."

The boy had taken down all the letters and was in the process of replacing them with new ones.

So far, the sign read: FORGIVENESS IS.

"Something sucky happens," I told Viv, "like Phyllis not wanting to have lunch with us. But look at what opened up. You get to learn to drive. In fact, you can drive us to Chick-fil-A. You better believe that's a one-time offer because of their politics."

"Mom," Viv said. "It makes me really sad for you."

"I survived," I said. "She loved me the best she could."

"You said Grandpa was worse."

"Did I ever tell you about Leadville?"

"No."

"Leadville is an old mining town in Colorado. We used to go every summer for the Shakespeare festival. One day, I ran in and said, 'Daddy! Me and a bunch of kids are going to go play in the abandoned mine!' Without looking up from his newspaper, my father said, 'Nice knowing you.'"

"That's sad, too."

"With the benefit of time," I said, "you can laugh at anything."

"That means nobody's ever loved you."

"That's not true," I said, puzzled. "Dad loved me."

"All I saw was you not liking each other. And now he has another family."

"Honey," I said. "Where's this coming from?"

"I'm really sad right now."

"But why?"

"It's like you don't know how it feels to be loved."

"You love me, baby."

"I don't count."

"Of course you count!" I said. "You're all that counts."

Viv covered her eyes and curled into a ball. "I don't understand what is happening right now! Why are we in this parking lot?"

"I'm teaching you to drive—"

"Why did we visit Grandma? Why are you acting like everything is normal? I don't understand what is going on!" She began hyperventilating.

"Let's calm down—" I said.

"Are you laughing at me right now?!"

I might have cracked a smile.

"Your daughter is saying she's scared and you laugh?!" She broke into open sobs.

"Viv! I'm smiling. Because you're so awesome and articulate and direct, so much more than I was at your age, and I've never loved you more than I do right now because you're a complete genius. I forget sometimes."

"Don't forget," she said. "That's your job as a mother."

"Tell me why you're scared."

"Because you're spending nights at a hotel and I don't know with who—"

"Wait— How do you know that?"

"I track your location."

"You do? Why?"

"So when you come home it looks like I'm doing homework."

"Viv, look at me. Yes. Something came up at work. I let it distract me. And I have not been present for you. The important thing is, it's resolved. I'm back. I'm here. We're here."

Viv pressed her back against the door. She screwed up the courage and said, "I saw the letter, Mom."

"What letter?"

"The one addressed to Layla Lockwood."

"What—" I said. "How?"

"After you went to sleep, I looked through your purse. It wasn't sealed. I read what it said." Her voice got tiny. "I'm really scared."

I needed to proceed carefully. "What did it say?"

"I know about the arms deal," Viv said.

"What do you know about?"

"That's what the letter said. One line. 'I know about the arms deal.'"

"Arms deal?" I repeated the words and felt my reality go topsy-turvy.

Years back, when I'd received that mysterious call offering me the job, I was given an address on Fifth Avenue. I asked for an office number or company name, but the voice said the street number was enough.

When I arrived and saw I'd been beckoned to the Lockwood Library?

I felt as if I'd been tricked.

Lockwood Industries, according to their website, dealt in "the steel trade," "government contracts," and "international logistics."

But the Lockwood billions came from weapons manufacturing. Everyone knew it. There had been much publicized die-ins at the Library during the Iraq war. The family's obsession with apples was an attempt to trick people into believing their fortune came from the Lockwood Red. "Apple washing," the activists called it, the ones who'd come to throw rotten ones at the building.

I distinctly remember standing under the Gothic arches and asking myself, What's the ethical thing to do?

Do I go in? Do I not go in?

I thought of Voltaire. "Once a philosopher, twice a pervert."

I was a philosopher. I went in.

And I never came out.

"And now," Viv said, "you're blocking calls and afraid of flowers and talking to yourself and pretending you like being with me—"

"I love being with you!"

"Mom, are you doing something illegal?"

"Of course not!"

"I know where you work."

"That's Lionel's father and sisters and grandfather. It has nothing to do with Lionel. He's a good guy. He makes the world a better place. That's the whole point. It's my moral obligation to support and guide someone with that much power, so he can use it for good."

Or so I'd convinced myself.

"Oh God! You're scared. I can tell."

"I'm not scared," I said. "I'm thinking. Whatever that letter may have said—"

"I told you what it said!"

"It could mean anything."

"Arms deal?" Viv said. "Really?!"

"Was it written in cursive?" I asked, remembering Digby's ornate penmanship.

"Yeah."

"They never taught you cursive in school. You can't read cursive, you can't write cursive—"

"I can't believe this!" Viv said. "You're gaslighting me right now!"

"Can we please not throw around top-trending buzzwords?"

"This is literally the definition of gaslighting," Viv said. "Denying someone's reality by blaming them."

Touché.

"I'm just having a hard time believing it. I need to see things for myself. That's how my mind works."

Ravi. I remembered his message, and the words "ethical dilemma."

I texted him.

Call me.

"René Descartes has this thing," I said to Viv. "He calls it the 'Deus Deceptor.' Which I translate as the Evil Genie. He came up with it one night when he was sitting by the fire contemplating reality. He asked himself, 'How do I know any of this is real, and not the work of an Evil Genie tricking me for his own amusement?'"

"Mom?" Viv sunk into her shoulders and added, "I took a picture."

"Of the letter? Let me see it."

"It's on my phone."

I started the car. "Let's get the dog."

"We're going home?" asked a shocked Viv.

"This had better not be a long con to get you reunited with your phone."

Viv was radiating too much joy to speak.

As we pulled out of the parking lot, the boy in black was locking up the sign, now complete.

FORGIVENESS IS
SWALLOWING WHEN YOU'D RATHER SPIT.

"Okay, juvie king," said Viv.

"And for the record," I told her, "my mother has much to recommend her."

Back at the Ansonia garage, Viv, Mr. Man and I loaded ourselves into the dog elevator. It stopped at the lobby. A man with a Shiba Inu got on.

"Hey, ladies!" called a voice.

It was Dante, standing at the front desk. One ankle crossed over the other as he chatted up a smitten millennial.

"What's the point of even having a doorman?" grumbled the man with the Shiba Inu, shaking his head.

Viv and I got out on seven.

"What's that guy's problem?" Viv shot. "I love Dante."

"Go, go, go!" I handed her the key. "We're going to beat the Evil Genie at his game."

"I can't with the Evil Genie."

"Too bad," I said. "I find it relaxing to talk about the Evil Genie."

I unhooked Mr. Man from his harness. "You're free, Mr. Man! Bust it loose!"

Mr. Man tore down the hall like a greyhound out of the box. When he got to the door before we did, he frolicked in victory circles.

"I know," I told him. "It's all very exciting."

Viv popped into her bedroom and returned, brandishing her phone. On it, the photo.

David Ignatius Beale stationery. And in Digby's cursive: *I know about the arms deal.*

"Oh," I said.

"You owe me an apology."

I still couldn't connect the words to Digby. Or Layla. Or Celine. Arms deal? It was too far-fetched.

"For gaslighting me by saying I can't read cursive."

"You still can't write it," I pointed out. "There must be an explanation."

My phone rang from the bags by the front door.

"Good! It's probably Ravi."

"Rude," said Viv, and slammed her door.

By the time I fished out my phone, it had stopped ringing. It wasn't Ravi, after all, but a 212 number I didn't know.

Ravi hadn't texted me back. I texted him again.

Call me.

And, to sweeten the deal, added . . .

I have gossip.

Clack-clack-clack!

The clash of metal-on-metal tore through the apartment. I leapt half out of my skin—someone was at my door and they weren't being shy about it.

Clack-clack-clack!

I stood there, my heart doubled and fluttering with dread.

What if it was Digby? What if he'd been waiting in the alcove? And seen us in the elevator? He could have easily slipped past a distracted Dante.

I crept to the door and positioned one eye over the peephole.

The view suddenly went from light to black. As if the person on the other side . . . had just covered it up?

The blackness became blurry . . . and started moving.

Suddenly—the door handle moved against my stomach.

I leapt back and watched, hand over mouth, as the insentient handle rattled back and forth, back and forth.

The fear filling my chest, it had started to spill down my inner arms.

I needed help. But I couldn't bring Viv into this, couldn't let her see me so scared—

I knew! I texted the coven.

Can someone go out and tell me who's at my door?

Immediately: a picture of Emily Ann sitting in the Dead Sea with mud all over her body.

Clack-clack-clack!

This was followed by voices. More than one. I strained to make out what was being said. Whoever it was, they weren't speaking English.

I carefully opened the coat closet and lifted out my aluminum bat. Minna had bought us each one, just in case. God bless the coven.

I checked the peephole again.

The black kept moving . . . and morphing into a shape . . . a hat . . . a flat-brimmed hat . . . gaucho-style . . . encircled in a band of silver medallions.

This person had just stepped back to confer with someone.

I could make out wild dishwater hair.

I flung open the door. "Blanche!"

"Welcome to you, too," she said pointedly.

I set aside the bat. "Please, come in."

Blanche was with a woman dressed in tight jeans, boots laced to the knee and black wool coat of copious fabric tossed this way and that. Her accessories were many and colorfully beaded: a cross-body tapestry bag, tassel earrings. Down her back fell a robust black braid. Blanche introduced her as Dorris, her contractor.

"She's Peruvian," Blanche said. "We were down the hall looking at the apartment. It's super crappy."

"I like crappy," Dorris said in a thick accent.

"She likes work," Blanche said. "Do you mind if Dorris looks around? Something about wanting to see how the plumbing sits in the walls."

"Be my guest," I said.

"You have a very beautiful apartment," Dorris said.

Viv emerged from her room to check out the commotion.

"Come here," I said. "Blanche is a landscape architect. I asked her to join the coven."

"Yeah," Viv said. "No."

"Viv is no fan of the coven," I explained.

"You have a very beautiful daughter," cooed Dorris.

"Blanche!" I said, realizing. "I have a question."

"Mom!" said Viv. "She just gave you a compliment."

"Thank you," I told Dorris. "She knows."

"May I see your room?" Dorris asked Viv.

"Show her your room," I snapped.

Viv, spotting a kindred soul in Dorris with her laminated brows and permanent lip liner, happily obliged.

"Yeah?" Blanche said. "What?"

"At dinner last night. How did Ravi seem?"

"Ravi? He wasn't there."

Hmm. The flag of India. I'd seen it being raised. "But he was invited."

Blanche shrugged.

"Did Layla mention why he wasn't there?"

"Never came up."

That was odd. If Ravi was a no-show, I doubted Layla would have been able to contain her peeve.

"*Nuestro trabajo aquí está hecho,*" Dorris announced, exiting Viv's room.

"That was quick," said Blanche.

"I am very good," Dorris explained.

Blanche turned to me. "Our work is done. A question about the coven."

"Sure," I said, my mind on Ravi's message. Which now made zero sense if he wasn't drunk—

"Who are the other women? Isn't there an interview process?"

My phone rang from the front hall table. Hopefully, Ravi.

"It's a benevolent dictatorship," I quickly told Blanche. "I say you're cool and you're in."

The phone rang again.

"You're the dictator?" Blanche considered it. "You do wear a uniform."

"Sorry—I'm expecting a call."

By the time I hustled Blanche and Dorris out, the phone had stopped ringing.

It hadn't been Ravi. But that 212 number. Trying me for a second time. And not leaving a message. I called back.

"Benjamin Moore," said a gruff voice.

"The paint store Benjamin Moore?" I asked.

"Last time I checked."

"You called me," I said.

"Order number?"

"I didn't place an order. My name is Adora Hazzard."

"Without an order number I can't help you."

"Would you mind asking around," I said, "to see who called me?"

The man put me on hold. In as long as it took to count to five and roll his eyes, he was back.

"Nope."

"Where are you located?" I asked.

"Eighteenth Street."

I hung up and went to Viv's room. She was sitting on her messy bed. (No wonder she came in to sleep with me at night. It wasn't because she loved me. There was no room on her own bed!)

Viv, who'd reached singularity with her phone, didn't see me.

"Viv. Look at me."

She coolly obliged.

"There is no chance I was involved, even in the tiniest way, in an arms deal. Do you believe me?"

"I guess."

"When I get back, I will have answers."

"Whatever."

"And you will have walked the dog."

She didn't respond.

"Viv?"

"You can go."

"I'm sorry for gaslighting you."

"I accept your apology," she said, ungracious in victory.

I stood in the empty Benjamin Moore and feigned interest in Historical whites.

"Let me know if I can help you find anything," said the man from the phone, looking up from restocking foam paintbrushes. A tabby cat rubbed cutely against his leg.

I nodded thanks and looked around, having no idea what I was hoping to find.

The phone rang. He went to get it.

"Benjamin Moore. I'll connect you."

Moments later, a distant phone rang.

In the corner, I spotted a spiral staircase.

"Design studio," came a voice. "This is Scott. I'm with a customer, can I call you back?"

That explained it. The design studio's phone was routed through Benjamin Moore.

Still. I didn't know a Scott from a design studio.

I climbed the tight metal stairs and found myself in a low-ceilinged land of shades. I instinctively ducked. The mezzanine must have been added to the paint store despite there being inadequate height. On display, every conceivable type of window treatment, and walls of fastidiously arranged fabric books.

At a worktable sat a preppy husband and wife. Spread before them, fabric samples that leaned surprisingly toward the animal print.

Scott sat at a desk in the far corner and had just hung up the phone.

He stood to reveal he was young, slight and right-sized for the low ceilings.

He wore an argyle sweater-vest over a crisp shirt, tight capri pants and Gucci loafers sans socks. His face looked weirdly polished, like a Polly Pocket doll that had been licked. Everything about him shined, his pomaded hair, planed skin and lips kissed with tinted gloss.

However this whole thing played out, I sure hoped it ended up with Scott being an integral part of my life.

"About the waffle shades," Scott said to the couple, picking up where he'd left off. "It's counterintuitive, but the brown is more transparent than the white."

Scott held a sample to the light and spotted me.

"Adora!" he said, wagging a finger. "You didn't have to come down!"

How did he possibly know me?

"I was—in the neighborhood—"

"Were you, though?" He held a finger to his lips and tapped.

On his ring finger, a band of 24 karat gold studded with rubies. The same ring as Ravi.

Scott was . . . Ravi's husband? (!!!)

"Is this about Ravi?" I asked.

"I've been trying to reach him. But he's not answering."

"Is everything okay?"

"He texted me last night that he was pulled out of town for work. I thought maybe you'd gone, too, and could give him a message."

"Sorry," I said. "No."

"Worth a try!" he said with a clap, and went to rejoin his clients.

I knew not what to make of Scott's information, but I wanted to keep him on the hook.

"If Ravi does call, what should I tell him?"

"That it's the surrogate's birthday. He should text her."

"Oh!" I said. "Okay. I'll let you go."

Before I left, I had one more question. "Have we met?"

"First time," said Scott.

"How did you know it was me?"

"Ravi told me you were a style icon. He thinks your look is kind of great."

"He does?" This came as a shock.

"I do, too," Scott said. "Obsessed."

I stood on the sidewalk in the Flatiron District, goosed by the unexpected compliment, but no closer to the truth.

Could Ravi have stumbled upon proof of an arms deal?

I remembered Digby's amusement when I'd mentioned Boy With Apple. "Is that what they're calling it?" he'd said.

Was Boy With Apple code for something?

Had Ravi opened the crates and seen there was no statue?

But weapons?

And he'd brought in that woman and her machine for verification?

Was that his ethical dilemma?

No, no, no. It couldn't be. Ravi was laughing.

I checked my phone to confirm I'd correctly read Ravi's voicemail.

> **"Adora, I'm afraid it's Ravi. Ha ha. I have an ethical dilemma. Ha ha. Call me. Ha ha. Please don't."**

Still. What was so funny about an ethical dilemma?

Only then did it occur to me: I'd never actually listened to Ravi's message.

I pressed play and held the phone to my ear.

"Adora!" Ravi choked out my name. His voice was unsteady, desperate. "I'm afraid! It's Ravi. Call me. Please don't—" He abruptly hung up.

What my phone had transcribed as laughter? The "Ha has"? They weren't laughter at all.

They were the double rings of a phone.

The Lockwood Library house phone.

Celine had been calling Ravi.

And he hadn't been heard from since.

What had happened in the Laundry that so terrified Ravi?

And what exactly did he please not want me to do?

I knew how to find out. But first, I needed to hit a cash machine.

It was the last weekend of Ravi's Black portraiture exhibit, and the Lockwood Library was packed.

I scanned the steps of wiped-out museum goers, water hawkers and ticket scalpers for a black V-neck sweater, black tie and gray slacks.

"Over here," called a voice.

"Dante!" I said, spotting him. "Thank you for coming."

"Sam's covering. He made sure I let you know, anything for Miss Hazzard."

"I'll make it quick." I hurried Dante towards the employee entrance.

"This is where you work? I thought you wrote books or something."

"I do." I pulled on the door. It was locked.

The guard at the main entrance scuttled towards us, beckoning.

"Come, come, come." He inserted us at the front of the line. "Go, go." He waved us through the metal detector. It beeped for Dante.

"Sorry!" Dante reached into his collar and pulled out a thick gold chain.

"No, no, no." The guard shook his head. "You're fine."

"Do you own this place or something?" Dante asked me as we cruised inside.

"He's a weekend guy," I explained. "They're all a little afraid of us Monday-through-Fridays."

"Word," Dante said, a weekend guy himself.

His eyes went to the masses swarming the punch bowl. "Is that free or something?"

Before I could answer, the guard had ladled cider into a cup and presented it, with napkin.

"*Gracias, mi amigo,*" Dante said, and took a refreshing sip.

"How many languages do you speak?" I asked.

"Me? Four. I grew up in Naples and learned English from watching *King of the Hill.* My mom's Russian. And I pick up Spanish from around." He drained his cup. "Tasty!"

"Frozen from a can," I said. "The secret ingredient is tonka bean. Which the FDA banned so we have to import it from Europe."

Dante marveled at the mural above the entrance, the story of Adam and Eve. "Would you look at this joint?"

"I can give you a tour someday."

"I'm good," said Dante.

I'd been scoping out the surroundings. A locked metal gate covered the stairs leading to the basement. I'd figured as much; it was weekend protocol. That meant I wouldn't be able to access the Laundry to get eyes on the crates myself.

The staff offices were dark. Nobody had gotten the bright idea to score Brownie points by working the weekend. And by nobody, I meant Hannah.

I led Dante into Command Central and closed the door.

I hit a button. Quiet as a whisper, the shades lowered over the windows facing the lobby.

"Cool," Dante said.

Our only source of light was the grid of monitors.

"This is the same system we have." Dante took a seat in front of the keyboard. "But way newer."

"What I'm looking for—"

"Are there any lights in here?" Dante reached for a desk lamp.

"Let's keep them off," I said, blocking his hand.

"You're the boss."

I watched the surveillance images cycle through. When the Laundry appeared, I pointed to it.

"That's the angle."

With a few deft strokes, Dante called it up on the desk monitor.

"Sweet res," he said.

We were looking at an eerily still image of the Laundry from a high angle. The four crates tantalized in the middle of the floor.

"This is it now?" I sat in Hannah's chair and walked myself over for a closer look.

"Live from New York."

"I want that angle, but yesterday, at around four."

In seconds, the identical image appeared: the four crates in dim light. Then, the lights flashed on.

"Showtime," I said.

The men entered from the freight elevator, pushing the machine, followed by Ravi and the woman. Just as quickly, the men pushed the machine out of frame. Ravi and the woman exited, too.

"Oh no!" I said. "Don't leave us!"

"Are you a reporter or something?" asked Dante.

"A philosopher. I wish we could zoom in to see what that machine was. Fast-forward until they return."

Dante did, and stopped when the woman reappeared.

"She's back," Dante said. "And dressed for success."

The woman's hair was up in a clip. She wore a white PPE smock, surgical gloves and mask.

Ravi stepped into frame, also decked out in protective gear.

I must have gasped.

"You okay?" Dante asked.

"Shh!"

I watched, riveted, as Ravi lifted the tops off the crates. The lighting and camera angle were such that the contents of the crates were obscured.

"She's holding something," I said.

"Looks like a credit card," offered Dante.

"And a fingernail tool?"

"Maybe," Dante said. "I don't know."

The woman leaned into the first crate as Ravi stood at attention. She slowly emerged and passed Ravi the credit card, careful to keep it flat.

"She must be collecting samples," I said.

"You could be a reporter."

Ravi carried the card out of frame. When he returned, the woman was doing the same to the second crate. And so on. After all four crates had been sampled, Ravi replaced the tops.

Both Ravi and the woman exited the frame. The four crates remained, as before, in the middle of the floor. But now they radiated danger.

"Zoom ahead," I told Dante. "Let's see if she comes back. Do you have time?"

"I have time." Instead of typing into the keyboard, Dante swiveled to face me. "I gotta say. I don't know why you're throwing in the towel."

"Throwing in the towel?"

"You, seven-fifteen, seven twenty-two."

"The coven?"

"You still got game." Imagine Ryan Gosling saying this. An Italian Ryan Gosling.

"I may have had temporary game," I said. "Not anymore."

"Don't be talking that way."

"I, very recently, had sex for the first time in years. What you're picking up now is the quickly fading afterglow."

"The night you went out!" Dante said, pumping a fist. "Dressed all, and you came back at five in the morning? I knew it!"

"Maybe I need to not live in a doorman building."

"Me and the guys, we're rooting for you, that's all."

"You sure know how to make a girl feel exactly her age." I pointed to the screen. "*Pronto*."

Dante fast-forwarded until we saw movement.

The men wheeled the machine back into the elevator.

"Oh no . . ." I said. "Is that it?"

The woman followed, back in black. She passed a piece of paper to Ravi. They exchanged friendly goodbyes. Ravi popped out of frame to hand her the bottle of tequila. The elevator doors closed behind woman, men and mystery machine.

Alone in the frame, Ravi studied the piece of paper.

"His expression," I said. "When he's reading. Wind it back."

Dante did.

"Am I imagining it?" I asked. "Or does he look scared?"

"He does look scared."

Ravi exited the frame.

"Hmmm . . ." I started to have a think.

"So," Dante said. "What's the meaning of life?"

"Me?"

"I've never met a philosopher. Isn't that what you do? Figure out the meaning of life."

"Some philosophers. I'm more interested in applying reason to achieve happiness."

"How do you do that?" Dante asked.

"By cultivating realistic expectations."

"What does that mean?" he asked. "Could you explain it?"

Dante was looking deep into my eyes. Too deep.

"Wait!" I said, scooting back. "You think we're in a porno!"

"An attractive woman invites a man to help her with a computer problem? It could be the start of one."

"I wouldn't know," I said. "I fast-forward through the beginnings."

"Damn!" he said. "You do have game."

"So this is how you do it?"

"This is how I do what?" Dante said. "What do you think I'm doing?"

I had to laugh.

"Don't make me become as obsessed with you as Viv is. But in a bad way."

"Wait," Dante said. "Viv's obsessed with me?"

"Viv is obsessed with Patti LuPone."

I gave Dante the crisp twenties I'd withdrawn on my way uptown. Without looking down, he shook my hand and took the money.

"Aww, you didn't have to."

Dante got up. Over his shoulder, on the desk monitor—which had continued running in fast motion—Ravi had reappeared.

"Look!" I said.

Dante wound it back.

In one of Ravi's hands, the piece of paper, now rolled tightly into a stiff tube. In the other, he was talking into his cell phone.

Ravi climbed the stairs towards the camera. His face was fear-stricken as he hung up and reached for something out of frame. He came back holding an old-fashioned phone receiver.

The house phone! It was at the top of the stairs, mounted below the camera.

The time stamp indicated 6:12.

When Celine had rung.

Ravi spoke feverishly into the phone and banged the white paper against the rail.

"Agh," I said. "If only we could hear him."

"Oooh. You know what you could do?"

"What?"

"I'm not saying you should," he said.

I put Dante in a cab and sent him back to the Ansonia. My parting words, "Stay away from Viv."

I hailed a cab.

"The Museum of Natural History," I instructed the driver. "Not the front. The entrance on Columbus, please."

Taxi TV was turned to the highest volume. The Final Jeopardy category was "Victorian Novelists." My wheelhouse. But I couldn't watch. Digby had ruined Ken Jennings for me.

Out the window, Central Park whizzed by.

Information was coming at me just as fast.

But I could go slow. My years of Stoic training had taught me to separate emotions from events, and perceive reality correctly. After a youth spent getting things wrong, I was now a woman who got things right. I would proceed carefully and not fall for the Evil Genie's tricks.

Four crates had arrived from France containing a statue Layla referred to as Boy With Apple.

According to Ravi's research, such a statue does not exist.

Celine, self-described "chateau rich but cash poor," brokered the deal.

Digby had come to New York to sit down with Layla Lockwood about something that had been stolen. He went so far as to claim, "Western civilization is on the table."

His note to Layla read: "*I know about the arms deal.*"

Ravi, for whom Boy With Apple had become a bugbear, stumbled upon an awful truth last night.

He called me in a panic about an ethical dilemma.

Before he could finish his thought, he received a call from Celine.

He was a no-show at dinner.

He hadn't been heard from since.

These were the facts as I understood them.

Nietzsche: *There are no facts, only interpretations.*

Yes, all arrows pointed to an arms deal. But with a huge asterisk: all my information came courtesy of a liar (Layla), a charlatan (Digby), an aristocrat with money troubles and a mean streak (Celine) and a man prone to blinding passion (Ravi).

I was still operating in the dark. It took all my mental strength to prevent half-baked conclusions from taking hold and distorting my ability to perceive reality correctly. There was more information to be had; I must remain clear-eyed.

The taxi emerged onto Eighty-First Street; it was down to one lane and clogged with traffic.

"Let me out here," I said.

Taxi TV now showed the news anchors at their desk. The chyron caught my eye.

"BREAKING: EMERGENCY MUSEUM CLOSURES."

I pushed the screen to unmute.

A woman identified as "FAYE LOWENSTEIN: FBI ART CRIME TEAM" was now speaking.

"We've received a credible threat—"

The screen suddenly switched to payment options.

"Agh!" I quickly paid and got out.

Standing on the sidewalk, I searched for "FBI New York museums."

Up came a story, hot off the wire.

> **Breaking News: FBI and DHS Warn of Terrorist Threat Against Museums**
>
> **New York, NY—In a rare joint intelligence bulletin, the Federal Bureau of Investigation and Department of Homeland Security have issued an urgent warning regarding a credible threat from the terrorist organization known as QUANDO, the group claiming responsibility for last week's devastating bombing of the British Museum.**
>
> **The four-page bulletin confirms they believe QUANDO has set its sights on New York City museums on Monday. While no specific museums were mentioned, the Metropolitan Museum of Art and the Brooklyn Museum have announced they will be closed for the day. Current assessments indicate that museums containing artifacts originating from Egypt, Turkey, Greece, and Syria are likely targets.**
>
> **QUANDO first gained international attention with last week's bombing of the British Museum, resulting in the destruction**

of the Rosetta stone. The group's motives center on the return of stolen and looted art and artifacts to their countries of origin. Little is known about the organization's leadership or specific ideological leanings. The extremists have vowed to continue bombing art institutions until their demands are met.

In response to the threat, the FBI and DHS have mobilized counterterrorism units and are working closely with local law enforcement and museum security to ensure public safety and the protection of all cultural assets.

Visitors to all New York museums can expect increased security measures including bag checks, enhanced surveillance, and a visible police presence.

My entire body was thumping.

Bomb threat. Arms deal. Were they one and the same?

Is this how the Lockwoods were still making their billions? Lionel, too?

And it was obvious to everyone but me?

Had I been so beguiled by money, status and proximity to power that I'd become corrupt to my core? (It wouldn't be the first time!)

Clinging to a shred of hope that there could be another explanation, I ran in the direction of barking dogs.

Bull Moose Dog Run, named after Teddy Roosevelt, was in the park off the Museum of Natural History, and a favorite of Ziggy's.

That's where I found him, leashes slung over his shoulder, throwing a tennis ball to a cattle dog.

I walked straight at him. He reacted with alarm.

"I need you to read lips." I held up my phone.

It was Dante's idea. "I don't want to rat out Ziggy or anything," he'd said, "but sometimes we get him to look at the freight elevator camera and tell us what Julio is saying to his girl. Just to mess with him. You know. It's all good."

I pointed to a bench in the shade. I could see Ziggy trying to figure out how much I knew about his shenanigans.

"Let's go," I said.

Ziggy followed uncertainly.

The cattle dog ran over with the ball, dropped it and gave Ziggy a life-or-death stare.

"Here." I swapped my phone for the plastic thrower and gave the slimy tennis ball a hurl.

Ziggy cradled my phone in his hands. Cued up was the video I'd taken of Ravi's phone call. Ziggy pushed play and watched it all the way through. He looked unsure.

"You won't be able to get the whole conversation," I said. "He's turning away for most of it. Just give me what you can."

The cattle dog returned. I threw the ball.

Ziggy sat and replayed the video, this time sliding the tracking button back anytime Ravi's face was clear. As Ziggy did so, he made the full complement of facial expressions: concentration, confusion, surprise, comprehension.

And the cattle dog was back!

"We are all you, little dog," I said. "We want what we want. Most of us just disguise it better." I chucked the ball.

Ziggy turned to me. "It's some pretty weird stuff."

"Yeah, I forgot to warn you."

"Who is this guy?"

"A work colleague."

Ziggy gave me a wary look.

"What?" I got out the pad and pen I'd filched from Command Central, and sat poised to write. Just then, I heard the approach of two panting dogs.

The cattle dog and . . . Mr. Man!

"Hey!" I said accusingly to Ziggy.

"Viv texted me."

"That little brat. I hope she paid you."

He shook his head to say it wasn't necessary.

"I'm paying you."

Now I had two dogs staring at me.

"Go away. Go play." But they remained fixed.

Ziggy patted the bench. Both dogs jumped up. (So that's where Mr. Man learned to get up on furniture!)

"What's he saying?" I asked.

Ziggy held the phone so we both could see and started playing back the video.

"The person he's talking to?" Ziggy said. "He had something to do with the Nazis?"

"It's a woman," I said, jotting down the word "NAZIS." "Her father saved the Mona Lisa from the Nazis."

"The Mona Lisa," Ziggy said. "And other stuff."

I wrote down "MONA LISA" and explained, "They smuggled it out of the Louvre and hid it in the family chateau until the end of the war."

Ziggy paused the video. "I saw a thing about that on the History Channel. Cool!"

I pressed play. "What's happening here?"

"The guy in the video is going on about the father's reputation. And the daughter's reputation. It's all reputation, reputation."

"That makes sense." I jotted down the word. Pierre Montford was a national hero. If his cash-strapped daughter had gotten involved in illicit activity, it would ruin the family legacy.

We were coming up on the part of the video where Ravi became particularly agitated.

"And now?"

"I'm not sure." Ziggy puzzled over Ravi's face. "He starts talking about . . . apples?"

"And that boys don't hold them?"

"Yes!" Ziggy said with a laugh.

"Long story."

Ziggy paused the video, hesitant to proceed.

"What's wrong?" I asked.

"This is where it gets weird. It becomes all about arms."

Arms. My body drained of strength as the reality set in.

"And," Ziggy said, "C-Four."

"C-Four?" I asked hopefully. "What's C-Four?"

"A plastic explosive."

I grew very still. The city around me rang with silence. It was imperative I move with extreme caution.

"How do you know that?" I asked Ziggy.

"I just do." He handed the phone back and raised his hands. He was done. Like, really done.

I searched "C4."

Images of a cutesy European-style car popped up.

"It's a Citroën," I said, showing him. "Their new model. The C-Four!"

Ziggy gave me a believe-what-you-want look, and gestured for me to keep scrolling.

Below the paid results, it was link after link to C-4, the plastic explosive.

How to make it.

How to detect it.

Its detonation mechanism.

Its blast yield.

My breath got caught in my throat.

I looked at Ziggy, but his gaze was stuck to the list in my hand. "NAZIS. MONA LISA. REPUTATION. APPLES. ARMS. C4."

At the bottom of the pad, the words "LOCKWOOD LIBRARY."

Ziggy waited for me to speak. I took my time.

"This simplifies things," were the words that came out.

The gray had separated into black and white. Right from wrong.

My next steps were clear. All four virtues would be required. Wisdom, courage, temperance and justice. Nothing about it frightened me. My whole life. It felt as if I'd been in winter training for this exact moment.

"That's all?" Ziggy asked, still strangely worried.

"That's it."

Ziggy wasn't so sure.

"What?"

"You're not mad I told that guy at the ballet where you live?"

"Oh, Ziggy." I tousled his hair. "Don't you know? You can do no wrong."

"He was hilarious," Ziggy said, and hung on my reaction.

"That's one word for it."

"He seemed really into you," Ziggy offered. "And I thought, maybe . . ."

"Yeah," I said. "I thought maybe, too."

"So," I said to Lucien and Lorenzo. "We've got a bunch of people living in a cave and chained in such a way that they can only face a wall. And projected onto that wall is a puppet show."

It was two days later, Monday morning, a school holiday, and we were back in the third-floor sitting room.

I'd loaded Book Seven of Plato's *Republic* onto an iPad. Having it on a screen guaranteed that, if nothing else, the twins would stare at it.

Out the window, maintenance men scaled Blanche's trellis and pulled out the many Havahart traps tucked throughout. Today's haul was impressive. Central Park was about to welcome a dozen new rat friends!

"And in this puppet show," I said, "the prisoners watch life play out before their eyes. Humans going about their day, animals in the forest. When Glaucon says, 'This is a strange bunch of prisoners,' what does Socrates say?"

"They are like ourselves," answered Lucien.

"This is what's called an allegory. It seems to be about one thing but really it's telling us about ourselves."

"Like a puppet show," said Lorenzo.

"I've never thought of that," I said. "The Allegory of the Cave functions the same to the reader as the puppet show in the Allegory of the Cave does to the cave dwellers. Well done!"

Lorenzo flushed with pride.

"So these cave dwellers," I continued, "they believe the shadows on the wall are the things themselves. They have no way of knowing otherwise. Until one day, one of them frees his chains and climbs out of the cave into the outside world. What's the first thing he sees?"

"The sun," said Lucien.

"This is painful at first. But eventually this man's eyes adjust, and for the first time, he sees the world for what it truly is. Humans in all their glory and foibles. Trees singing with birds. Flowers, fragrant and colorful. He gets so excited, he rushes down and tells the others to come up. They do. But when these cave dwellers step into the sun, it hurts their eyes, too."

"Like when you walk outside after a movie during the day," said Lorenzo.

"Exactly! Which is just too uncomfortable, so they all rush back into the cave where they continue to watch the shadows. Our free man, he's so enraptured by the wonders of the outside world that he chooses to live there. But he keeps returning to the cave to try to get the others to join him. And what do the cave dwellers do?"

"They laugh at him," said Lucien.

"And even what else?"

"They kill him," Lorenzo answered.

"Because they'd rather be left in peace staring at shadows."

I gave this a moment to sink in.

"Now," I said. "Why do you think that is?"

"It's easier?" suggested Lorenzo.

"It's what they're used to?" said Lucien. "It's what everyone else is doing?"

"And they don't want to look stupid," added Lorenzo.

"I have a question for you boys. Where do you think you live?"

"The cave!" they happily answered.

I had to laugh. "Why do you say that?"

"You're always telling us how bad we are," Lorenzo said.

"That's not true! Let me ask you another question. If you genuinely appreciated all the beauty of the outside world, where would you rather dwell?"

"The cave," they said.

It was official: I'd taught them nothing.

Ding.

A text came in. The one I'd been waiting for.

"FL" was the sender.

Here.

"Lesson's over," I said. I took a good look at my precious miscreants. "I love the two of you, you know that. You're never bad. You're only good. Come here. Give me a hug."

I'd never asked for one before. The boys eagerly entered my open arms. I pulled them close; they released into my embrace. I kissed the tops of their crusty, over-moussed heads.

That morning, I'd woken up and said to the universe, "Surprise me."

Whatever happened next, I was certain this moment with Lucien and Lorenzo would be the sweetest.

To return to the Library, I had the choice of tunnel or street, darkness or daylight. As I headed across Seventy-Sixth, I noticed a black sedan with government plates parked in the No Stopping Zone.

"You're walking tall," called Tony, approaching from Madison on one of his routine perambulations. I waited for him to catch up.

"Catch any crazies?" I asked.

"Whatever you're on," he said. "I need some."

"Virtue. More powerful than any drug."

A pair of NYPD cars screeched up to the Library and stopped.

"What's this?" Tony said, and trotted over. I headed up the steps.

"Adora!" called a voice across the Fifth Avenue traffic.

Gravelly, deep. Days before, the sound of it had rendered my bones jelly.

I refused to turn. I refused to slow down. I refused to rush.

I arrived at the Library entrance. From behind, a hand grabbed my arm.

"Adora." Digby's face was puffy. A shirttail hung from his sweater. "Talk to me. You don't know what you're doing."

"I know exactly what I'm doing."

I glared at his hand. He quickly released it.

"You have to talk to me," he said.

Our eyes met. That's all it took; everything else fell away. My stomach thumped with want.

I steeled my voice. "I don't have to do anything I don't want to do."

"You deserve peace, Adora. I'm the only one who can give it to you."

I had to scoff. "Don't you remember, David? I stopped falling for your bullshit."

"Tell me what's going on. Please. We can go back to the hotel. We can talk, we can—"

"What do you take me for?" Fearing his answer, I quickly added, "I saw your note. Arms deal?"

With that, I entered the Library and instructed the guard, "He stays out."

The lobby was empty but for Hannah, who was taking on Faye Lowenstein in her FBI windbreaker.

"We are closed today," Hannah told her.

"I have a warrant." Faye handed one over.

"My head of security is on his way. You can discuss it with him."

"There's nothing to discuss," Faye said.

"Dr. Hazzard!" Hannah called, spotting me. "Maybe you can reason with this woman."

Without stopping, I headed to the basement stairs. Faye peeled off and followed.

....

I'd spent the day before in Faye Lowenstein's dingy office in Federal Plaza, laying out everything I knew. I endured an unpleasant hour of being spoken to like a mental patient. Slowly, though, Faye called in her colleagues. By the end of the day, they agreed my information was credible. A plan was put in place.

"No!" Hannah yelped. "That's a restricted area!"

Faye and I hustled down the stairs.

"The crates are still there," I informed her. "As of an hour ago." I'd seen them through the Laundry window on my way to tutoring.

"The mayor is a personal friend of the Lockwoods!" Hannah cried, racing to catch up.

I fobbed open the Laundry door. Hannah gasped.

"Dr. Hazzard? What are you doing?" She stepped in front of me to block my entrance.

Faye took care of that with a jab of the elbow. (Yesterday, Faye had described herself as "being in touch with my inner impatience.")

"Hey!" Hannah said.

I hit the lights.

The fluorescent rods flickered on one by one, revealing below . . .

A sea of concrete.

The crates were gone.

"Where are they?" I said.

"If this is about the statue," Hannah said to Faye, "I can give you all the paperwork. Follow me upstairs and—"

"Where did they go?!" I demanded.

"The parterre," answered a perplexed Hannah. "Everybody's outside for the unveiling."

"Ravi, too?" I still hadn't heard from him.

"Mrs. Lockwood gave him the day off," Hannah said. "To prevent a scene. You know. Now could you please tell me—"

Faye had her walkie-talkie out. "All units. Move into the garden."

"Because of the statue?" asked Hannah. "What's wrong with the statue?"

Faye and I stepped out of the gloriette elevator into blinding sun and a chaotic parterre. It looked as if a baseball bat had been taken to a beehive and men in uniform were released. FBI and NYPD in dark blue. Gardeners in khaki. Art handlers in Lockwood Red. Ex-Mossad in standard-issue black.

Standing among them, perfectly still, Layla and Celine. They looked caught, as if awaiting the inevitable.

The four crates were at the center of the bedlam, tops on the ground.

Lionel, spotting me and Faye, tore across the grass at top speed, his wheelchair making mulch of pansies and yew borders alike.

He intercepted Faye and pulled a one-eighty. "I'm Lionel Lockwood. This is my family library."

"I'm aware." She continued her march straight for the crates.

"May I gently ask what this is about?" Lionel said, riding alongside. "I'd like to cooperate—"

He'd spotted a pair of agents whose vests read, "FBI BOMB TECH." They were up ahead examining the crates with handheld devices and a jacked-up German shepherd. It, too, wore a vest. "DO NOT PET ME."

"Another bomb scare?" Lionel stopped and looked at me to share in the irony. "This is some strange karma."

I kept going, following Faye to the crates.

"What you got?" she asked a bomb tech.

"*Nada,*" he replied. "All empty. And clean as a whistle."

Hannah breathlessly arrived and presented Faye a fat folder. "Here's everything. Bill of sale. Provenance. Customs documents."

"You know about this?" Lionel asked Hannah.

"Mr. Lockwood," she said. "I have no idea what's going on. It's apparently the statue."

"What about the statue?" Lionel looked towards me, but not at me.

Over me.

"What's wrong with it?" he asked, puzzled.

Towering above, at my back, I felt a nauseating presence. Oversized and white. I turned.

Standing on the plinth, a marble boy, with tight curls and smooth, blank eyes. His hips were cocked. His arms were delicate. One fell at his hip; the other was raised, offering . . .

An apple.

"No . . ." I sputtered. "There's no way."

I gripped the statue by his legs. The chill of the marble shot up my arms.

"There it is," said Faye, looking none too pleased. "A statue, all right."

"The note said arms deal . . ." I muttered.

"Arms deal?" asked a confounded Lionel.

"I thought it was an arms deal," I said softly.

Celine stepped forward.

"Arms deal!" she said. "Indeed! There was an arms deal. And a legs deal and a torso deal and a head deal!"

"How could this have happened?" I heard myself say.

"Adora?" It was Lionel again. He'd raised his chair so we were eye to eye. "Did you . . . ?" The rest of the sentence was too horrific for him to utter.

"Mystery solved," announced Faye.

She pointed her foot in the direction of the empty crates. As I'd remembered, they were covered with stickers, stamps and plastic pouches.

But I hadn't seen that each was numbered.

"C1," "C2," "C3," and "C4."

"There's your C-Four," Faye said with a rueful grunt.

"C-Four," said Celine. "*Caisse numéro quatre.* It's how we label them in France."

"C-Four?" Lionel said. "The plastic explosive?"

Faye stepped in and took the bullet. "We received a tip about a shipment of C-Four that I deemed credible."

"A tip?" Lionel said. "From whom?"

Faye dipped her head towards me.

Lionel's eyes begged me to say it wasn't so. "Did you call the FBI on us? For plastic explosives?"

I had no words.

"Adora," said Lionel. "Why?"

"Baby." It was Layla, putting a tender hand on Lionel's shoulder. Sylvia was at her side. "Let's get you out of here."

Sylvia lowered his chair to seat height. Lionel slumped, as if his whole world came crashing down, too.

Layla waited until Lionel and Sylvia were out of earshot before she got in my face.

"You had one job," she snarled. "To help my husband. Do you have any idea the level of betrayal? To him? To me?"

"I'm so sorry," was all I could say. "I got it wrong."

"We treated you like family."

With a flamboyant wave of the hand, Layla was off. Security knew what to do next.

By the time I was escorted upstairs, my key had been deactivated, my laptop stripped of any trace I'd ever worked at the Lockwood Library, and an empty cardboard box placed on my desk.

Tony had been tasked with standing outside my office for the five minutes I'd been given to clear it out.

I looked around. Bookshelves lined with foreign translations of my books. Gold medallions on wooden stands. The framed letter from Barack Obama thanking me for my edition of *Meditations,* which had made his year-end list. An honorary degree from Barnard College describing me as a "Public Intellectual." A candid photograph of Lionel and me sitting in the garden, Lionel's head thrown back in laughter, the early days, visible behind us a bare trellis; neither of us having an inkling of the growth and kinship to come.

The drawing Viv had done for me in second grade, of us hugging. Me in blue. She in pink. "I LOVE MY MOMMY VERY MUCH. SHE GIVES ME HUGS. SHE GIVES ME KISSES." She'd written all her Y's backwards.

I'd grown frustrated trying to teach Viv the correct way to make her Y's, but it never took. Until one day it did, and the backwards Y's were gone, forever. All the Stoic training in the world can't prevent that punch to a mother's gut. I loved Viv's picture for the obvious reasons, but hung it prominently to remind myself how quickly it can all vanish.

I removed it from the wall.

"This is all I want," I told Tony.

Out on the steps, FBI and NYPD stragglers remained, shooting the breeze and eating street tacos.

Pedestrians were slowing down, traffic, too. The Taxi TV news van was on the scene, Faye Lowenstein again being interviewed.

I didn't even try to stay out of the shot. Tony was at my side, keeping a respectful distance as he walked me to a town car waiting to ferry me on my one-way trip away from the Lockwood family. A restraining order was already in the works.

"Bye, Tony," I said. "I guess you finally caught your crazy."

"Goodbye, Adora," he said. "I'm going to miss our mornings."

Over the town car, across Fifth, Digby. Standing at his bench, looking haggard and small. A scrap of toilet paper fluttered on his neck, stuck there with blood.

For him I'd lost everything?

The sound of glass shattering. Viv's picture. I'd dropped it.

I made a mad dash for Digby. Cars screeched, invectives were shouted. What did it matter? It was all over, anyway.

"You did this to me!" I screamed. "Why?! Why me?!"

I beat on Digby's chest as he stood, eyes closed, absorbing my violence.

"I had everything!" I said, tears flowing. "I was happy! I was free!"

It took Tony and a guy eating a hot dog to pull me off.

I entered the Ansonia a zombie.

"Hello, Miss Hazzard," said Sam from behind the mail desk. "You have flowers."

The peonies. They hadn't even started to wilt.

"Give them to your wife," I said.

"You sure? Here, a package came."

Sam handed me a manila envelope. Next to my name and address: "FROM DAVID BEALE, BY HAND."

I didn't care.

"Whoa," said Sam. "Let's see that hand."

It was dripping blood. I looked down. A trail of crimson across the black-and-white tile. From Viv's drawing. I must have cut my finger on the broken glass.

"I'll clean it up," I said.

"No, you won't." Sam tore a paper towel off a roll and wrapped it around my sliced finger. "This should hold you until you get upstairs. And don't forget this."

He handed me the envelope. It was unsealed and upside down. The contents spilled onto the floor.

I stood there computing the colors.

Black, white, blood red . . . sky blue.

A contract? Why would Digby be sending me a contract?

I bent over to pick it up. The pages were yellowed and stiff.

It was my NDA.

"What the—"

Two loose pages had fallen to the floor, too. I read the first.

EVELYN STEELE-BROWN
55 Pavilion Crescent
Winnipeg, Manitoba R3P 2N6

Dear Adora Hazzard,

My name is Evelyn Steele-Brown and I'm writing you on behalf of my dead father. I will not do him the dignity of saying his name. I was just informed by your associate, Mr. David Beale, that my father, POS for short, put you under an NDA for sexually assaulting you. I wish I could tell you I was surprised. But after constantly cheating on my mom, the deadbeat abandoned us when I was three. I didn't write to dump on you. I wanted to tell you, as his only (known) surviving spawn and heir, that I am formally releasing you from your NDA. Do me a favor, please, and speak, let your hammer ring out across the land what an asshole the guy was. I would find it comforting. Joking aside (although I wasn't joking), this angry mother-of-three wants to help in any way she can. Call her (me). My mom is happily remarried and she's not interested in trashing the dude. I'm always up for it, day or night. Help me. Please, kind lady? All I have is you. (You don't know me well enough to know that was a joke.) In closing, sorry for your pain and fuck that guy, right?

Yours until my glory passes,

Evelyn S-B
(Oh, by heir I mean the person who had to pay off his gambling debts. Family sucks!)

I read the letter again. It made no sense.

Why would Digby have my NDA? How could he have even known? And why was he contacting TJ Steele's daughter on my behalf?

The other piece of paper lay on the floor. It was the same yellow as the pages of my NDA, and just as brittle.

IDELSON, BRADSTOCK, TOLL and MILLER
2930 Avenue of the Americas
Suite 2200
Century City, California 90032

May 21, 1998

Travis,

Here's the latest Steele/Hazzard. I'm still waiting on dollar amounts. Please look over and let me know if you have any adjustments. Otherwise, see you today at three.

Best,

David

David? I flipped to the last page of the NDA. Past the notarized signature pages, to the appendix. It was two lines long.

APPENDIX [A]

Per item 7b, all communication regarding this Agreement shall be conducted exclusively through the law offices of Idelson, Bradstock, Toll and Miller, with David I. Beale as the point of contact.

The lawyer in the room.

It was Digby.

It had been thirty years. I hadn't recognized him.

He'd written up my NDA.

This whole time, I hadn't known him, he had known . . . me.

It was Dante who found me. Collapsed in the dog elevator.

—PART FIVE—

RELEASED PARTIES

Our Parisian flat was in a medieval building—literally, built in 1430—and the staircase leading to it tightly spiraled. Its triangle treads, even at their widest, could barely accommodate the ball of my foot. I considered it a small miracle I didn't tip backwards and take Viv with me. The white plaster walls were irregularly embedded with rough-hewn logs of different lengths at haphazard angles. Structural or cosmetic, I knew not.

"This staircase," I said to Viv, "has more charm than anything back home!"

This was both sincere and a sales job. Viv had balked when she'd seen it was a fourth-floor walk-up. What she didn't yet know was that in France, a fourth-floor walk-up meant a fifth-floor walk-up. I carried both our suitcases in anticipation of her pitching a fit.

"What?!" Viv, on cue, as I continued past the fourth-floor landing.

"One more," I huffed. "We're going to have the most amazing calves!"

I let us in with the key that had been left at the falafel place downstairs.

Inside, an achingly sweet living room. Out the window, dappled trees and Notre-Dame peeking through.

"Already Monet!" I said. "Can you believe this place?"

Viv had located the larger bedroom of the two.

"I'm never going back down," she informed me.

"Yes, you are."

The door slammed.

Back in New York, Viv had always been signed up to take the bus to school. However, I'd long suspected that Tessy—who had unchecked privileges on Daddy's black Amex—would pick Viv up from the bus stop in a cab. My suspicions were confirmed the day after my firing.

I received a call from the school nurse saying Viv had thrown up in the bathroom and wanted to come home. Turns out, on the way to school, Taxi TV was running a story with the chyron, "DISGRUNTLED LOCKWOOD EMPLOYEE CALLS IN BOMB SCARE." They'd managed to capture me getting perp-walked to the curb.

That night, I went into Viv's room to check on her and found her in bed, red-eyed, staring.

"I'm really sorry I embarrassed you, baby."

"Yeah, well."

"We can talk about it whenever you're ready."

"I never want to talk about it," Viv said without looking up.

I sat on her bed. "I made a mistake. I was wrong about something. I thought I was doing the right thing, but it turns out I was really, really wrong. I don't know how, but I—"

"Mom, I literally just said I never want to talk about it. Please respect my words."

I walked to the window. Looky-loos swarmed the art stalls lining the Seine. Joggers and bicyclists breezily abounded. Laughter and tinkling floated up from a pair of shaded cafés below. In the glasses, I counted more orange than red or white. It was spritz o'clock in the Fifth.

I knocked on Viv's door. "What's important is you don't fall asleep—"

She had fallen asleep.

"I'm waking you up," I said, shaking her. "For your own good. Let's get some fresh air."

"I don't want to."

"You know what this reminds me of? When you were a baby and we'd be in the car and it was almost nap time. I didn't want you to fall asleep before we got home. So I kept M&M's in the cup holder and I'd pass them back, one by one, to keep you awake."

"That's child abuse," Viv said. "Controlling a baby with food."

"Here's the Wi-Fi password." I texted it to her. "I'll be back in a couple of hours. My lecture isn't for two days, so tomorrow is free. In the morning, we'll do what I want. In the afternoon, we'll do what you want. Have you figured it out yet?"

It wasn't the first time I'd asked. In exchange for bringing Viv to Paris, I'd expected her to research things she wanted to do.

Her silence said she hadn't gotten around to it.

"There's an easy solution to me repeating myself," I said. "That's for you to do things the first time."

"Fine, I will."

"We're in Paris, girlie! Let's make some memories. And I'm not talking about visiting Jim Morrison's grave and we're done."

"Who's Jim Morrison?"

The Assemblée nationale was a straight shot down the Seine, a thirty-minute walk. I set out, Notre-Dame on my right, Shakespeare and Co. on my left, the Louvre was there, too. But all I saw was Digby.

I racked my brain trying to remember anything about the man in that conference room thirty years ago. I always came up blank. He was an incidental character in an episode I'd spent half my life trying to forget.

How would Digby, the man who'd written my NDA, end up involved with the Lockwoods? He said he'd come to New York on behalf of a client. But who? To what purpose? And why on earth would his note have read, "I know about the arms deal"?

I now understood Digby's shock at seeing my name printed on the ballet ticket. The woman he'd targeted thirty years ago was the same one he'd chosen to target again. What were the chances?! He'd seen firsthand how easily she could be manipulated. His lucky day! This time, for sport and giggles, he'd get her naked. And when she proved incalcitrant, mock her for how she'd managed to bounce back from a sexual assault to create a life worth living.

Nah, that wasn't sick enough.

To really mess with her head, how about he contact her abuser's family and get her released from her NDA? By identifying himself as her "associate"—

That always made me swallow the hardest.

I didn't want to be Digby's associate.

I wanted to be his one and only.

I wanted him to want what I wanted.

To walk around naked in front of each other, gloriously at ease.

It felt ancient because it was ancient. He'd known the girl before she became trapped in amber. He'd experienced the strength and light of the woman who'd broken free.

After we had sex for the first time that night, neither of us dared close our eyes. We didn't want the other snatched by sleep. We reviewed our every moment. Digby's favorite part, my vocalized pleasure at his various tricks. To which I quoted Socrates, "Hunger is the best sauce." My least favorite part, when he baby-slapped my butt. To which Digby protested, "But the girls in the movies like it!" Our total lack of self-consciousness. The amazement at our total lack of self-consciousness. The recognition that being amazed at our total lack of self-consciousness was totally self-conscious. I told him about my dry spell. We laughed at his dry feet. When the sheets burned our skin from all the rolling around, we changed venues to the couch for three A.M. goat cheese omelets and fries in hotel bathrobes. We pulled out our phones and showed each other our favorite YouTube videos. His, an anniversary concert of *Phantom of the Opera.* In it, all the actors who'd ever played the Phantom came together to sing "Music of the Night." "Oh!" I'd said, "You have bad taste!" I then saw the performance had moved him to tears. I regaled Digby with Phyllis's greatest hits. He wanted to jump in a taxi then and there and experience her for himself. Sex again and again. I worried I was bad at it, that I only knew how to do what Hal liked. I wanted to learn what Digby liked, wanted to become a model student of his every pleasure. He said he'd teach me. How fun that would have been, to—

Oof!

I'd hit the ground. I must have rolled my ankle on the uneven stones.

Americans lined up at a crepe stand looked over in concern. I waved them off and got back on my feet.

This is all to say I was in a weakened state when I arrived at the Assemblée nationale, a stately and solemn affair fronted by a forbidding row of king-sized columns.

On the street in front idled a row of high-end buses. Placards in the windshields read, "AARC," and told me I'd timed my walk just right.

I'd read in the paper that an emergency meeting of Celine's organization, the Art and Antiquities Recovery Council, had been called for that afternoon. Days before, the terrorist organization QUANDO had blown up a Mesopotamian horse at the Nationalgalerie in Berlin. Their next target was thought to be Paris.

I climbed the steps just as snooty yet somber European types began to stream out and board the buses. I stood off to the side and waited.

Celine saw me before I saw her. Doing nothing to mask her vexation, she marched over.

"To what do I owe this honor?"

"I'm sorry," I said. "But I need to say something to you. In person."

Celine looked around. She had distinguished colleagues on one side, me with gravel in my palms on the other.

"Quickly." Celine walked us behind the far column. "I've got a dinner."

I launched in. "I need to apologize. I reported you to the FBI for bringing explosives into the country. I have no excuse, other than to say I made a mistake. I genuinely believed I was doing the right thing. I am deeply sorry for the disrespect and embarrassment I caused. If there's anything I can do to make it up, tell me. Whatever you have to say to me, I'm here to listen."

If that sounds like AI, it was.

First thing on my agenda after the fiasco at the Lockwood Library was to make amends. But anytime I tried to think of what to say, my brain got scrambled. What had I done? Why had I thought what I'd thought? How could I have leapt to such an outrageous conclusion?

"Americans," said Celine. "You do love your feelings."

"*À bientôt?*" said a man who'd broken away from a chatting cluster.

"*Tout va bien. Merci.*" Celine watched the man leave and turned to me.

"I do have a question," she said, "seeing as they're on offer. *Pour l'amour de Dieu,* what made you think I would bring explosives into the United States?"

"Well, okay." I could already feel my head fogging up.

"Digby told me he was working for a client who'd had something stolen. Then I saw his note to Layla. Arms deal, it said."

Celine sparkled at the memory. "That I will be dining out on for a very long time."

"There was more," I said, hating the desperation in my voice. "Ravi called me, and he was so scared. I'd seen him with the crates and a machine and a strange woman—they were both in these hazmat suit things. He said on his message he had an ethical dilemma. And all I can think is because the Rosetta stone was in the air, it must have gotten into my subconscious or something—and also how the Lockwoods made their money—because when it said New York museums were being targeted, I jumped to the conclusion. It seemed so rock solid. Even the FBI believed it. But hearing it now . . ."

I was starting to get dizzy. "I'm sorry. I need to sit down."

Using my hands, I walked myself down the pillar and sat cross-legged on the ground.

The museum directors were largely gone. A lone assistant with a clipboard stood at the last remaining bus waiting to catch Celine's eye.

"*Continue sans moi!*" Celine called down.

"I'm really sorry to do this," I said, tears forming.

Celine braced herself for the unthinkable and lowered onto a limestone step.

Only then did I realize: I hadn't tracked Celine down to apologize. I tracked her down because I was the one who needed answers. About Digby.

"I'm really confused," I said. "Maybe you can help me?"

This came out so *misèrable* it would have made Fantine blush.

I reached into my pocket and pulled out the paper with the list of Ziggy's key words from Ravi's call.

"NAZIS. MONA LISA. REPUTATION. APPLE. ARMS. C4."

I handed it to Celine.

"What am I looking at?"

"The words," I said, "from surveillance camera footage. Ravi talking to you on the phone. I had a kid lip-read it."

I wiped my tears and snot with the apron of my dress.

"Your aesthetic holds one advantage," Celine remarked.

"I know, it's gross."

Celine straightened her arm to read. With each word, her left brow ratcheted higher. She turned to me, eyes brimming with reproach. I felt my whole being quail.

"You want to know what happened?" Celine said. "I'll tell you what happened. But then we're done."

"*Je promets. Fini.*"

"I called Ravi," Celine flatly began. "Before the dinner party. To see if we could start over after a scene we had in the garden. Neither of us had been at our best. The moment Ravi heard my voice, he launched a fresh attack. About knowing my father. The reputation of which Ravi spoke so passionately? It was his own. He didn't want Boy With Apple figuring so prominently in his statuary. C-Four, as you found out the hard way, would refer to *Caisse Quatre*. Ravi had spotted a clerical error in the customs documents for that particular crate, C-Four. C-Four held the statue's arms. He was threatening to use the technicality to sic the authorities on me."

"For what?"

"Who knows?" she said. "Customs fraud? You know the man. He really didn't like that statue."

I let it sink in.

"Maybe that was Ravi's ethical dilemma," I said. "Whether or not to blackmail you with a trumped-up charge."

"Which he decided in favor of," said Celine. "Last thing I heard, he was off to a customs office on Long Island."

"That explains why he wasn't at dinner," I said, putting it together.

"As for David Beale's mysterious client? The one claiming to have something stolen from him? Which your Digby had so gallantly arrived in New York, cape unfurled, to repossess?"

“Please!”

“That would be my half-brother. He learned I was selling the statue and wanted to split the proceeds. What can I say? I didn’t feel like it.”

I sat there while the information arranged itself in my brain and body, forming something coherent and concrete. For the first time in weeks, a peace settled in.

“Thank you.” I took both her hands in mine and shook perhaps too vigorously.

“Let’s get you home.” Celine rose to her feet. “My driver will take you.”

By the time I arrived back at the flat, light shot up the sides of Notre-Dame, bleaching its gray stones.

I let myself in and was met by the odor of gelatinous lunch meat. Specifically, turkey.

“How was your walk?” Viv asked. She had found Paris’s nearest Subway, and was sitting at the table, eating a five-euro footlong.

Viv and I ate breakfast at a café on the Place Maubert. We sat under a striped awning, shoulder to shoulder, watching Paris pass by.

"Every seat is the best seat," I said.

We ordered the *petit-déjeuner*: *café crème*, fresh orange juice, baguette with butter and jam, and croissant. All for nine euros! Mind you, these were the best croissants in Paris, from a patisserie across the street. The line stretched around the corner.

"Mom!" Viv said, eyes bugging as she took her first bite of what was essentially hot, flaky Normandy butter.

"Right?"

As we ate, we watched a waiter periodically cross boulevard Saint-Germain with an empty wooden box and pile it high with croissants taken directly from the patisserie's oven.

"I love it here," Viv said.

I filled her in on some Paris basics. They don't bring you the check until you ask for it. You can sit down, order one cup of coffee and stay for hours. It's what they expect, they'll never give you the stink eye. There's barely any tipping. When you go into stores, you must overstuff every interaction with *Bonjour, madame; Merci, madame*; and *Au revoir, madame.*

"All the things," I said. "Otherwise they consider you rude."

"That's so interesting. Thanks, Mama."

Down the block, I noticed a stationery store with bold signage that read, "EYROLLS."

"Look," I said, pointing. "In case you run out."

Viv wasn't laughing.

"Come on. I had to."

"Did you?"

The morning was Mom's choice, and I wanted to visit the Panthéon. It was only a few blocks away. Carbo-loaded and overly caffeinated, Viv and I climbed the hill to arrive right when it opened. Already, the Place du Panthéon was teeming with tourists.

"What is this place?" Viv asked.

"The literal pantheon," I said. "People who were revered by the French but couldn't be buried in the Catholic church are buried here. Victor Hugo, Emile Zola, my homie Voltaire. Rousseau."

The Panthéon was surrounded by a black fence, but nobody was going up the main steps.

"The entrance must be on the other side," I said, leading Viv around.

Viv, who'd been half-listening, stopped at a gate where a dozen people had gathered around a sign. She held up her phone.

"Rousseau invented Romanticism," I said. "Which changed the way people saw the world and themselves. He believed man was born good. This was a radical departure from the Church's doctrine of original sin, which taught man was born bad. Rousseau believed we came into this world happy, moral and curious, only to become corrupted by civilization itself."

"Mom!" Viv turned to me, her face lit up.

She'd been using a translation app on the sign, which read, "SUITE À UN MOUVEMENT DE GRÈVE, LE PANTHÉON EST FERMÉ AUJOURD'HUI."

"It's closed!" she cried.

"Another thing about France," I said with a sigh. "The workers are constantly going on strike."

"Can we be done doing what you want?" Viv asked.

At the end of a wide boulevard, I recognized the iron gates of the Luxembourg Gardens. Hovering behind, the Eiffel Tower.

"First, let's go sit down," I said. "There's something I need to tell you."

You know how when you see an attractive couple walking down the street in New York and you wonder if they're having hot sex?

The Japanese twentysomething man rocking the Meg Ryan hair and wearing the widest bell bottoms you've ever seen, with the girl in the oversized blazer? Or that bald man in tight down vest and expensive sneakers who looks like he bio-hacked around the fact he's eighty, holding hands with the girl in the short skirt who turned eighteen yesterday?

In Paris, you don't have to wonder. You know they're having hot sex.

So hot it spills out onto the sidewalk, where they kiss passionately, gooeyly, obliviously. To get around them, you have to step into the street.

That's what I saw: lovers everywhere.

Viv, on the other hand, all she saw were laughing packs of American teens. None were alone in Paris with their moms.

I led us through the pristine Luxembourg Gardens with its manicured emerald grass, easter-egg hued bulbs and abundance of red chairs.

"In New York," Viv said, "these would totally get stolen."

I found two in the shade.

"Why do all the statues have metal pokeys coming out of their heads?" Viv asked.

"To keep the pigeons off."

I'd been hoping to avoid white marble statues, for their obvious triggering effect. Now I was encircled by them. Maybe Paris hadn't been such a good idea.

"Okay, what?" Viv asked. "Because I told you I don't want to talk about it."

"A long time ago," I began.

Viv let out a groan. "Can this please not take forever?"

"Before you were born, I was a comedy writer."

"I know."

"You do?"

"I looked it up when I was eight. I've never heard of any of the shows."

"Okay, Phyllis."

"Just, what?"

"Something happened. One of the actors on a show I worked on—"

"Was he famous?" Viv asked, interest spiking.

"No. He's dead now. I'll tell you his name. TJ Steele."

"Never heard of him," Viv said.

The pigeons here were black with bright yellow beaks and wings with multicolored tips. They hopped cutely and industriously just like at home.

"He sexually assaulted me," I said. "I was young and naïve and didn't understand what I was doing and I ended up signing an NDA. Do you know what that is?"

"Yeah. . . ."

"That the whole idea is you're not allowed to tell anyone what happened. In my case, if I did, I'd have to pay a million dollars."

"Mom!" Viv cried. "Why did you just tell me? We're already poor!"

"Okay, we're not poor. And the reason I can tell you about the NDA is I just got released from it. I'm free to talk about what happened. Which I don't need to do in any urgent way. You don't even need to care. But I wanted you to know. And if you ever do want to talk about it, I'm here."

Viv's eyes instinctively dropped to my wrist. The tattoo.

I'd never told her what was under those words, or indicated they were to cover a scar. There are some things a child should never know about her mother.

"Did you get raped?" she asked, her hands in a white-knuckled clasp.

"No." I placed a hand over Viv's. Immediately, I felt her tension release and drain into my body. Its warmth felt solid and right. I made sure to enjoy it.

"And I'm okay," I said. "Genuinely."

She gave her head a sideways toss. "Now can we do what I want?"

I didn't even have to look at my wrist for the reminder. In that moment, I not only accepted what Fate had just delivered, I actively loved it. The Luxembourg Gardens + me + Viv = life's ultimate anti-climax.

"What's on tap?" I asked.

"I want to go to the Café de Flore."

"Good choice, sweetie."

"I know," she said, and hopped up.

When we arrived, there were seats available in the café proper, but we waited in line for the perfect table inside a glass atrium, facing out, to better enjoy the passing parade.

The woven bistro chairs were comfy, the forest-green tables tiny. Atop each was a paper doily with a charming Sempé sketch depicting life as it once was along the boulevard Saint-Germain. It was no less charming today: on the median between us and the Brasserie Lipp, waiters in short black jackets and long white aprons gathered to smoke and chat while on break.

"Ah, Paris," I said.

The waiter arrived with menus. Viv didn't need to look. She ordered the hot chocolate.

I ordered the same because . . . why not?

The maître-d' crossed in front of us, leading a man to an empty table. The man wore a plaid button-down, ripped jeans with cuffs turned well above the ankle and a white belt. On his feet, Keds.

"Who's that?" I asked Viv. "You know."

"What?" She discreetly looked. "I don't."

"Jeans, Keds. White belt. You can do it."

Viv was all smiles as she thought hard. "Mom! Who?!"

"Troy from *High School Musical 2*." It was our favorite *High School Musical*.

"Oh my God!" she said. "You're right. That's pretty genius."

Hal and I hadn't wanted Viv to watch TV when she was a kid; we managed to make it until she was six. We were at a friend's house for dinner. The adults were having a great time until we realized things had gone eerily quiet, never a good sign with a house full of children. I went down to the basement to check and found them all watching *High School Musical*. Viv was in a trance. I called her name several times before she heard. When she did, she gave me this look, like, What other amazing things are you depriving me of, Mom?

"I hope you haven't outgrown *High School Musical*," I told Viv.

She looked genuinely hurt. "Mom, I'll never outgrow *High School Musical*."

Suddenly, Viv was lost to a girl walking by. A basic American teenager in a Nirvana T-shirt.

"What?" I asked.

"Her shoes," said Viv gravely. "I need them."

The girl was wearing Adidas Gazelles, ones that all teenagers wear, including Viv. But the girl's? They were a new color: persimmon. Just like Layla's workout top. I'd called it!

"What's so funny?" Viv asked.

I explained how Layla had been wearing that color two weeks

ago, and it had finally trickled down to the unwashed masses, aka Viv.

Viv found it less funny than I did.

"You want your mind really blown?" I said. "You wouldn't believe who's buried in that church across the street." I pointed over Viv's shoulder. "René Descartes. Of Evil Genie fame."

Viv shrugged.

"Turn around," I said. "It's right there."

"You're the one who's into the Evil Genie, not me."

"I am asking you to turn around."

"My body, my choice."

The hot chocolate arrived, accompanied by champagne glasses erupting with whipped cream.

"Yay," said Viv, doing demented little claps.

It then dawned on me that half the tables were occupied by replicas of Viv: girls with hot chocolate. Teenagers, all colors, all sizes. This hot chocolate was their international language.

"What is this?"

Like them, Viv was taking selfies with her cup.

"Emily's favorite," she answered.

"Emily who?"

"Emily Cooper," she said. The name meant nothing. Viv added, "*Emily in Paris,* dummy!"

"Wait," I said. "That's why you wanted to come to the Café de Flore? I thought it was because of Hemingway and Picasso. Or Simone de Beauvoir and Jean-Paul Sartre."

"Nope!"

Across the aisle, a table of Americans had been listening. A man and his two hot-chocolate-drinking daughters. He and I exchanged hapless looks.

"This café is the birthplace of existentialism," I told Viv. "It was by watching a waiter here that Sartre came up with one of his most consequential insights. In fact . . ."

I'd been watching our waiter since we arrived. He had black hair, a close-shaved head, little wire-rimmed glasses and pimply face. He wore a bow tie, vest and shin-length apron. His demeanor was one of a clown; there was an elasticity to his facial expressions. But his concentration was fierce. He greeted every request with enthusiasm and a smile, as if hearing it for the first time.

"Watch that waiter," I told Viv. "See how he moves around the restaurant?"

She gave it a few seconds.

"He takes the exact same route from the kitchen to the front. It's like a maze, the way he weaves around the tables. But he only ever goes in one direction. Even if he's close to the kitchen, he doesn't go back, he goes the long way around. It's like he's on a slot car track."

"So?"

"My mind is getting totally blown right now. This is literally how Sartre came up with existentialism. Here, at the Café de Flore. By watching what he called the 'bad faith waiter,' or the 'robot waiter.' Sartre observed that the waiter was nothing more than an automaton. Who goes through life pleasing people, never deviating from his sad little routine."

"That's rude."

"It inspired Sartre's rallying cry, 'You are free. Go choose.'"

"Maybe if you're rich," Viv said. "But I like the waiter. Maybe he's happy. Maybe he has a family to support. It's mean to sit around cafés all day smoking cigarettes and mocking people who have to work for a living."

"Maybe I didn't explain it right." I spooned whipped cream into my hot chocolate.

"You explained it fine. I'm just saying it's mean."

"Sometimes great concepts come from bad people. Sartre was a little judgey."

"Congratulations," said Viv. "I'm glad you found each other."

"I am literally trying to teach you about Paris because you couldn't be bothered to look it up yourself."

"I did, too!" Viv slammed down her cup. "I learned a lot about Paris! Maybe it's not what you know, but who cares? I know there's something called Paris Derangement Syndrome. It's where Japanese tourists have spent their whole lives building up Paris in their imaginations and when they get here, they go into shock. There's a whole hospital wing devoted to it. I know it's where Princess Diana died in a car crash. And the robbery occurred that left Kim changed forever. I know it's where Carrie and Big reunited. I know the Mona Lisa is a fake—"

"I have to stop you there."

"I read it in *National Geographic*!" Viv cried. "There was a whole article."

"Then *National Geographic* has gone seriously downhill." I waved down the waiter. "*Pardon, monsieur. L'addition, s'il vous plaît.*"

"I'm not done," Viv said. "You're mean."

"And you're a low-information person."

I took a sip of my drink. Cold cream followed by hot, smooth chocolate. The hype was real.

I pointed over Viv's shoulder. "Oh my God! It's Jennifer Aniston."

Viv whipped around.

"René Descartes," I said. "Made you look."

Viv's eyes became wet with tears.

"I'm sorry," I said. "That was mean."

"Do you realize that all you are right now is a bitter, old woman making fun of her daughter? I don't even think you know you're doing it."

"Okay, that's enough," I said, looking around. I was grateful to see the man and his daughters were huddled over his phone and hadn't heard.

"We're even," I told Viv. "Truce."

"What's especially twisted?" Viv said. "Is adults are always like, *Enjoy your youth.* Because they know it's a short, fleeting time, and the joys attached to it are fleeting, too. Like how you loved Rob Lowe—"

"For the record, I never loved Rob Lowe."

"Or whatever in the Brat Pack. And you know you'll never feel that way about those people again. Because it belongs to a dead part of your life. You know that who I am right now is going to be a dead person, too. What you're making fun of is a beautiful tiny sliver of my life I'll never get back. When it's gone, it's gone forever."

I fell in love with Viv all over again. But this was not the appropriate venue.

I lowered my voice to reset the volume. "You're right. Maybe you didn't hear me. I'm sorry."

"Nobody is looking at you, Mom. This main-character energy is super gross and millennial."

"Viv." I put my hand on hers but she whipped it away.

"It's why I get so upset when people are mean about the Eras tour."

I could relax. The gun Viv had been waving at me was now pointed at Taylor Swift haters.

"Tell me," I said.

"It's pure misogyny. You never see anybody telling little boys they're idiots for playing with dinosaurs. They will tell it to an eight-year-old girl crying over 'Love Story' with friendship bracelets on her arms. Who, pretty soon, will start being bullied and think she's fat and boys at school will show her deepfake porn with her face on it. But everyone's like, Fuck you, little girl, for liking Taylor Swift."

It was the first time I'd heard Viv swear. Worse, I could sense that at hearing the name Taylor Swift, the army of girls had turned to listen.

"Isn't that what parents are trying so hard to preserve?" Viv said. "That innocence? It's why they don't want their kids watching R-rated movies. I'm fifteen, Mom. I'm innocent, too. Maybe I don't play with baby dolls anymore. Maybe I go to school with my Stanley cup, and me and all my friends compare colors. Maybe I want the new Adidas. I know it's stupid and capitalistic, and billionaires are buying private islands because we have our parents' credit cards. But I want to belong. Let me belong."

"I do want you to belong."

"You think I'm so stupid I don't know the world is about to get worse? You just told me what happened to you. Let me care about the things I want to care about in this moment. But you're like, Ha, ha, it's not Jennifer Aniston, it's a real philosopher, you dumb bitch."

I dared look around. If Viv wanted to start a cult anytime soon, now was the time. I'd never seen such adoring gazes.

"Real," the girl across from us told her sister.

"Felt," the sister said back.

The dad? He distanced himself from me with a sad shake of the head.

"I never called her a dumb bitch," I felt compelled to clarify.

"I don't know why you have to be so mean to me," Viv said, tears spilling down her cheeks. "Maybe you're just being careless, but it has such grave implications. Shame is the single worst thing a person can feel. And you flippantly try to inflict it on your own child for liking the things I like."

I tried to look unbothered. It was awkward, as I was shaking so hard I couldn't pick up my cup without spilling its contents all over my hand.

Viv dried her eyes and composed herself. "I'm going to sit here. And I'm going to drink my *Emily in Paris* hot chocolate. I'm going to enjoy it. I'm going to post about it, hashtag-Viv-in-Paris. I'm even going to tag Darren Star."

The waiter, who was not a robot at all, but a man who possessed exquisite emotional intelligence, arrived with the check.

"Apple Pay?" he asked in flat English.

I reached for my phone but realized I'd left it at home. (I'd been that determined to spend quality time with Viv!) I handed the waiter my credit card; he set out on his appointed rounds.

"We can leave after we pay," I told Viv.

She finished her hot chocolate and set it down. She scraped her spoon into the whipped cream and came out with a cumulus cloud. She turned the spoon upside down and stuck it in her mouth. It emerged clean.

"Bye, Mom," she said, getting up. "We'll always have Paris."

I could only sit there and watch her walk away with dignity, strength and fantastic posture.

By the time I'd paid and stepped outside, ten minutes had passed and I was something of a wreck. The street Viv had headed down was narrow, pristine and daughter-free.

I hastened along it, hoping to catch a flash of Viv on a side street. Each time she wasn't there, my stomach twisted tighter; it required all my concentration to will the hot chocolate to stay down.

Paris is safe, I reminded myself. Viv has her phone. I'd texted her our address in case we got separated. She could Uber back.

Figuring that's where she must be—back at the flat because where else would she know to go?—I pointed myself towards the Fifth and picked up my pace.

Why couldn't I have been kinder to Viv? Why the compulsion to put her down? To always rub it in her face that I find Ziggy's character superior to hers? A child of divorce, too! Why didn't I stick with Hal? For her sake. It's what mothers did, sacrificed for their children. My whole life was a farce, one big delusion. Delusion I'm a good mother. Delusion I possess basic wisdom. Delusion this menopausal body would be desirable to any sighted man on the planet—

The street had taken a sharp turn like something out of Mr. Toad's

Wild Ride. I put on the brakes before I crashed face-first into a store window.

"Don't do this!" I said, squeezing shut my eyes.

I opened them; the store sold nothing but antique globes.

In the reflection, a plaid shirt, jeans and white belt. Troy from *High School Musical 2*. He was a block back and striding towards me . . . with purpose?

I turned. He was gone.

I blinked to reestablish connection to reality. My only concern was to get back to the flat and apologize to Viv, to start our relationship over, this time being unfailingly kind.

I started to jog, my limbs loosey-goosey.

On a hunch, I spun around.

Troy from *High School Musical 2* was back. And he'd gained ground. Seeing me, he froze, as if playing Red Light, Green Light.

For (an eternal) split second, we both stood there. My pulse hammered throughout my body as I frantically mapped my surroundings.

On my left, a cutesy car airbrushed blue, white and red, and the words "RENT ME." Just ahead, a café, a real tourist trap, one with a human-sized teddy bear wearing a beret sitting at a table out front. (Even in my panicked state, pride wouldn't allow it.) On my right, a *parfumerie*.

I ducked inside and was immediately enveloped in floral notes and tomb-like silence.

The lone salesperson leaned over a glass case, arranging an Easter display.

I forced a swallow and attempted a belly breath.

The woman straightened and sized me up.

"May I help you?" she asked in (passive-aggressive!) English.

"Non, merci."

Her bun was slick and smile dry. Over a pink blazer she wore a white lab coat.

The small shop was apothecary-themed. Dark wood shelfing, floor-to-ceiling drawers. Dramatically staged beakers, each holding a single, poetic stem. A tassel of vanilla beans. A spun-sugar orchid. A sprig of flowering rosemary.

Behind the counter, a mottled mirror faced the street. I dared look into it.

Reflected back, a plaid shirt.

Troy from *High School Musical 2*. Now standing in front of the shop. His back to the door.

"I am here to answer your questions. Every scent is custom. Mixed for you."

I perused the scented offerings while scanning for an escape. Back exit? No. Side door? No. Troy from *High School Musical 2*? Yes.

A display of perfume bottles—accompanied by framed photos of French luminaries—caught my attention.

I knew what I'd do! I'd beckon Troy from *High School Musical 2* inside, making out like I wanted to have a chat, lead him to a corner out of the shopkeeper's sight line, pump Francois Truffaut into his eyes, knee him in the balls and—

Wait—what was I thinking? Had I lost my mind? Why was I hiding in a perfume shop?! What was even happening?

I blamed Viv.

I was a serious person, capable of having a direct conversation with a stranger. If he indeed wanted one.

I reset my posture to that of someone in full command of the situation.

"*Au revoir, madame*," I told the shopkeeper. "*Merci*."

I opened the door and, acting "as if," slipped past Troy from *High School Musical 2* with a friendly but forceful, "*Pardon, monsieur.*"

"Adora Hazzard?" he said. "We would like to speak to you."

So that was a shocker! Compounding my confusion, his French accent was so strong it was hard not to think he was out to seduce me.

"I'm sorry—" I sputtered. "No."

Head down, I scooched past him and took a few steps.

Suddenly he was standing in front of me, blocking my path—right where the sidewalk bottlenecked: café chairs on one side, little French car on the other.

"Excuse me," I said, voice low and determined. "I'd like to get by."

Just then, the little French rental car—its passenger door creaked open from within. A shadow moved in the driver's seat.

"This way," said Troy from *High School Musical 2,* motioning towards it.

The only way out was through. I assumed the rope-a-dope stance and body-butted Troy from *High School Musical 2.*

Caught by surprise, he stumbled back and hit the ground. The crack of tailbone-on-ancient-stone is a sound I hope never to hear again.

"*Pardon, monsieur!*" I gasped and started to run—

When a black blurry figure swooped in and grabbed me from behind. I tried to wrestle free—elbows and black fabric flying—

"Help!" I screamed. "*Aidez-moi!*"

Nobody could hear. The café was completely empty. The only pedestrian—a woman in a green dress and giant headphones—rounded the corner and disappeared.

In a flash, I was shoved into the car, my attacker stuffing themself in behind me. Troy from *High School Musical 2* jumped in the passenger seat. With a screech, the tin can careened onto the teeny street.

"Please!" I pleaded. "I'm a mother!"

"Take it down, will ya?" said a familiar voice.

The driver turned around.

"Blanche?!"

The person in black sitting beside me, smoothing out her jacket? The Peruvian contractor, Dorris.

"I know," Blanche said. "It's weird."

"I lost Viv!"

"She's ubering to Sephora on the Champs-Élysées," Blanche said. "We've got time."

I didn't want to be Interpol," Blanche was explaining. "It just happened."

She'd driven us to a concrete government building made even uglier by contrast to its Haussmann neighbors. We were now gathered in a borrowed office, judging from the family photos depicting nobody in our group.

Troy from *High School Musical 2,* focused on his laptop, sat as far from me as possible on a tired wooly sofa. Under each butt cheek, a ziplock bag of ice.

Dorris had helped herself to the leather swivel chair and kicked her knee-high boots on the desk. Blanche was left standing.

"I'd been hired by the Aman resort in Dubai," she explained. "There I was, doing what I normally do, which is installing a garden and fucking up my back. When I started noticing some weird shit."

"What kind of weird shit?" I asked.

"Can't say. But I realized it was about to go from weird shit to bad shit. The kind you don't want to go down."

"Wow, okay," I said, as if comprehending, which I most certainly was not.

"Luckily, I was able to prevent it."

"She's very modest," added Dorris.

"Let's just say," Blanche said, "you are now living in a safer world for it."

"Me, personally?" I asked.

"You." She pointed to Dorris. "Her. Him."

I turned to Troy from *High School Musical 2*. "What's your name, by the way?"

"Mathieu," he said without looking up.

Blanche vaguely motioned out the window. "Them."

"Are you saying you saved the world?" I asked.

Blanche: "So they tell me."

"Who? Interpol?"

"It's probably just flattery to keep me in."

It was a lot to absorb!

"Sorry to be all me, me, me—"

"But how do you fit in?" Blanche said.

"That."

"You're being followed."

"I know." I pointed at Mathieu. "By him!"

"No." Blanche passed over some photographs. "This guy."

The photos depicted a small, masked man picking the lock on a crooked wooden door.

"That's my flat," I said, and looked up. "When was this?"

"A couple of hours ago. Right after you left this morning. Mathieu took them."

"How do you even know where I'm staying?"

"We cloned Viv's phone onto an emulator." Blanche held up an iPhone. Its home screen was one I knew well . . . Viv squeezing Mr. Man half to death when he was a puppy.

"You've got to slow down." I was getting machine-gunned with information, each piece more surreal than the last. "When?"

"That day in your apartment," Blanche said.

"How?"

"Like most things in life, all you need is the will and good Wi-Fi. That's what Dorris was doing in Viv's room."

"Your daughter is very beautiful," Dorris said.

"Okay, okay," I said, my head officially exploding. "What?!"

"I was sent to New York to track QUANDO," Blanche explained.

"The terrorist group," I said. "And you were sent by Interpol."

"They'd been on QUANDO for months. Chatter pointed to a private plane leaving from an airstrip outside Paris. It flew to Nova Scotia. There, four crates were transferred from it to a seaplane that landed in Sag Harbor."

"The Hamptons Sag Harbor?"

"It's an official point of entry into the US. And tiny. Most people don't know about it. It's basically run by kids with summer jobs. In other words, someone was being deliberate about getting those crates into the country legally but way, way under the radar."

I considered it. Celine had said Ravi was heading to a customs office on Long Island, which now made sense.

Blanche went on: "When it was discovered the crates were headed to the Lockwoods, I got activated to oversee the operation."

"By Interpol," I said.

"Because of my history with the family."

"You've got to admit, that's some happy coincidence."

"For Interpol maybe," Blanche said. "Not me. I was on my way to Orlando with my grandkids."

"And you?" I asked Dorris. "Are you Interpol, too?"

"Me?" she responded with a frown. "Oh no."

"She's just a contractor," Blanche said. "But when you find a good one, you don't let go. This woman can, and will, do anything."

"I am very good price," Dorris told me. "I am on schedule. I never bother you with my problems. I sign a contract. But all my clients they trust me. We never have to look at the contract."

"Good to know," I said.

"Next time I bring a card."

"So," I said, back to Blanche. "You just show up at the Lockwood residence."

"I texted Lionel I had a sudden opening and mentioned the hydroponic project he always wanted. You know Lionel. He'll roll with anything."

"Philosophy in action." It had to be said.

"The idea being I'll keep my eyes open and assess if a tactical intervention is necessary. The first thing that happens is you ask me to move in with you. It makes me wonder if my cover is blown. You become a person of interest."

"Because of the coven?"

"You have to admit," Blanche said, "it's pretty weird."

"Not terrorist-threat weird!"

"Agree to disagree. Then I catch you sneaking around Annoying Girl's office and hiding that letter in the mail cart."

"Well, okay."

"I go to your apartment to bug it—"

"Which I'm assuming is illegal."

"—and you greet me with a baseball bat."

"That was weird."

"We cloned Viv's phone just to be safe. The next morning, they're yanking me out of New York. The tip about QUANDO hitting a museum? Turned out to be erroneous. New information urgently pointed to Berlin. So they sent me over there."

"The Mesopotamian horse," I said, recalling the news reports. "That got blown up."

"I'm trying not to beat myself up about it."

"So far, I'm following. I'm shocked, and I'm pretty sure I'm angry. But I'm following. Still, I don't understand. If you moved on from the Lockwoods and the crates, why are you staking me out in Paris?"

"Ravi Bhardwaj has vanished," Blanche said.

"I know. . . ."

"Leaving no trace. We're talking next level."

"You're not implying . . ." I couldn't bring myself to finish the thought.

"Ravi is QUANDO? That's a maybe."

"*Regardez ça,*" Mathieu said, turning the laptop for us to see.

On it was a live feed from Sephora. Getting out of a makeup chair, wearing a red beret: Viv.

"Are those fake eyelashes?" I asked.

"We set it up," Blanche said, "so when she spun the wheel at the register, she won a free session."

"Even more beautiful," Dorris marveled.

I'd never seen Viv look happier nor more terrifyingly adult.

"She's leaving," Mathieu told Blanche.

"I've been sending her TikToks," Blanche said. "For that cookie-croissant place. The line's always at least an hour long."

She checked "Viv's" phone and held it up for me to see. The blue dot indicated she was heading south on the Champs-Élysées.

"And she's off!" Blanche said.

"You can do that?" I asked. "Force someone to go somewhere by sending an ad?"

Blanche, wistfully: "There's a part of you that wishes it was harder."

"Ravi is QUANDO?" I said, still reeling. "What even is QUANDO?"

"A radical group that splintered from AARC."

"Celine's organization," I said. "The Art and Antiquities Recovery Council."

"Which was formed about twenty years ago. When museums were coming under intense pressure to return all the art they stole."

"I remember that," I said.

"Celine Montford and some pals from the Getty, the British Museum and the Met formed AARC to 'study and put forth recommendations.'" Blanche's air quotes shot venom.

"Sounds fair," I said, confused.

"But Celine and her ilk were a bunch of snobs with businesses to run and a bottom line. They had no interest in their cash cows going bye-bye."

"Also sounds fair."

"AARC was one giant stall tactic. They'd meet quarterly in European capitals, fire off angry letters and dine out at Michelin-starred restaurants. On their museums' dime."

"Good scam," Dorris put in.

"Until it wasn't," Blanche said. "AARC was finally forced to add museum directors from these other 'lesser countries.'" More air quotes. "No dummies, they immediately grokked to AARC's bullshit. It's believed they broke off, radicalized and formed QUANDO."

"QUANDO," I said. "What does it mean?"

"Latin for *Quibus Amissa Non Dici Omnia.* 'All Things Refusing to Be Lost.' Their goal is the same as AARC, to repatriate stolen treasures. But QUANDO will do it by any means necessary."

"And Ravi?" I asked. "You think he's one of them?"

"Ravi Bhardwaj was one of the founding members of AARC," Blanche said. "He spent years negotiating the return of a Greek urn to Athens. At zero hour, AARC recommended against it. Ravi, seeing what he was up against, quit in a snit."

"That I believe. But he's no terrorist. He has a baby on the way." And I remembered. "Poor little Scott!"

"Yeah," Blanche said. "He's not taking it well. So this is where you come in."

"Please," I said. "Tell me."

"That day in your apartment. You asked me about Ravi. You said you were waiting on a call. I assume it was from him."

"Yes. But he never called back."

"Here's what I need from you," Blanche said. "I need you to tell me everything you know about Ravi." She turned to Mathieu. "How's the wee one?"

"Stopped a block away from the Maison Louvard."

Blanche motioned for the laptop. He handed it over. She started pressing keys.

Soon, a CCTV camera showed Viv. She stood in line regaling a bunch of spellbound girls, talking fast and with her hands.

"We've got an hour," Blanche informed me. "Start spilling."

One of the benefits of having excoriated myself by obsessively reliving every second of the last ten days? I was able to deliver for Blanche.

I walked her through how I'd seen Ravi in the Laundry with the woman in black. How they'd rolled in a mysterious machine—

"That was nothing," Blanche said.

"You know what they were doing?" I asked, literally jumping to my feet.

Blanche searched the desk. "Boots off," she said to Dorris. "I'm looking for the thing."

From her tapestry bag, Dorris produced a piece of paper rolled so tightly it was practically solid.

"That's it!" I said. "The paper Ravi was holding! What's it say?"

Blanche started opening drawers and came out with a pair of drugstore half-eyes. She put them on. "Good enough."

She began to read. "Stable isotope analysis using the Drakoulias-Warner Ratio Mass Spectrometer blah blah." She tossed aside the readers. "Straightforward marble analysis. To date it and whatnot. Standard procedure for new acquisitions. The Lockwood Library's was broken."

I plopped back down with an "Ugh." Next came a fresh tsunami of self-reproach that I'd ever convinced myself it could have been . . . a machine to test for chemical weapons?! Double ugh.

"What else?" said Blanche.

I continued my yarn, recounting to Blanche the voicemail Ravi had left me, and the video I'd taken of his call with Celine.

"A video?" Dorris said. "You are very good, too."

Blanche held out her hand. "Gimme."

"Oh," I said. "My phone is back at the flat."

"You don't carry your phone on you?" she said.

"Blame Gandhi."

Here's something not fun: the prospect of walking into your apartment—even if it is an Airbnb—after you learn someone, possibly a terrorist, has broken in while you were off sightseeing.

I had my key in the lock. Before I turned it, I asked Mathieu, "Should I be warned? Did it get trashed?"

Mathieu, sandwiched on the stairs between Blanche and Dorris, shrugged.

"You didn't go in?" I asked.

"Mathieu?" Blanche said. "How would he get in?"

"Doesn't he work for Interpol?"

"Oh no!" Blanche said. "Mathieu's a trendspotter. Dorris met him in a wine bar last night. He told her he follows stylish people around and takes pictures of them. She asked if he was free today."

"And you said yes?" I asked Mathieu.

"Her style, it's . . ." He kissed his fingers.

"You are good," I said to Dorris.

"I have availability in September," she offered. "First, finish a big job in Tribeca. Everything custom."

"How can I say no?" Mathieu said of Dorris, to Dorris.

"You are very kind," she replied.

"Mathieu," I said. "Now I feel really bad about your tailbone."

Blanche: "Uh-hum!"

I opened the door.

The apartment was exactly as I'd left it.

Towel hanging on the shower rod. Cosmetics lined just so on the shelf. Dirty clothes in the empty suitcase on the closet floor. The glass of water on my bedside table, half-full. The bottle of eye drops that had fallen to the floor and I explicitly remembered not picking up.

It took on the significance of a museum diorama, as if frozen in time for posterity.

"Nothing's been touched," I reported with confidence.

"Phone," Blanched said.

It was on the fireplace mantel, charging.

My screen was a rash of credit card alerts. Viv had spent two hundred euros at Sephora. Twenty at Starbucks. A hundred at Brandy Melville. And ten on the beret.

I shook off my irritation and opened my photos.

I thumbed through the images. Viv on the plane asleep with her mouth hanging open. (Ha-ha!) Mr. Man looking cute in the back of Emily Ann's car. A glam shot of Marry Me Tofu.

"This is the night Ravi called." I swiped to the next photo. But it wasn't there. "Oh, right." I realized I'd taken the video the next day. I swiped forward in time. Still, the video wasn't there.

"This is weird," I said. "It's gone."

I navigated to voicemail. There was no sign of Ravi's call.

"The voicemail, too." I turned to Blanche. "They've been deleted. Both of them."

"He got what he was looking for," Blanche said. "The good news, you're probably safe. I really didn't feel like putting in a work order for twenty-four-hour protection."

"Maybe I want twenty-four-hour protection!"

"Worth a shot," said Blanche.

"You don't need work order," Dorris told Blanche. "I protect her."

"It's like the coven!" Blanche said, making the raise-the-roof gesture. "Women helping women. I like it!"

Just then, a knock on the door.

Mathieu screamed and hugged me. Definitely not Interpol.

"Go check who it is," Blanche instructed Dorris.

Dorris clomped over.

"See what I'm saying?" Blanche remarked. "No fear this woman."

Dorris opened a little hinged peephole and announced, "Nobody is here."

She unlocked the door.

Sitting on the landing was a flower delivery.

Tented in clear cellophane: peonies. With a card that read, in the hand that had caused me so much pleasure and pain, "*Adora*."

Blanche and crew had left by the time Viv—wantonly eyelashed, laden with shopping bags and topped with a beret—made her grand entrance.

"You must take a bite," she announced as she handed over the cookie-croissant she'd bought me. "It's divine."

She had turned into Auntie Mame. It was as if our entire fight at the Café de Flore never happened.

Worked for me!

That night, we climbed into bed, opened my laptop and fired up *High School Musical 2*.

"It doesn't get better than this," I said to Viv.

"Yeah, Mom," she said. "Sorry for being a brat."

Tomorrow's speech was written and ready to go. Viv was at my side. We were safe. (Thanks to Dorris; she'd engineered a way to bar the door from the inside using a fireplace poker, vacuum cord and Mathieu's white belt.) Pressed to my heart, Digby's letter. I didn't need to read it again. I could recite it from memory.

Dear Adora,

You asked me who I am.

I am one in a long line of carrot farmers from the Sacramento Valley.

My first memory is of wanting to get out, and I did. I graduated USC Law into one of LA's top firms. There, I became "the NDA guy."

I'd like to tell you this moniker filled me with shame. The opposite was true. I'd have put it on my license plate if discretion allowed. I was the coolheaded nexus of impossibly sensitive and high-stakes negotiations: boldfaced names with reputations hanging in the balance; corporations one wrong move away from going up in flames; women suddenly possessing the match with which to burn it all down. My job: to navigate the panic, rage, denial and greed in such a way that everyone left feeling as if they'd gotten off lucky. This required fortitude, empathy, and a gambler's intuition for when to go all in.

When you own the secrets of the world's most powerful men, they keep you close. We golfed at Riviera, watched the World Series from private suites, vacationed on the Vineyard. Whenever someone asked what I did for a living, I told them, "contract law," an instant conversation-killer. I could easily tolerate the dismissiveness because inside I was a Hindu god. (A Hindu god who kept having to pop up to Modesto for the latest carrot crisis. My parents had died a year apart. My brother's first crop came out of the ground humongous and misshapen. We were perpetually one growing season away from going under.) The more secrets I learned, and the more I kept locked in the vault, the more powerful I felt. It was like tantric sex. A philosopher once put it thusly: "the pleasure is in the self-control."

When Travis Burden called me back in '98, here's what I remember. He had a mess that needed to be cleaned up on behalf of WAC client TJ Steele. The woman in question was also an agency client and wouldn't have a lawyer present. It would be straightforward, but had to be wrapped up quickly. The woman was fragile, unpredictable, but sure to roll. I wrote up a contract overnight and arrived at the appointed hour.

I'd been in a lot of these rooms. Never before had I seen the woman walk in and offer to get herself and me a Diet Coke. Later in the meeting, you stood up to get a coaster. Do you remember? How you didn't want to ruin the table? And you wiped the water off with the front of your shirt? And sat through the next hour with a wet splotch? I knew right away she was not like other girls.

Something came over me. For the first time, I wanted not what was best for my client. I knew there was an extra $100k sitting there, and I wanted the courteous, pliable girl to get it. Hindu god that I was, I tried telepathy. I aimed all my mental powers across the table: *Don't sign it. There's another contract.*

It worked. Or were you just that good?

Weeks later, Travis called to say the woman still hadn't cashed the check. Was that a problem? I told him, no. But I found myself picking up the phone to call her. All I had to do was speak my name. Fifteen minutes later, the check was cashed. Hindu god, anyone?

Years passed.

One day, I was at my favorite Tesla charging station on the way to Modesto—Pea Soup Andersen's, Santa Nella—when the phone rang. It was a *New York Times* reporter. She said she was doing a story on Harvey Weinstein. She asked what I knew.

"Off the record?" I asked.

She confirmed we were.

“That he raped Rose McGowan in a hot tub,” I answered between bites of my Reuben.

It was an open secret; I’d never had anything to do with Harvey Weinstein. Even in the world of NDAs, he was considered a real *paskudnik.*

“How long have you personally known this?” the reporter asked with a flatness I found no fun.

“Forever?” I said.

“I’m wondering if you’d be willing to speak to me. On background.”

“Can’t help you.”

We exchanged friendly goodbyes.

A year later, rumors swirled that a *New York Times* story on Harvey Weinstein was about to drop. I read the whole thing the moment it posted. To this trained eye, it was a whole lot of nothing. My reaction? Poor reporter, she didn’t get the goods.

You asked me who I am.

I am a bad man.

Hindu gods don’t give up without a fight.

There were the Kübler-Ross stages of grief. Denial, bargaining, anger, depression. Highlights included: joining in the choir whenever Harvey Weinstein’s name came up, feigning horror and disbelief; going to a sweat lodge ceremony in Ojai; converting to a raw diet; raising the paddle at charity auctions, always for an amount that made the whole place turn and “ooh” in hallowed respect; marrying a woman I met at the sweat lodge; drinking too much; getting arrested for it, to my credit, I was going 30 in the slow lane; flying to Thailand for a year-long silent retreat, only to spend the night before check-in at the bar of the Bangkok Mandarin Oriental jabbering to anyone who would listen—who cared if they didn't speak English?—and flying home the next day; acrimoniously divorcing the woman I met at the sweat lodge; embracing AA; attending regular meetings in Venice; one day at the Farmshop, seeing a woman whose NDA I'd written and walking over to apologize—she'd been an up-and-coming TV exec and was now a successful jewelry designer—but when she saw me coming, she yelled, "Predator!" and, after being sucker punched by her husband, I was escorted out and told never to return.

To put it in philosophical terms, when a man lives a cliché Westside life and is banned from setting foot in the Brentwood Country Mart, does that man exist?

During all this, my phone kept ringing. Friends and former colleagues wanting advice. They'd come to know me as smart and discreet. An inveterate strategist, I offered what I could. Sometimes it meant picking up the phone to talk to a spouse, neighbor or coworker. Intractable problems were smoothly solved. Word spread I gave good counsel. Some called it genius; on my good days, I had to agree. I determined not to throw my talent away with the bathwater.

Acceptance, the final stage of grief. I bid adieu to the past and decided to put myself to use. This time, for the greater good. This time, for free.

See, on one of my trips to Modesto, my brother showed me a last-ditch attempt he'd made to save the farm. He'd engineered a machine that cut our giant, misshaped carrots into smaller carrots. We called them "baby carrots." In a month, the orders were coming in too fast to keep up. Because I thought like a lawyer, and was a lawyer, I had the machine patented. You might not think it's much, getting one ten-thousandth-of-a-cent each time someone bites into a baby carrot. Trust me, it adds up.

You asked me who I am.

I am the filthy rich Baby Carrot King.

A week ago, I received a call from France. Someone I'd never met. How this person had found me? I'd stopped asking years ago. My job was to be of service. This person proceeded to lay out a fantastical scenario that required deft, discreet diplomacy, and it was time sensitive.

To pause here. My work is my living amends. This letter is the most I've spoken about it to anyone. Do not take it personally that I will not reveal more.

I will fill in details of the aspects you already know. I took the red-eye and checked into the Lowell. My goal, to sit down with Layla Lockwood. But there was no way to get within a mile of her. Or, I should say, the traditional ways would require others finding out. I feared this might spook her into doing something rash. I needed someone on the inside.

I sat across the street from the Lockwood Library with a *New York Times* and waited for a sign. From behind, I heard a conversation.

"Catch any crazies?" asked a woman.

"Whatever you're on," answered a man, "I want some."

"A life of the mind," said the woman so cheerfully, I couldn't help but turn.

My eyes followed her as she tripped the light fantastic across Fifth Avenue and into the employee entrance of the Lockwood Library. Whoever she was, I had a hunch she'd be my ticket to Layla. I waited all day for her to leave, and followed her across Central Park to the ballet.

And then. And then. And then.

"ADORA HAZZARD," read the ticket.

Was it really you? Aged into a gorgeous, self-possessed woman and world-class flirt?

During the ballet, I caught you studying my face. And then you ran away. Had you placed me?

Next up: a real dark night of the soul. (I am still afflicted.) I didn't know whether to jerk off or pull out the hairshirt. When you arrived at dinner wearing that dress, I realized you hadn't connected me to your NDA. Added bonus, in addition to your banging looks, you were stone-cold brilliant! I didn't know if I wanted to fuck you or put you to work. I tried to do both. After our night of priority-shifting sex (I can call it that, right?) you walked into my hotel room and—in so many words—informed me that my mission had gone horribly awry.

I panicked.
I lost my temper.
I dismissed you.
I underestimated your strength.
I mocked your principles.
I wanted to fuck you.

You asked me who I am.

I am a man.

Here comes the hard part. Your life has exploded and I am responsible. The man who set out to do only good has once again caused the winsome, credulous girl irreparable harm.

What does a man do?

He can get you released from your NDA. He does. It strikes him as small beer.

He can accost you. He does. And wishes he hadn't.

He can punish himself. I hope it doesn't disappoint you that I have chosen not to. I've tried it before and it doesn't work.

He can run into you in another twenty years and cross his fingers that time has healed.

But I'm restless. I feel the bulk of my years behind me. Time is running out.

What do I do?

The Welsh poet would advise me to "burn and rave at close of day."

But I've decided to let the wise men, the good men, the wild men, and the grave men rage, rage against the dying of the light.

I've raged enough for one lifetime, and I suspect you have, too.

You and me, Adora. How about we try something new? How about we go gentle?

Yours in all the ways,

Digby

The next morning I sat in an anteroom off a lecture hall, doing last-minute tweaks to my speech, when came a knock at the door.

Blanche entered, followed by Dorris.

"Uh-oh," I said. Some things you just know.

Blanche: "Are you the type of person who insists on hearing bad news immediately?"

I set aside my pencil. "I am now."

"It's Ravi," Blanche said.

"They found him?"

"At the Lockwood residence. Last night. The brats went to go lay down some tracks—"

"In the screaming room?" I was on my feet and pacing the tiny chamber.

"He somehow got locked inside," said Blanche. "He'd been there a week."

"He's okay, though?"

"In a word," Blanche said, "we don't know. His kidneys were beginning to shut down. He's in the hospital. They put him in a coma to try to stabilize him. Wouldn't have been my first choice. But they're the experts, right?"

"For a whole week?" I let the horror of it sink in. "He was trapped. . . . And nobody could hear him call for help?"

"It's pretty awful. Best not paint yourself a picture."

It made no sense. "How could that happen?"

"Last thing we saw," Blanche said, "Ravi was heading through the tunnel from the Library to the main house. When he got there, he personally informed Layla he wouldn't be at dinner."

"Layla told you this?"

"Just spoke with her. She said the night of the dinner party, Ravi told her something had come up."

The customs document and the trip to Long Island. This explains why the Indian flag was raised before dinner, but Ravi wasn't there.

"On his way out of the residence," Blanche said, "Ravi must have taken a wrong turn. The door closed behind him and the knob broke off."

"Poor-quality materials," Dorris said. "Never pays to cheap out."

"I feel bad about maligning the guy," Blanche said. "He was nothing but nice to me. Kind of."

"Poor Ravi." I put the heels of my hands to my eyes and pressed.

Dorris whispered to Blanche, "I said wait until after her talk."

"There's no way we'll ever really know." I looked up and saw blotches.

While the Lockwood Library had more electronic eyes than *1984*, Layla had insisted the residence be their sanctuary.

"Right? The house has no cameras."

Blanche shook her head.

"Dr. Hazzard?" The director of the Alliance Philosophique de Paris had stepped in. Marie Chantal was her name. She wore a butter-yellow pantsuit, beige suede heels and printed silk shirt. “We are ready.”

I sat back down, staring at the floor with glazed expression.

“You have very bad instincts,” Dorris said, shaking a manicured finger at Blanche.

Marie Chantal, sensing the torpor in the room, adopted the air of a brusque nanny.

“You will be pleased we have a full house!” To prove it, she opened the door to the lecture hall. Feel-good chatter roared into our feel-bad chamber.

Lecture in hand, I willed myself to rise and began a disembodied walk into the former anatomy theater, built in the 1700s.

The audience sat at a steep incline in semicircular rows of benches. Wooden desks served as rails. Overhead, a soaring dome inlaid with rosettes. A hole at the top was the primary light source. It was noon sharp; a column of dusty daylight shot directly down and filled the space with a comforting glow.

The room grew progressively quiet as the audience spotted me. Their equidistant faces beheld me with benevolence, their eyes trusting and curious.

But all I felt was cruelty.

The images I’d been able to hold back now flashed freely. Ravi, an accomplished and elegant man banging on a padded wall, crying out for help, growing weak, hoping against hope as nobody came. Collapsing into unconsciousness. His last thoughts of Scott and the baby he’d never meet. And for what? Because boys don’t hold apples?

“Welcome,” said Marie Chantal into the mic.

I felt myself uncoupling from reality. Marie Chantal blurred on me, her words wavering in and out.

"It is my great honor to introduce Adora Hazzard. Dr. Hazzard is a devoted classicist who we can thank for re-introducing the ancient wisdom of the Stoic philosophers to our ailing, modern world. Dr. Hazzard likes to call the Stoics the original gangsters of self-help."

Laughter from the audience.

"Their advice is appealing," Marie Chantal continued. "In her introduction to Epictetus, Adora Hazzard boils it down to this. 'Use your head, people!'"

Salvation through reason.

It had worked for me.

Stoicism had flourished from 300 BC to 100 AD. The reason it even had to be reintroduced by the likes of me? Because Christianity came along and wiped philosophy off the map.

Jesus was offering something better.

Salvation through love.

The Stoics never spoke of love. They spoke of ridding yourself of emotions. They spoke of going hard on yourself. The spoke of inoculating yourself against disappointment. They spoke of accepting, with relish, life's cruelties.

Projected on the wall, the title of my talk.

THE BLIGHT OF HOPE: THE STOICS, NIETZSCHE AND A NEW INNER FREEDOM

Marie Chantal was now running through the list of sponsors.

Had Stoicism worked for me?

Where had it left me? Feeling intellectually superior to others. Knowing how to throw in that extra dig at Viv. Blaming myself for what TJ Steele had stolen from me. Coldly turning on Hal for having different politics than I did.

When I first met Layla and she told me there was nothing she wouldn't do for the love of her husband, I'd laughed out loud. That's how far gone I was. I assumed she was doing a bit!

Maybe that's why Layla had gotten under my skin so. Because she had something I didn't. Not money. Not status. Not a ridiculous wardrobe.

Love.

"And now," Marie Chantal said, "please welcome Adora Hazzard."

Applause rang through the dome. I walked to the lectern. On my way, I passed through the column of light.

This whole time, I'd been jealous of Layla.

I'd created the coven to prove to the world, and myself, I didn't want love.

But I did want love.

I craved love.

Love as fearless and flamboyant as Layla's. The architectural undertakings and the foot rubs. The pecks on the cheek and the private viewings of the *Venus de Milo*.

I looked into the audience and found Viv. I saw Blanche, high up, standing against the back wall.

"Imagine it. Eat it."

That's the sign Blanche had seen in Las Vegas, for the Mirage buffet. It's how she'd summed up Layla's love for Lionel. Layla was so rich that all she had to do was imagine something, and it would magically appear.

And then, it started happening.

Breakthrough ideas—and I'm talking on the level of Newton, Curie and Einstein—are portrayed in movies as arriving fully formed in one spontaneous burst. The truth is, these people have been pondering the big idea for years. When the aha moment does come, it's only ever a tip-in.

I locked eyes with Blanche and began to smile.

Titters from the audience.

Viv, in the front row, glared at me like, *Don't you dare.*

I looked back at Blanche. She knit her brows, asking what was going on.

I stepped up to the mic. My eyes fell to my lecture. But the words were swimming. A greater truth had just locked into place.

"Fuck me," I said. I turned to Marie Chantal. "*Pardon, madame.* There's something I have to check."

I barreled down the stairs to the lobby. Blanche, Dorris and Viv followed, breathlessly demanding answers to all iterations of WTF.

I burst onto the quai Voltaire and madly pounded the pedestrian button.

"Mom!" said a distraught Viv. "That was so bad in there!"

"I'm aware."

"What do you have to check?" she asked. I was too popping with connections to answer. She turned to Dorris. "Do you know?"

"Your mother is a very smart woman," was the best Dorris could offer.

The light turned green; I took off for the wooden footbridge that crossed the Seine to the Louvre. The four of us raced across, our footfalls pounding like thunder, the sea of tourists parting to make way.

At the other side, I waited for the light at the quai François Mitterrand.

"Tell me!" Viv pleaded. "What are we doing?"

"I figured it out," I said. "I was wrong before. I want to make sure I'm not wrong again."

"Oh no," said Viv, looking as if fighting sudden onset nausea.

We dashed along a chunky stone path and under a high, narrow arch. A carriage entrance, from days of yore. The smell of horses somehow remained.

It landed us in a secondary courtyard, one relatively unpopulated. To the left, a sliver of webbed steel and glinting glass.

I took off for it, running, checking behind me that the others were keeping up. They were, Blanche holding her boobs. Good idea, I thought, and grabbed mine.

I entered the main courtyard of the centuries-old palace. In its center, the glass pyramid.

I couldn't help but pause to honor its courage and wit.

When it was first built, a scandal had ensued. I. M. Pei's solution for a new entrance was seen as sacrilege. There were calls for the pyramid to be demolished. Now, its fame has surpassed the palace itself and become the symbol of the Louvre.

"Never ceases to stir the soul." It was Blanche, having her own moment.

"Felt." I turned to Viv. "Is that what the kids say?"

"Yeah." She managed to pack into the one syllable a shotgun blast of contempt, embarrassment and pity.

Dorris weighed in. "Me? I don't understand the lamp." Indeed, alone in the plaza was a randomly placed, old-timey streetlamp.

Viv had spotted tourists posing atop low stone walls, pretending to pluck the pyramid while their friends snapped highly postable pics. Viv realized what they were doing—at the same moment she realized there was no way I was stopping to let her do it herself.

"No fair," she preemptively whined.

I headed for the pyramid. When I got there, the entrance was mobbed and the lines weren't moving.

"Damn!"

"The Louvre?" Blanche asked. "You want to go inside? Follow me."

Of course! Blanche could play her Interpol card.

Under a different carriage entrance—this one acted more like a wind tunnel—was another point of entry, and its line relatively short.

Blanche bypassed it for the guards at the front. I followed.

"Mom." Viv had slowed, made uncomfortable by the daggers being stared at us.

I gave her a shove. "Go!"

Blanche was at the head of the line, getting into it with a pair of guards. Her perfect French—who knew?—was coming fast and furious.

"She's saying some really bad words," said a wide-eyed Viv.

"We don't know that."

"I do. In French we listen to rap music from the Côte d'Ivoire."

"You're changing schools when we get back."

The guards relented and held the line, allowing us to go straight through security. One shouted after us in disgust. Words I knew were bad.

We all waited for Dorris's bag to make its way down the conveyor belt.

"This country," Blanche grumbled. "Your French is ninety-nine percent perfect and they hate you for it. You're much better off speaking English and getting condescended to."

"You told them you're with Interpol?" I asked, not understanding the controversy.

"I said we were American and if it weren't for us, their quisling asses would have put France on a platter and handed it over to the Nazis."

"Oh," I said.

"It was actually worse," Viv sidled up to say.

"She's sorry!" I called to the guards. "It was a time of moral relatives!"

Dorris retrieved her bag. I led the charge, sprinting towards the stairs—

—but didn't see the sensor-operated glass doors.

And smashed into them before they had the chance to open.

I saw stars; it felt like my nose was sideways on my face.

"Oh my God!" Viv doubled over, laughing in ecstasy.

"I'm glad I amused you." I blinked a few times and descended the escalator into the belly of the Louvre.

We entered into a shock of light courtesy of the pyramid above and white tile below. Through the overhead glass, the palace façade loomed, storm clouds behind.

"Marvelous," I said.

"Timed entries only," announced a voice over the loudspeaker. "We are sold out for the day."

"Crap!" I said. "How are we going to get in?"

"Let me," Blanche said, and stormed ahead.

"No!" I said, yanking her arm.

There were entrances at each of the three wings; all hanging with banners depicting the iconic treasures within. Each entrance was heavily fortified with ticket takers, armed officers and metal detectors.

Over at the Sully wing, I spotted a sign.

ENTRÉE DE GROUPE

There, distinctly bunched tourists waited to clear security. At the front, a mob of purple, red and gray. Old ladies, dressed in purple . . . wearing red hats.

The Red Hat Society! You see them at all the bucket-list tourist destinations.

Their guide waved them through with one hand and held up a red-hatted stick with the other.

"Stay close," I told my crew.

"Nice." Blanche had read my mind.

I steeled myself for what had to be done. I walked to the woman at the back of the group. From behind, I snatched her red hat and whipped it to Blanche. A second woman's hat, I flung to Dorris. A third, to Viv.

The geriatric adventuresses didn't comprehend what was happening until I grabbed hat number four. This, I pulled onto my head and hustled to the front of the line. Behind me, elderly voices, crackling and braying for help.

"Why are the hats?" Dorris asked. "Who are these people?"

"When I am an old woman, I shall wear purple," said Blanche, quoting the poem. "With a red hat, which doesn't go."

"Why for?" asked Dorris. "The ladies look ugly."

Viv seemed genuinely hurt. "I think they're cute."

By the time the tumult had made its way to the authorities, we four had slipped into line and past security.

I picked up my pace. Sensing we were down one, I turned back.

Viv was frozen in place, shoulders hunched.

"Mom," she gasped, barely able to speak. She had just realized: "Mine has hair."

Viv's hat hung with gray curls. I swiped it off her head, and my hat, too. I flung both onto an empty guard chair. Dorris and Blanche followed suit.

We ran-walked through a brightly lit corridor of excavated stone walls. It was once a moat, according to the artistic renderings we whizzed by.

"Wow, Mom," Viv said. "I'd go to all the museums if we could go through them this fast."

We turned a corner to a smallish staircase. At the top was a stone sphinx.

"Whoa," Viv said. "Is that the Sphinx from Egypt?"

"Think about that for a second," I told her.

Viv did. "Oh."

At the top of the stairs, a sign.

GREEK ART

I entered a dog's dinner of marble. Columns, inlaid floors, walls and plinths in different varieties, all heavily veined. The statues, of course, a pristine white.

The sound was cold and deafening. Tourists milled about. Some on their own, others with audio tours raised to their ears. Those who'd been able to snag a spot on the rare bench checked their phones to the overt envy of others. (Viv.)

At the far end of the gallery was a soaring rotunda, and the largest concentration of people.

I calmly headed through the cool white forest of goddesses and athletes, nymphs and angels.

As I drew closer to the throng, I stopped and closed my eyes.

I knew I was about to cross a line. Of before and after. I wanted to fully experience, for the last time, what before felt like. To say goodbye to it. To thank it for the good times.

". . . All but one statue in this gallery is a copy," came an Italian-accented voice. "They are dated from the first, second and third century BCE."

Speaking softly to the floor, and walking in small circles, was a woman wearing a flowery dress. Her highlights had grown out a good four inches.

"The originals were in bronze that the Romans melted."

I thought she might be a crazy person. Until I saw a microphone on her lapel. She was giving a guided tour to a group wearing wireless headphones, deep in the rotunda.

"They came to Rome by ship," she continued. "And many fell to the bottom of the sea. We have seen how the Greeks depict man not as he is, but how he wants to be seen. The ideal of man. They are naked to emphasize their perfection. And now, of course you see one of the Louvre's most beloved treasures."

I raised my eyes.

Standing on a pedestal, in a room all to herself, the Venus de Milo.

"The Venus de Milo, or Aphrodite of Melos," the woman said, "is the only original statue in the gallery. She was discovered by accident, and given as a gift to Louis the Eighteenth."

I had come to check her size. My heart quickened. She was larger than life. But not that much larger than life.

The same size as Boy With Apple.

I took out my phone. My fingers trembled so badly I couldn't type.

"She is the first mutilated statue," the guide was saying. "The first statue to engage our imagination."

I was finally steady enough. I texted Digby.

It *was* an arms deal.

Immediately, bubbles. The longer they lasted, the wider my smile. Suddenly, they stopped.

Next, simply: the fire emoji.

"You've got to fill me in here." It was a breathless Blanche.

"That's what was in crate four," I said. "The arms of the Venus de Milo."

Blanche had no words.

"Ravi was right," I said. "Boys don't hold apples. Aphrodite holds apples."

"I'm not getting it," Blanche said.

"Boy With Apple never existed. The statue was a composite, Frankensteined in an elaborate ruse perpetrated by Celine. Its body was a boy. But his arms had been replaced. With the arms of the Venus de Milo. So Celine could smuggle them out of France and into the US."

"What are you even talking about?" Blanche said.

"The Paris cure. Years back, Layla brought Lionel to Paris. It was their first trip after the accident. When Lionel saw the Venus de Milo, it had a profound effect on him. Her armless beauty, it gave him permission to see the beauty in his own amputation. Layla marks it as the moment Lionel snapped out of his depression. The myth of Lionel being saved by the Venus de Milo grew so large—in Layla's mind at least—she even had it emblazoned on the family crest. If the arms of the Venus de Milo were to get reattached, Layla feared it could plunge Lionel into another suicidal depression."

"Is this what a philosophy degree gets you?" Blanche asked. "You just figure shit like this out?"

"Thousands of years of men's wisdom . . ." I said. "Turns out it's no match for female intuition."

"This is why they hate us," Blanche said. "I am joining your coven."

"Thanks for the assist," I told her. "Imagine it. Eat it. You understood before I did the insane lengths a person will go to for love."

My phone was in my hand. I pressed it against my heart and felt it buzz. I looked down.

Turn around.

I did.

A family of four posed with a selfie stick. A man, wearing tiny rainbow shorts and a poncho of pink net, was so entranced by the Venus de Milo he wiped sweat from his brow. A Japanese tour group paid scrupulous attention to their guide.

And standing twenty feet away, Digby.

"Fine, I'll tell you," he said over the din. "I was working for the Louvre."

"Not Celine's brother."

"Is that what she told you?" Digby said through the tourists passing between. "Celine Montford has proven herself to be a woman of many liberties."

"So Western civilization was on the table," I said.

"And you just saved it." Digby wouldn't budge. I could feel him willing me to take the first step.

"It was all you," I said, denying him the satisfaction.

"How did you do it?" Digby asked.

"I went gentle."

Digby breathed in my words.

We drank each other in with all the things: joy, solemnity, regret.

"Promise," he said. "From now on, you'll only go gentle."

". . . with you?" I asked, showing my hand, my voice small with hope.

Digby looked utterly confused.

"Of course with me!"

"I didn't know!"

I ran into his arms. He held me tenderly, desperately. His smell, his skin, his strength.

"Hang on," came Viv's voice. "This is the guy from the hotel?"

I stepped back and said, "Yep."

Digby took my hands in his. Our fingers couldn't stop exploring.

"Mom!" Even to a fifteen-year-old, the man was gorg.

"Didn't I make it clear enough?" Digby asked me. "I fucking love you."

"Stop saying it that way," I said.

"You're right," he said. "What I meant to say—"

"No space and time crap, either. I want mortal coil."

"So you . . . forgive me?" Digby tentatively asked.

"For being a man?" I said. "Yes. Turns out, I love men. This man."

"So no coven," said Blanche.

She'd been watching, too.

"I love you," Digby told me. He threw his hands in the air. "This man loves Adora Hazzard!"

It wasn't just Blanche and Viv. It was the family of four, the man in the net poncho, the Japanese tour group, the Italian guide and everyone else who'd come to check the box on the Goddess of Love and instead had stumbled upon us.

I threw my arms across Digby's shoulders. He held me by my hips.

"I have a gross question," I asked.

"Open book," said Digby.

"Are you really that rich?"

"Obscenely so."

"So I'm rich?" gasped Viv, cutting in.

"Up to this one," Digby said, looking at me.

Viv squealed.

"This is Viv, by the way," I told Digby. "Viv Weymouth, David Ignatius Beale."

He shook her hand. "Call me Digby."

He returned his gaze to me. His eyes, shining bright. Or was it the reflection of my own radiance?

"You have to promise," I told Digby, "to be extraordinarily nice to me. You got angry at me that last night and you said mean things and it scared me. It still scares me. Please, never be mean to me again."

"Only," he said, "if you promise to keep quoting Socrates."

"Only if you promise not to make me watch that cheesy Phantom reunion concert."

"Only," Digby said, "if you promise not to make me watch that number from *Smash*."

"'Let Me Be Your Star'?" cried Viv. "Oh, Mom, you didn't!"

Digby mouthed to Viv, *Over and over.*

Viv walked off shaking her head. I turned to Digby.

"Only if you promise to cut your toenails."

"Sorry," Digby said.

"Only if you promise—"

"Hey!" Digby said. "Still my turn."

"What?" I asked, slowing things down, wanting to wring every bit of happiness out of this daisy chain of wonderful, wonderful, wonderful moments.

"Only if you promise to not change a thing," he said.

"She can, though!" Viv called from a bench. "She can change anything! She needs to change!"

"Only if you promise," I told Digby, "to kiss me on command. And not a *mwa*. A real kiss."

"*Peut-être,*" Digby said. "*Un baiser français?*"

He found Viv and warned, "Avert your eyes, child."

Digby kissed me, big. I yielded to his soft, intimate, searching pleasure.

I was inside a kaleidoscope. Triangles of gold marble became red hats became rainbow shorts became Paris out the window became purple jackets became grown-out highlights became the Venus de Milo covered in net became a man's bare chest—

I let out a cry, right into Digby's mouth, and shoved him off.

The Venus de Milo—she was draped in pink netting!

Down the corridor, I spotted a bare-backed man in tiny rainbow shorts running away. His pink poncho—he'd thrown it over the Venus de Milo—

"Get back!" I shouted. "Bomb!"

Chaos erupted in the rotunda. Screams echoed, audio tours clattered onto marble. Paper maps tossed, backpacks abandoned, a panicked Tower of Babel as desperate families and friends called out for loved ones.

I fought the tide of fleeing, flailing tourists and hurtled myself towards Viv—who still had hands securely over face on account of Mom making out.

And then, the explosion.

This time, a real one.

In an instant, my insides compressed and a force threw me onto Viv.

Next, silence. But for the ringing in my ears. My eyes stung inside my head. My mouth, dry as death, tasted of chalk. The acrid stench of gunpowder.

"Mom?" came a whimper. "What's happening? Are you okay?"

"I'm fine, baby," I said, and knew I was, having heard Viv's voice, felt her warmth.

Warmth, too, draped across my back. I fumbled and felt cashmere. Digby. He had shielded us from the blast.

I creakily peeled apart my eyelids into a dim realm of white dust and black smoke. Murmurs, coughs and cries. In the distance, racing footsteps, an alarm, shouted French.

Digby straightened; I did, too. Underneath me, the ground tilted. One hand still on Viv, I grabbed Digby's arm.

The two of us, unsure on our feet, white-haired, hunched and cautious, it was as if we'd skipped ahead to our dotage.

A gust blew through the shattered window; with it, a slice of sunlight.

I didn't dare turn.

I turned.

In the center of the rotunda . . . an empty pedestal. Where once had stood the enigmatic emblem of beauty and resilience was now a deafening void.

The Venus de Milo. She was gone.

The rotunda had been taped off and cleared of visitors. As with the Rosetta stone and Mesopotamian horse, there were no casualties. QUANDO, they did one thing right.

Authorities poured ceaselessly onto the scene, footprints across a virgin layer of white powder. The air was thick with disbelief, even as there was no doubt what had just happened: the Venus de Milo was no more, blown up by terrorists.

I stood alone as a carousel of Venus de Milos whirred in my head.

Lawn statues, restaurant frescoes, dangly earrings, MTV videos, pizza boxes, those giant bronze replicas on Sixth Avenue, cat memes, silk scarves, fleece blankets, a dry cleaner sign, figurines hawked on a beach in Mexico.

And she wasn't even a Michelangelo or a Da Vinci. Who could name the artist? The Venus de Milo claimed no artistic innovation or historical significance.

She'd reached icon status for . . . taking you by surprise. She was special, that's all. She brought joy. The purity of that, also obliterated. Now, even the memory of the Venus de Milo would be tied to the maniac impulse of one man.

My chest hollowed at the senselessness of the loss.

There was no consolation to be found. Stoic aphorisms seemed puny by comparison. Jesus, too.

A new shudder. The way I'd patronized Ravi that day on the stairs. "It's a hunk of marble," I'd said. "What's it to you?" How misguided of me! How vain! And now I might never get the chance to apologize.

Digby was deep in conversation with museum higher-ups. Even in the midst of such shock and despair, Digby remained lighthearted, instilling ease in others.

Viv, caked in marble, took selfies. I walked over and reached to wipe her face.

"Mom!" She swatted my hand. "Stop!"

On a nearby bench, Dorris was looking to comfort a dejected Blanche. I joined them.

"Man, I suck at my job!" Blanche was saying. "I told them to find someone else."

"When you thought QUANDO," I said, "you could hardly have pictured a guy who looked like he took a wrong turn to Pride."

"Literally in front of my eyes!" Blanche said. "I am about to get so shit-canned."

"You get what you pay for," Dorris said. "They should pay you more. Me, they pay nothing."

"You know one person who's having a good day?" I said, as the thought occurred to me. "Layla Lockwood. What she wanted most in the world was for the Venus de Milo to never be reunited with her arms."

Blanche: "Careful what you wish for is the moral of that story."

Digby approached. At his side, a young man in a tan suit and aura that blazed with pride. His unruly blond curls could have been an artistic expression of all within him wanting to burst out. It was hard not to be buoyed by his youthful enthusiasm.

"Ladies," Digby said, "I'd like you to meet the true hero of our story, Benjamin Montfort."

I recognized Celine's cheekbones and green eyes.

"Tell them," Digby said. "From the beginning."

In a highly appealing French accent, Benjamin launched in.

For Benjamin's senior-year internship, his aunt Celine had hooked him up at the Louvre. Benjamin was given busywork, responding to emails that came in to the museum's tip line.

Benjamin Montfort loved his job. When he received his first stipend, he insisted on taking Aunt Celine to dinner.

Over a bottle of Sancerre, Benjamin recounted in lively detail all the quacks who had written in. There was the schoolteacher in England who was in possession of Napoleon's taxidermied rooster. The priest who'd walked past the window of a mansion in Düsseldorf and spotted the legendary missing Raphael. The Greek fisherman who'd been trawling for sardines off the coast of Milos and pulled from his net a pair of marble arms belonging to the Venus de Milo.

Celine interrupted. "The hardest part about ordering one bottle of wine at dinner? Deciding whether or not to order the second bottle of wine. Let's shall."

As the night unfolded, and Benjamin grew quite drunk, Celine said she'd love to see these silly emails for herself. Could Benjamin access LignedeDénonciation@louvre.fr on his phone? He did; they shared more laughs.

Aunt and nephew kissed goodbye. Back home, Benjamin crashed on top of his sheets, too drunk to take off his shoes.

The next morning, he arrived at work, logged into his Louvre email account and noticed something peculiar.

The email from the Greek fisherman.

It had an arrow next to it.

Benjamin opened the "sent" folder. Last night at 22:33—while he and Celine were at dinner—the email from the Greek fisherman had been forwarded. To Celine Montfort.

Would . . . his aunt have forwarded the email to herself without telling him?

Of course not. Still, Benjamin found himself in a dilemma. If his supervisor caught him forwarding emails, he'd certainly be fired. Even if the recipient was a museum board member. Figuring it had to be a mishap of his own drunken fingertips, Benjamin erred on the side of honesty. He walked into the office of his direct superior, outed himself and figured that was that.

What Benjamin didn't know was that his superior notified her boss. Who notified his boss. Who notified the curator of Greek art. The curator studied the attached photos and was adequately intrigued; he contacted the Greek fisherman.

By then, a week had passed. The Greek fisherman emailed back to say he'd already sold the arms. To a Frenchwoman who'd appeared on his doorstep out of nowhere, and paid in cash.

"Celine?" I asked.

"She flew to Athens the day after our dinner," Benjamin breathlessly explained. "She took the ferry to Milos. The fisherman identified her from a photograph."

"That's where I came in," Digby said. "The Louvre called and asked me to sort things so as to minimize embarrassment to all parties."

"Who even are you?" Blanche asked.

Digby: "When I'm feeling pretentious, I say I make people whole. But really, I'm just a carrot farmer with a Batphone."

"I can't," said Blanche.

"Ask this one," Digby said, and pulled me in close.

But I'd gotten to thinking. I pushed him away with an annoyed, "Stop that."

"Ooh," Digby said. "Our first fight?"

He and Benjamin peeled off; I turned to Blanche.

"Interpol knew nothing about this?"

"First I've heard," she said. "We knew something about the crates was shady. But we were thinking QUANDO."

"So Celine Montfort went all that way to buy what most likely weren't the arms of the Venus de Milo. And sold them to Layla Lockwood? Why?"

Blanche was quick to answer. "I can think of a million reasons."

"A million dollars?" I said.

"I saw the bill of sale when I was going through Annoying Girl's desk."

"I don't mean to be like this," I said, something within me stirring. "But only a million dollars?"

"These days it buys very little," Dorris agreed. "I tell my clients. Cost of material. I have to pay my guys."

"Let's say," I told Blanche, "Celine Montfort is cash poor. Her access to power, admiration and world travel depend on her family's reputation. If anyone discovered she'd sold the arms of the Venus de Milo out from under the Louvre—the museum her father risked his life for—it would cost her more than a million dollars. It would destroy her good name. Celine Montfort would die in disgrace."

Time passed.

There it was: my barely perceptible shift.

"Or," I said.

"What's happening?" Blanche asked.

"Dorris," I said, and pointed to her sling bag. "Hand me the thing."

The chateau Montfort was ninety minutes by car from Paris, in Chantilly, a town of stone houses with painted shutters. The chateau announced itself from a half mile away by a high wall topped with wrought iron, lacelike in its delicacy, and punctuated with gold M's.

Its gate was massive and wide open. The imposing gravel drive lined with rose geranium hedges, aromatic from a recent pruning. Combined with the scent from the lavender fields on either side and the wisp of smoke curling from a chimney, I couldn't help but think: this would make a great candle.

I rang the doorbell. After a long while—of what I imagined was chaos within—the door opened.

"I suppose I'm inviting you in?" said Celine.

"I suppose you are."

I stepped into the grand entry. The walls were plaster, the color of cream, and enriched by an exuberance of gold molding. Crystal chandeliers danced abundantly from on high. Underfoot, polished wood floors inlaid with marble. If Liberace had a mood board, this would be it.

Through three spectacularly large windows, acres of manicured lawn and a pond.

"It's been quite the day," Celine said.

"The news is shocking," said I, playing along.

"I've got reporters calling." Celine led me through the entry. "I'm helping the Louvre with a statement. I've got a Zoom with AARC." She checked her watch. "You have ten minutes."

She opened a door into a library of dark wood. Behind glass, color-coded books with faded spines covered every wall. Stairs led to a balcony, which provided access to a second story of books. In the center of the room, a pair of leather couches sat perpendicular to the cavernous fireplace, which crackled with burning wood. At the far end, a desk fit for Louis XIV, perhaps once his. A narrow table populated by family photos ran the length between fireplace and desk.

Perched on a stiff chair was a woman with a servile effect, pen and paper in hand.

Celine addressed her. "*Pourquoi ne vas-tu pas commencer à faire cette liste, Mimi.*"

"*Oui, Madame*," said Mimi. "*Je serai dans la cuisine.*" She left, shutting the door behind her.

Now that we were alone, Celine's tone grew more pointed.

"What brings you to these parts?" She sat at the desk, fingers woven behind her head, elbows out. An animal's instinct to appear big, but really a sign of fear. "In the market for lace?"

"I wanted to go over my list one last time," I said, and produced the one I'd made of Ziggy's key words, by now well crumpled. "You remember."

"I do."

"May I borrow a pen?" I asked. "I promise to return it."

Celine pointed me to a heavy, orange Montblanc, its weight pleasing to the hand.

I flattened the list against the mahogany. “May we start at the top?”

“Why not?”

“Nazis,” I said. “Your father saved the Mona Lisa from the Nazis.”

“For which he was awarded la Légion d’honneur. It’s over there if you’d like to take a look.”

“Nazis, check. Mona Lisa, check.” I drew lines through both.

“Next up,” I said. “Apples. In Ravi’s words, ‘Boys don’t hold apples.’ We both witnessed how strongly he felt about that one. Check. Then we come to C-Four, the misunderstanding which will live in infamy.”

Celine gave a rueful cluck.

“Whoops,” I said. “I seemed to have skipped one. Reputation.”

“Aren’t you having fun?”

There should be a word for the particular amusement that comes from being insulted by a patently inferior person. Pregnant with such emotion, I stood up and made my way down the row of family photos, scanning for the perfect one.

“The Stoics were big on reputation,” I said. “They wrote about the madness that can ensue from trying to preserve one’s own. Not so much Epictetus, who was born into slavery. But Seneca—a playwright, banker and senator—was all over it. Marcus Aurelius—literally the most powerful man in the world—you couldn’t get him off the subject. It seems the bigger your reputation, the more it consumes you. The more extreme the measures you’ll take to preserve it. To be honest, I always found the topic off-putting, the purview of powerful men.”

I picked up a photo. In it, an elderly Pierre Montfort flanked by family members, among them an ageless Celine and a butterball Benjamin.

"Your father," I said. "He was a powerful man. He had a big reputation. Here he is with your nephew, Benjamin."

Celine's eyes darted nakedly between me and the photograph. Catching herself, she took a beat, from which emerged an enigmatic smile. She rose from her desk and approached.

"Oh?" She glided into my personal space.

"I'll admit," I said, holding ground, "it struck me as odd when I heard you'd happened to run into Lionel and Layla at the Louvre. Why would you, Celine Montfort, be ambling about the Sully wing at eight in the morning?"

"I have a sense you're about to tell me," she said, her face so close I could feel her hot breath.

"Because you planned it that way. Everyone at the Louvre knew Layla and Lionel were in town for one of their private viewings of the Venus de Milo. Including you."

"Their quarterly pilgrimages did provide for amusing fodder."

"To Layla, the limbless Venus de Milo was responsible for curing her husband of his depression. In her, you identified a kindred spirit. Someone as motivated as you to ensure the arms of the Venus de Milo never got reattached."

Celine stepped back and forced her best baffled look.

"It's why you flew to Greece and bought the arms off that fisherman," I said. "To protect the Montfort family secret."

"We have a family secret?" Celine said. "This is exciting."

"That the Mona Lisa wasn't the only famous work of art Pierre Montfort smuggled into this chateau during the German occupation.

He also took the Venus de Milo. And when the war was over, he replaced it with a fake."

Celine became statue-still.

"If those arms ended up at the Louvre, a pro forma marble analysis would prove the arms didn't match the body. And that the Venus de Milo, the one standing in the Louvre, being worshipped, gawked at and photographed from 1944 up until a few hours ago? It was a fake."

I crossed the last item off the list.

"Reputation," I said. "Check. Where is she?"

"The Venus de Milo?!" Celine cried. "Are you serious? You think I have it? Here at the chateau? Forgive me, but aren't you known for getting things spectacularly wrong?"

"This time I have proof."

"Proof?" she said. "Of what? There is no proof! What you're saying didn't happen!"

"The same proof Ravi had. The proof he presented to you when you called him up to your room. And when you fully understood its implications, you pushed him into the soundproof room. The one Lionel had just shown you on the house tour. The proof you feared I might have, so you had someone break into my flat. Proof so indisputable, you sicced your pals at QUANDO on the fake Venus de Milo. To destroy her, just to be safe."

I pulled out the tightly rolled piece of paper. The one Ravi had been waving in the phone call. The one Blanche had referred to as a nothing marble analysis. The one Dorris handed me, back at the Louvre.

"It's a lot of technical blah-blah," I said. "Enough to make you stop reading before you get to the good part. Page two, the conclusion. Skip ahead if you like."

I handed it to Celine.

STABLE ISOTOPE ANALYSIS USING THE DRAKOULIAS-WARNER RATIO MASS SPECTROMETER III™

Performed by: Isobel Ruiz

For: Ravi Bhardwaj of the Lockwood Library, New York, NY

Purpose: To Determine the Age and Origin of "Boy With Apple" Based on Samples Labeled C1, C2, C3, and C4

1. METHODOLOGY

1.1 Sample Preparation and Initial Analysis

The marble samples were ground to .001mm. X-ray diffraction (XRD) was used to identify the mineral content. Scanning electron microscopy (SEM) coupled with energy-dispersive X-ray spectroscopy (EDS) was employed to analyze the distribution of trace elements within the samples.

1.2 Thermoluminescent Dating (TL) and Sediment Dating (SD)

The samples were subjected to increasing doses of artificial radiation and measured for thermoluminescence. (290 C activation energy 1.7–2.0EV, minimum spurious effects, high intensity, linear response up to 50Gy, bleachable down to the residual level in 1h.) The glow curves were analyzed to determine activation energies and frequency factors to indicate the date of carving, as opposed to the age of the marble itself.

2. RESULTS

2.1 Composition Analysis

- Samples *C1, C2,* and *C3*: The chemical composition analysis revealed these samples to be homogeneous, consisting of 94% calcium carbonate ($CaCO_3$) with trace amounts of quartz (SiO^2), mica (TOT-c), and iron oxide (Fe^2O_3).
- Sample *C4*: This sample displayed a composition containing 91% calcium carbonate ($CaCO_3$), 8% magnesium carbonate ($MgCO_3$), and trace amounts of potassium feldspar ($KAlSi_3O_8$).

2.2 Origin Determination

- Samples *C1, C2,* and *C3*: The homogeneity and mineral composition of these samples are consistent with marble quarried from the island of Paros, Greece.
- Sample *C4*: The composition of this sample, particularly the presence of $MgCO_3$ and $KAlSi_3O_8$, suggests it originated from a different geological source. The characteristics align with marble found in the quarries of modern-day Turkey.

2.3 Age Determination

- Samples *C1, C2,* and *C3*: TL and SD results indicate these samples were carved during the Roman period, with an estimated date range of 150–180 AD.
- Sample *C4*: The analysis suggests that this sample was carved earlier, around 170 BC, during the Hellenistic period.

3. CONCLUSION

Due to the heterogeneity between Samples *C1, C2, C3* and Sample *C4,* in composition, date of carving, and quarry of origin, it is determined that the statue "Boy With Apple" is a composite of two different statues.

Or," I said, "boys don't hold apples."

Celine stared wide-eyed at the paper, calculating its implications.

"Don't try to swallow it or anything," I said.

Celine quickly threw it into the fire.

"We have copies," I said. "Plus, you're surrounded."

I opened the door. Digby was standing there, bouncing like a kid waiting to open his presents.

"Found her!"

I handed the Montblanc to Celine. "Your pen."

I walked out, passing the gendarmes on their way in. Before I closed the door, I turned to Celine.

"Since you asked. Ravi is alive."

Digby took my hand and led me to a room of tapestries depicting the 1533 marriage of Catherine de Medici to Henry, dauphin of France; both were fourteen. One tapestry had been removed and tossed into a corner.

Where it had hung, a secret door, now open.

I turned to Digby in disbelief.

He nodded.

"Okay," I said. "This one was all me."

"I'm giving it to you."

"How did you find her so fast?"

"Dorris did," he said. "Knocking on walls."

Dorris walked up, her eyes gleaming with visions of all the contracting work this would land her.

"It's how we do it in my country," she said. "I keep looking."

She made her way into the next room, knocking on walls as she went.

The gallery was rapidly filling with officials. Static from walkie-talkies periodically pierced the hushed amazement. Amazement at the surrounding opulence, but also the secret concealed behind these walls for the past sixty years.

"Wait here," Digby said.

He went to the gathering at the open door and asked that the area be cleared. He returned and walked me to the threshold. "Take as long as you need."

I stepped over it.

"Open or closed?" Digby asked, of the door.

"Closed."

The room was small, about ten by ten. It was dank and dark but for a single spotlight set on a stand and pointed at the Venus de Milo.

She wasn't on a pedestal. She was at my level. Her large nose, her cut abs, her twisting form. I looked directly into her eyes. Peaceful and far-off, she refused to engage.

The only furniture was a folding table on which sat an ancient record player, and a white chair of molded plastic, the cheap ones you see everywhere. Strewn across the floor, empty wine bottles.

On the record player, a 78 with a peeling label. Jascha Heifetz playing Tchaikovsky's Violin Concerto in D.

I toggled the old-fashioned switch, dropped the needle and took a seat.

The term "irrational joy" came to mind.

One of Stoicism's *principia primas* is to renounce externals. But even Seneca recognized this wasn't humanly possible. As a workaround—and perhaps as justification for he himself being one of the richest men in Rome—Seneca divided externals into two categories. "Preferred indifferents" and "dispreferred indifferents." (Don't shoot the translator!) Money, fame and status were "preferred indifferents." Sickness, destitution and ignominy, "dispreferred indifferents." You were allowed to possess and enjoy "preferred indifferents" as long as you could maintain tranquility with or without them.

Sitting there, having rescued the Venus de Milo, was peak preferred indifferent.

I let beauty and the sense of a job well done take it from there.

I stepped back into the gallery feeling wildly, ridiculously happy and found Digby scratching his head like a dog with fleas.

"For the rest of my life," he said, "I'm going to have the goddamned Venus de Milo coming out of every orifice."

I rested my elbows on Digby's shoulders and swayed.

"Do you consent to a kiss?" I asked.

"Always and forever."

We kissed again and plunged straight into the depths of euphoria that was carnal, pleasure-seeking and all ours.

"Please stop." It was Viv, quickly approaching.

She'd driven out with me, Digby and Dorris. Blanche, she'd remained behind to get yelled at by Interpol.

Digby and I stepped back and sheepishly wiped our mouths.

A man ran in from the next room flapping his arms.

"*Cette vieille salope folle!*" he cried. "*Dorris! Elle a retrouvé le Raphaël disparu!*"

"Ew," Viv told me. "What he just called Dorris, that was really misogynistic."

"They're just excited."

"No excuse."

A delegation of officials had arrived and was pointed our way.

A man in a crisp suit and lapel pin of the French flag introduced himself as Régis Toussaint, the minister of culture.

"Madame Hazzard," he said in extreme deference. "I have just learned what you have done. I thank you. The prime minister thanks you. He has sent me to ask what France can do for you."

"The pleasure was mine," I said, then corrected myself. "Maybe not pure pleasure. But it's what my ethics required. Which is a pleasure in itself. So thank you."

"Like," Viv said, stepping in and addressing Monsieur Toussaint, "what are you thinking?"

"And who is this?" asked the charmed official.

"My daughter, Viv."

"If it weren't for me," she informed France's minister of culture, "none of this would have happened. I'm the one who told her half the stuff in the Louvre is fake."

"Then I shall direct my question to you," said a stoic Monsieur Toussaint. "What can France do for Viv?"

That night, after dinner for three at Le Jules Verne, in separate rooms in the Ritz Paris, mother and daughter made the most of France's appreciation.

Me and Digby . . . going gentle, and not.

Viv, FaceTiming her friends from the exact suite where Dodi proposed to Diana and where she said yes and immediately called the Queen and then the Queen sent paparazzi assassins to kill her.

According to her podcasts.

A month later, we were back at the Ritz, and, like Lady Di herself, stepping into the back of a limousine. Viv had staged it so she'd go in first and get the window.

"Nope," I said.

I got in, followed by Viv. And of course, Digby.

I looked out the window as we drove out the Place Vendôme, past the Palais Garnier.

Don't even think about it, Paris. Don't even think about turning me against New York. Paris, with your government-subsidized baguettes and café culture, your dirt-cheap fresh orange juice and tombs of the philosophers, your grand boulevards and giggle-inducing side streets. Your lopsided police sirens that make every emergency seem quaint. Your shrimpy pedestrian wait times. Your bookstores, chocolate shops and pâtisseries, one to a block. In New York, when you pass men on the sidewalk standing with their backs to you in a certain way, they're pissing on a wall. In Paris, they're looking into the window of an antiques shop, admiring a display of nineteenth-century signet rings. Nope, Paris. I love New York and the scaffolding we've all become resigned to, the strangers walking up to you and hitting you in the face with cell phones. The waking up to poop-smeared sidewalks and smashed planters and walls of garbage piled like body bags, dripping with ooze, a bouncy house for rats.

"We might have to move here," I said over Viv to Digby.

Digby: "As you wish."

"Really?" asked Viv.

"After she goes off to college," I clarified.

"No fair!" said Viv.

We pulled up to the Louvre.

"Baby's first red carpet," I remarked.

And it was a banger. Télévision Française was broadcasting the unveiling of the Venus de Milo, live. Reporters, politicians, the who's who of the art world. Select Kardashians were in attendance with their own film crew.

Our limo waited in line. Ahead of us, flashbulbs galore for the trio of men Viv identified, through squeals, as Emily Cooper's love interests.

"Busy girl!" noted Digby.

When it was our turn to roll up and hit the red carpet, the photographers dropped their cameras in disappointment.

"In the old days," Digby said, "I could understand not wanting to waste film. Now, it literally costs them nothing. Still, they don't want a picture."

We passed Benjamin Montfort giving interviews to an enthralled press. He'd just vaulted from lowly intern to France's Most Eligible Bachelor, as per *French Vogue.*

Digby, Viv and I entered the pyramid and descended the escalator. A red carpet led us to the grand staircase. I remembered it from my days of youth hostels, Eurail passes and *Europe on Five Dollars a Day.*

At the top, the Winged Victory of Samothrace. Her base, a ship's bow, her head and arms, missing.

I must have paused.

"Don't get any ideas," Digby said.

The air grew electric as we approached the Salle de la Vénus de Milo.

Standing tall, under a silk shroud, the statue.

Digby had made sure I could invite anyone I wanted; I did so with abandon.

The first familiar faces were Dante and Ziggy.

Dante approached a man in black tie admiring a pair of marble cupids, and asked, "How much do you think they could get for one of those?"

Ziggy was going from statue to statue, carefully reading every inscription. Love that kid.

Dorris wore a high-necked, black muslin gown. She was adorned with statement jewelry from her country. A Peruvian goddess. Mathieu the trendspotter, her tuxedoed consort.

Two nondescript men approached me.

"Adora Hazzard," said one with British accent. "We heard what you did. You have a real talent. We'd like to explore the possibility of you—"

Suddenly, Blanche was there. "They're Interpol. They're about to flatter you into accepting a job. Don't fall for it. It's a trap."

"I must demure," I told the men. They walked away, no fans of Blanche.

I'd made her promise to dress for the occasion. She wore a shapeless print frock that did nothing for her.

"I got it at the farmers market." She gave it a twirl. On her feet, gardening clogs.

Across the way stood Hal and his wife. Last night, at a family dinner, I'd met Claire for the first time. She taught yoga. She had a quirky sense of humor.

Viv ran straight to them and swooped up their three-year-old little girl.

Lionel and Layla made a grand entrance.

(Layla's part in the affair had been conveniently forgotten. A legacy pledge to the Louvre helped.)

Layla had spent all week at the atelier for fittings, and all today in her suite at the Georges V with a team of stylists. The result: a warrior princess with studded epaulettes, high ponytail and maximum side-boob. Which was kind of great? I didn't know anymore. I was sticking to blue.

Lucien and Lorenzo tore past me, straight for Viv. They'd finally met last night, at the family dinner. (Yes, the Lockwoods were family again.) Viv, apparently, the newest external the boys desired.

Phyllis was there with Haruto, whom she'd brought, along with his wife and mother. Standing by a statue of a naked archer and soaking in the admiration of her sushi chef, I'd never seen my mother so happy. Not since the *Laugh Riot* wrap party.

". . . You know who else has a giant nose?" she told her guests. "Barbra Streisand."

Haruto's eyes glazed over as he released the desire to be elsewhere. Enough time with Phyllis, and he had mastered what the Stoics call "the art of acquiescence."

Digby returned from his lap around the room.

"How we doing?" he asked. "You good?"

"Only good," I said. "Only ever good."

This is what Digby does. He cares for people.

"Finally," he said. "I'll be able to meet the famous Minna and Emily Ann. I've never seen them with my own eyes. I'm beginning to think they don't exist."

"They're here somewhere," I said. "I just saw them."

As the unveiling of the Venus de Milo approached, I found Lionel. It wasn't hard; Layla had positioned him directly in front. Basking in the drama and attention, Layla took his hand and emoted grandly if nonspecifically.

I went to Lionel's other side and stood just behind.

Digby watched from afar. The architect of what we were about to see, he didn't seek credit. He was more at home in the shadows.

Speeches were given. The crowd pushed in. The silk shroud, attached to invisible wires, flew up to dramatically reveal the Venus de Milo.

One hand holds the drapery at her hip. The other offers an apple.

My main concern is Lionel. Of course he's fine. I never had any doubt. It isn't the unveiling I want to be present for. But for what comes after.

I watch it ripple across Lionel's face. The initial fear that he will be unable to handle an event in the future. The bracing for the worst. The event itself. The awareness that he, in fact, feels nothing. The surge of joy that he feels nothing.

Lionel looks around for a witness. It's not Layla, who's succumbed to her own emotion. It's me. I am there.

"I feel you," I say, and hold up my tattoo.

Thunderous applause. A needle drop. Tchaikovsky's Violin Concerto in D. The party really begins.

I find Viv. She is standing alone, absorbing the Venus de Milo with endearing seriousness. I stand at my daughter's side and look, too.

More than two thousand years ago, Venus had been set free from the stone. She was seized by looters and chopped to pieces. They put her on a ship sailing for Rome. When a storm hit, she fell to the bottom of the sea. Only parts of her were recovered. She was given to a king and set on a pedestal. And admired by all for what she left to the imagination. She was rescued from the Nazis. And locked in a dark room for decades. Returned to her palace, she is once again admired. This time, for offering an apple.

"So?" I ask Viv. "What do you think?"

"I liked it better before."

As with all things Viv, I kind of have to agree.

I find Scott, standing in the corner, looking smaller than usual. He is dressed in tight raw-silk pants and jacket with sequined lapel. On it is a button of Ravi's face. Ravi is recovering. There is no organ damage, but he is still being monitored and is forbidden to travel.

At Scott's side, the surrogate—six months pregnant—wears a matching button. They've taken the *Queen Mary* so the baby can be here for Daddy's big night.

They name the baby, a girl, Ravija. Daughter of the sun. When she gets older, Ravi and Scott drop Ravija off and pay Viv to babysit. (I am the one who babysits.)

Blanche joins the coven and moves into the apartment down the hall. "The apartment that started it all," as it is forever known.

I make clear to Digby there's no way I'll ever move out of the Ansonia.

Soon after, he rides the elevator with a crying woman. She's impossibly chic and insanely nice. She apologizes and explains she's having a hard time; her youngest has recently flown the nest. Now it's just her, alone in a giant apartment.

Digby sits with her. They agree to a price. The insanely nice woman moves to Gramercy Park. Everyone wins. This is what Digby does.

We hire the Seattle architect for the remodel. She creates a separate wing with its own entrance for Digby to conduct his business. Dorris does the work. The only thing not very beautiful is her price. Digby is amused.

After Digby, Viv, Mr. Man and I move up to sixteen, the Seattle architect takes my old apartment. The coven is thriving.

I will spend my days the same as before. I will walk across the park to the Lockwood Library. Out my office window, Boy With Apple. When his arms are sent back to France, Layla has an identical pair carved. Few of us will ever know the truth.

My circle is small, but inside I feel vast.

I study philosophy.

I love well and I am well loved.

I am whole.

ACKNOWLEDGMENTS

Thanks to . . .

Anna Stein, crack agent and stellar human. Lindsay Sagnette, instantly adored editor whose bubbly brilliance and exquisite care has felt like coming home. Ivan Held, more long and deep lunches, please! Alexis Welby, miracle worker. Katie McKee, for making every interaction an efficient pleasure. Ashley McClay, for the vision and can-do. Lettice Franklin, deliverer of the right notes at the right time.

The village: Maija Baldauf, Steven Barclay, Olivia Checchio, Gaelyn Galbreath, Sarah Harvey, Madeline Hopkins, Megha Jain, Ruth Leibmann, Jazmin Miller, Zoe Mohaupt, Vi-An Nguyen, Claire Nozeries, Lorie Pagnozzi, Sofie Parker, Molly Piper, Anthony Ramondo, Almudena Rincón, Erica Rose, Tarini Sipahimalani, Claire Sullivan, Lynsey Sutherland, Lindsey Tulloch, Virginia Woolstencroft, Blythe Zadrozny.

The stalwarts: Kate Beyrer, Maya Forbes, Holly Goldberg Sloan, Crystal Liu, Melissa Oman, Julia Sweeney, Leta Warner.

From their mouths to my page: Michael Blum, Chip Brown, Richard Day, Sasha Emerson, Mitch Hurwitz, Brett Johnson, Jodi Kantor, Henry Kaplan, Jenji Kohan, Gretchen Rubin, Sam Sussman.

Barbara Heller—for whom I could write a book—I set you apart.

For the early reads, time invested and saving me from myself: Mark Driscoll, Sarah Dunn, Hannah Mensch, Matthieu Miljava, Katya Minn.

You're true blue and cherished: Julie Anthony, Chris Barton, Kate Betts, Taffy Brodesser-Akner, Judy Clain, Gigi DePourtales, George Drakoulias, Maria Eitel, Dennis Erdman, Aya Hamilton, Dan Harris, Branden Jacobs-Jenkins, Ken Jennings, Mindy Jennings, Ali Krug, Peter Mensch, Miwa Messer, Sue Naegle, Chris Pavone, Darren Star, Sarah Stern, Katherine Stirling, Jess Walter, Tiffany Wendell, Meg Wolitzer, Wally Wolodarsky.

A showbiz shoutout: Josie Freedman, Shaun Gordon, Will Watkins.

The fam: Susie Bradstock, Lorenzo Semple III, Oliver Semple, Patrick Semple, Sheridan Semple, Phil Bradstock, Mimi Falcone, Phil Falcone, Anthony Falcone, Charlie Falcone, Ann Vitti, Jon Vitti.

George Meyer, as ever and for always.

The shows *Illinoise*, *Stereophonic* and *Sunset Blvd*, which I saw thirty-plus times while writing this book. (Presented without comment.)

The philosophers and teachers, and their teachers, whose paths I tread every day with seriousness and gratitude: Alain de Botton, Ward Farnsworth, Luc Ferry, Stephen Hanselman, Ryan Holiday, William Irvine, Sharon Lebell, Daniel Ogilvy, Massimo Pigliucci, Donald J. Robertson, and Stephen West, my philosopher king.

y Meyer, Poppy Meyer, Poppy Meyer, Poppy Meyer, Poppy Meyer, Poppy Meyer

Photo by Beowulf Sheehan

Maria Semple is the bestselling author of *Today Will Be Different, Where'd You Go, Bernadette,* and *This One Is Mine.* Her novels have been translated into forty languages. Before writing fiction, Maria wrote for TV. She lives in New York.

mariasemple.com

MariaSemple